Ker Seymer

**Since first I saw your face**

Ker Seymer

**Since first I saw your face**

ISBN/EAN: 9783744738750

Printed in Europe, USA, Canada, Australia, Japan

Cover: Foto ©Andreas Hilbeck / pixelio.de

More available books at **www.hansebooks.com**

# BEECHAM'S PILLS

FOR ALL

# Bilious & Nervous Disorders

SUCH AS

## SICK HEADACHE, CONSTIPATION,

## WEAK STOMACH, IMPAIRED DIGESTION,

## DISORDERED LIVER & FEMALE AILMENTS.

*Annual Sale, Six Million Boxes.*

In Boxes, 1s. 1½d., & 2s. 9d. each, with full directions.

# BEECHAM'S TOOTH PASTE

## RECOMMENDS ITSELF.

It is Efficacious, Economical, Cleanses the Teeth, Perfumes the Breath, and is a Reliable and Pleasant Dentifrice.

In Collapsible Tubes, of all Druggists, or from the Proprietor, for ONE SHILLING, postage paid.

*Prepared only by the Proprietor,*

THOMAS BEECHAM ST HELENS LANCASHIRE

# 'SINCE FIRST I SAW YOUR FACE'

# SINCE FIRST I SAW YOUR FACE '

BY

MRS. KER SEYMER

LONDON
GEORGE ROUTLEDGE AND SONS, Limited
BROADWAY, LUDGATE HILL

# CONTENTS.

vi                        CONTENTS

# 'SINCE FIRST I SAW YOUR FACE'

## *PART I*

### CHAPTER I.

#### THE TWINS.

'EIGHT o'clock, sir, and it's raining.'

The well-trained hunting valet then proceeds without more ado to draw back the curtains and pull up the blinds of two large windows in the luxuri-ously-furnished room he has just entered.

'Eh, what?' says a sleepy voice from the bed; 'eight o'clock? Why, Patterson, I told you not to call me till nine; what's the use in getting up at eight in a frost?'

'Beg pardon, sir, you didn't hear me say it was raining,' replies Patterson.

'Raining!' cries the voice, no longer sleepily; 'why didn't you say so? Have you called Mr. Algy?'

'No, sir; but I am going to him directly. Mr. Freeman says he thinks it must have been raining since about two o'clock this morning, and that, as there was not much frost in the ground, the hounds will most likely meet at eleven, certainly at twelve, so I thought I had better call you. Mr. Freeman says that he has got ready the Steamer and Largie for you, and Practitioner and Rose for Mr. Algy. If you want to make any change, he says, will you let him know as soon as possible?'

'All right, Patterson, I'll think it over for a few minutes; meanwhile go and call Mr. Algy and tell him the good news.'

'Eight o'clock, sir, and——'

But Patterson has no need to finish his sentence. Mr. Algy is wide awake, and exclaims at once:

'I have just heard you come out of Mr. Evy's room; but it's only eight o'clock—the stable clock struck five minutes ago: he isn't ill?'—this with a look of anxiety on his face.

'Ill? No, sir,' replies Patterson; 'but you wouldn't let me finish, Mr. Algy. It's *raining*, and Mr. Freeman has got ready Practitioner and Rose, unless you wish any change for second horse.'

'No, that's all right, Patterson. What is my brother going to ride?'

'Steamer and Largie, sir.'

'Good! I'm glad Freeman hasn't given him that new brute; I don't half like him. Now, look sharp,

Patterson, with the hot water; we shall have to start at ten-thirty, and Mr. Evy hates to be hurried over his dressing and breakfast.'

'Well, I'm blowed!' says Patterson to himself as he goes downstairs; 'if ever I saw anything like them young gentlemen! If I was to wake up one of them in the middle of the night, he'd say, "Holloa, Patterson! anything wrong with my brother?" That comes of their being twins, I suppose, and orphans; for they don't seem to care for anybody *really* except each other—though, goodness knows, they are kind enough to everyone. And popular? Why, that ain't no word for it. Oh, Lord! I hope they will never be separated it would pretty well settle the one that was left.'

It must here be mentioned that Patterson, being the son of the old family butler, through having been brought up with his young masters, was more interested in them than servants generally are in these days. To him they had always been 'Mr. Evy' and 'Mr. Algy,' and he had been 'Tom' to them. Lately, however, it had been decided, as the twins stayed about a great deal in country-houses now they had left Oxford, that 'Mr. Patterson' would ensure to their faithful servant a better reception in 'the Room' than would be accorded to plain 'Tom,' endeavouring themselves, though with many a slip of the tongue, to help him to keep up his position.

Hardly had the valet got to the basement than the loud ringing of Mr. Evy's bell caused him to drop the smoking suits he had over his arm on the nearest chair and run up the stairs again. A head, with tumbled curly hair, was thrust through the door, and a voice cried :

'Tom—I mean Patterson—ask Freeman to come up and speak to me at once.'

'Very well, sir;' and in a few moments Mr. Freeman, the stud-groom of the world (as he considered himself—and he was not far wrong), was walking slowly up the stairs, quite determined to do battle should any change in his programme be suggested.

A few words of description concerning this remarkable man will not come amiss, for Freeman's character is drawn from life, and as, alas ! his prototype's career was cut short some ten years ago, in the prime of life, he cannot come forward to contradict any statement which may appear in this book, as he most assuredly would have done—whatever it was—were he still in the land of the living. But here be it said that no better stud-groom ever laid his hand over the glossy quarters of the hunter which he had brought to the pink of condition, although no man was more fully convinced that he alone was capable of arriving at such a result. A tall, heavy man, with a considerable amount of what might be politely termed 'second chest,' a long body on short legs, not the best of hands, and a loose seat

—notwithstanding these drawbacks, Freeman was firmly under the impression that the light-weight hunter, which his art had made so fit, could only be done full justice to if he himself were in the saddle. A Scotchman to boot, with a strong North of the Tweed accent, Freeman was wont to say, after preparing a new purchase for either of his young masters, ' I would just like to ride him myself, and get him into good ways, before you get on his back.' In this he was generally indulged by the twins, with the result that either the horse—wiser than his teacher—declined the first fence, or deposited himself and his burden—no light one—in the nearest ditch.

After this introduction we will follow Mr. Freeman into his young master's room.

'Good-morning, Freeman. I hear you say that it has been raining since two o'clock.'

'Ah, I didn't say two o'clock, sir; I said about half-past one.'

'Well, never mind, Freeman. Anyhow, it will be good going by eleven.'

'Hounds will hunt, sir. I don't say it will be good going.'

'All right; we will chance that,' laughs Evy. 'Mr. Algy will ride Practitioner and Rose, and I will ride the Steamer first horse; but I want to try the new one second horse.'

'You can't do that, sir.'

'Why not? There's plenty of time; it is only

half-past eight, and I shall not want him, say, till one.'

'No, sir,' says Freeman; 'but I haven't ridden him myself yet, and I don't know how he will go in a bank country. I have got him ready, and was going to take him out myself this morning.'

A smile passed over the face of the young man of twenty-two, fresh from Oxford grinds, and probably as good a man to hounds for his years as could be found anywhere. Knowing, however, that to get his own way it would be necessary to put his foot down resolutely, he attempted to dispose of the autocrat by saying rather severely:

'I am sorry to disappoint you of your schooling this morning, Freeman, but I want the new horse for myself,' adding, after a moment's reflection: 'And, by Jove! as he is ready, I'll ride him first horse, so that, if he doesn't do, I've always got the Steamer to fall back upon. Send him on, and have the dogcart round with May at half-past ten.'

Freeman had one more try to get his way, for, on turning to leave the room, he said:

'I believe this is a dangerous horse, sir. Let Mr. Algernon ride him; he falls very light, for he is more used to it than you are. Besides '—hesitatingly —' you are the eldest, Mr. Evy, and your life is the more precious of the two.'

Could those soft blue eyes grow hard and stony? Could that smiling mouth draw itself into hard, almost cruel, lines? Yes! With a severe look which there was no mistaking, Evy dismissed the stud-groom, saying curtly:

' Do as I tell you, please ; if either neck is to be risked, it shall be *mine*—not my brother's.'

# CHAPTER II.

THE scene recorded in the preceding chapter took place at Huntingford, a beautiful Elizabethan mansion in Blankshire; the gray stone walls, the stone tiles and gables, had all mellowed down to the same shade, and the harmony was complete. Like most of the houses of that epoch, it was built in a valley, and rising out of the small park were two hills, each with an encampment at the top where the fortunate mortal who was allowed to dig could still find Roman and Saxon weapons, coins, etc., in profusion, not to speak of relics of a much earlier period. Two old avenues led to the house, and a narrow but deep river wound round one of the hills, running through the park within three hundred yards of the house—a peaceful, lovable old home, and as such it was loved almost like a living being by the brothers Everard and Algernon Somerville.

They were twins who at the age of fifteen were left orphans, their parents having gone down in a yacht which, in a dense fog, ran upon a rock and

foundered with every one on board. The shock to
the boys was great, and their grief painful to
witness, for they tenderly loved their parents; but
at that age sorrow has not the power over us that it
obtains in later years. Moreover, these lads had
that all-absorbing love for each other which occasionally exists between twins, to the extent, even, of
making them one in thought as in appearance.
After a fairly successful career at public school and
college, we find the brothers at twenty-two their
own masters, with plenty of money, and life lying
smilingly before them. What wonder, then, that
death, or even sorrow, should seem far removed from
that happy home and its joyous inmates?

'Algy, do look sharp; you've had four kidneys,
three eggs, and——'

'Shut up,' retorts Algy; 'you've had two mutton
chops, and they are quicker to eat, though there's a
lot more solid stuff in them; anyhow, I want some
marmalade; the dogcart won't be round for ten
minutes. But I say, old chap, do be careful with
that new horse, for I don't half like the look of him;
he seems to me one of the sulky sort.'

'Oh, he'll be all right,' said Evy; 'Mason told
me that he was good at everything except water, so
I'll look out for a bridge if I see we are coming to
the Fordham Brook; it would be deuced disagree-
able to tumble into half-frozen water.'

As the brothers sit at the breakfast-table, it would
be almost impossible to tell them apart—the same

oval face with long gray eyes, dark hair and a slight moustache. The only difference was in the expression of the mouth, that tell-tale feature which physiognomists declare reveals with unfailing truth the real character of man or woman. Everard's expression was *weak;* it was the face of an irresolute man who yields to temptation, however much against his better judgment. With Algy, on the contrary, the mouth was strong, and, without being a Lavater, you could predict of him unhesitatingly that no ordinary force would turn him from whatever purpose he had in view.

'The dogcart is at the door,' announces the footman.

Great-coats are brought out, and aprons to protect their immaculate buckskins from the mud, and in a few minutes the brothers are bowling along the rather hilly road behind a well-bred cob, who can be warranted to do the five miles in five times as many minutes. Arriving at the meet, and the usual morning greetings having been exchanged, coupled with congratulations upon the break-up of the frost, a move is made towards a covert not very far off, which is the chosen abode of a certain heroic fox who has furnished more than one great run, at the end of which he has saved his brush by getting to ground in a neighbouring country.

Horses are fresh after the late frost, and sportsmen extra keen to get to work again, so that nearly all the members of the hunt on the effective list are out, together with a few strangers, noticeable among whom is a beautiful young girl accompanied by an elderly, soldier-like man. They are riding two smart hacks, useful in their place, but with no pretensions to negotiate the very stiff line of country likely to be taken from this favourite wood, which generally sends the field over the cream of a very celebrated vale.

' Oh, father !' says the fair girl enthusiastically, as her eager and appreciative gaze takes in the well-mounted field and the business-like look of hunt servants and hounds. ' It is a pity the Melvilles don't know any of these people. What a sporting lot they look, and how they would despise our harriers ! I wish we lived in a hunting country. The fences about here seem enormous ; but don't you think we could get over *one* of them ? If the hounds find at once, I should dearly like to follow for a little bit.'

' My dear child,' replies the soldier-like man, ' you are always anxious to try anything; but as you dance, and ride a bicycle, and play golf and lawn-tennis, I think you may leave hunting alone for the present. If you marry a hunting man, who would like you to hunt, by all means take to it ; you ride admirably as it is, and will find hunting far more satisfactory than any other form of what you call " sport." But for the present, as these pretty hacks are pig-fat, they would probably be pumped out at the end of the first field, and undoubtedly subside

over the first fence, so we must content ourselves
with trotting about until hounds find and go away.
Remember, we have the best part of seven or eight
miles to ride back. When we came to stay here,
Melville warned me that, owing to his wife's ill-
health and his own, they had almost lost sight and
touch of their neighbours, and that our only excitement would be a meet of the hounds within distance;
so make the most of it. Let us see as much as we
can of the fun, and don't get kicked in the gateways.'

Father and daughter, for such is their relationship, ride on with the large field down the highroad
until they come to a bridle-path, so narrow that it
almost becomes a case of single file for horsemen
and horsewomen. Such, however, of the latter as
are near the front find themselves, by the courtesy of
the men, invited to pass first through the gate at the
end of the bridle-path.

Hounds and hunt-servants are through when the
Master, on a rather restive horse, though trying to
keep the gate open for the ladies following him, is
obliged to let it swing back with a bang, which
closes the latch and makes it somewhat difficult to
open from the other side.

In a moment, however, Algy Somerville, grasping
the situation, jumps his horse out of the bridle-path
and into it again on the other side of the gate, which
he reopens in a moment, and invites the ladies to
pass through. All do so with the exception of the
fair girl, who, being a stranger in this, and, indeed,

in any other, hunting field, hesitates and looks
anxiously behind to see if her father is coming ; upon
which Algy, bowing to her, for he could not well
take his hat off, both hands being engaged, says,
smiling :

'Please come through.   There are plenty of
people behind you to hold the gate open, and I think
you had better get forward.'

Flushing slightly, she thanks him and obeys, at
the same time giving rather a long look at the
speaker, for she wishes to remember the face of
this young paladin who succours damsels in distress,
and it seems to her wondrous fair.

# CHAPTER III.

HOUNDS had not been five minutes in covert before the uplifted cap of the whip stationed at the further end of it 'proclaimed him away.' Of course, hats were 'jammed on,' 'cigars and cigarettes were thrown away.' Was ever a run described without these incidents being mentioned? Too often the sacrifice is found to be premature, and the fact emphasized by a little unparliamentary language, when a plough team, or a shepherd's dog, or a man digging potatoes, has headed the fox back into covert, from which he declines to emerge a second time, meeting in the end with the ignominious, but—from a sportsman's point of view—well-merited fate of being chopped, which is better fun for the hounds than for their followers.

However, no such untoward incident awaited the eager and hard-riding field with which we are concerned on this occasion. The fox who broke covert as soon as the hounds gave tongue was one of the right sort—bold, stout, and with all a fox's share of cunning. What cared he for ploughs and shepherd's dogs, or digging labourers? Why, he saw them every day, and knew that they boded him no harm. No, *his* enemies were behind him, and behind he meant to keep them, heading for a friendly earth, an eight-mile point, quite straight, where he had already twice taken refuge.

It is marvellous how an old dog-fox, who has 'travelled' in the spring, will remember the line of country, and, when the day of emergency comes, never stops to look at small covert, thick hedgerow, or open drain, but goes straight for his point, and generally gets there. What true sportsman will grudge him a triumph so well earned?

'Gone away! Forward! forward!' is a welcome cry, and here there is no necessity for the Master to say, 'Give them time, gentlemen,' for hounds are still in the middle of the large wood; everyone knows that the fox has got a fair start, and that now it is a case of 'catch who catch can.' The brothers are riding abreast, and make straight for a rather formidable stake-bound fence, with a wide ditch on the take-off side. Everard's new horse clears it with several feet to spare, and, as he spurts up alongside of Algy, he cries:

'How about your croaking, Algy? This horse jumps splendidly.'

'Yes,' replied Algy, with his eyes fixed on the next fence; 'but look out for the Fordham Brook, for it's straight in front of us.'

After this there is no time for talking; the scent

is burning, the pace tremendous, and, hounds having
the best of it, every man has his work cut out to
solve the difficult problem of how to live with the
flying pack.  Some of them make for weak places
in the fences in order to save their horses, but
generally find, to their cost, that they would have
done better to have taken the fence where it came ;
for the ground was sound, and a big jump would
have taken less out of their horses than having to
bustle them to make up the hundred yards they have
given away by their want of judgment.

The line is a stiff one : fair banks, stake-bound
fences, and a little useful timber here and there, but
so far no water.  Then comes the cry, 'The Fordham Brook !'  Hounds are into it at once, and as
they scramble out, shaking themselves, it is evident
that, swollen with the recent snow, it has overflowed
its banks considerably ; otherwise the hounds would
at any rate have jumped at it, hoping to get clear
without swimming.

'Isn't this glorious ?' cries Evy, as side by side the
twins clear the small fence into the meadow through
which the brook runs, and they concentrate all
their thoughts on the formidable obstacle in front of
them.  Where is now the prudent resolve to look
for a bridge ?  The excitement of sport, the young
blood coursing through their veins, have sent all
thought of prudence to the winds, and, as they
charge the brook together, it does not occur to
either of them that the new horse is under suspicion

as regards water. Over goes the huntsman first, where he generally was, being a really good man to hounds, riding under eleven stone and splendidly mounted. Nevertheless, the ominous 'Come up!' is heard as the horse lands with a struggle, his nose very near the ground.

After him comes a rough-rider, the scion of an old Blankshire family, who now makes horses for other people to ride over land, much of which his fore-fathers owned. To-day he is qualifying an accom-plished steeplechaser for hunt races, and the horse throws the brook behind with a good six feet to spare, recalling the methods of the historic Chandler, though, fortunately, without having to clear the legendary thirty-nine feet.

Next to the leading pair come the twins, a set look upon their faces, combined with a happy smile as they realize that, once over that brook, the four of them will probably have the run pretty much to themselves; for giving one glance behind them, as they set their horses going in grim earnest, they see several men who have hitherto been in the first flight pull up and look anxiously for some means of getting to hounds, without the great likelihood of an ice-cold bath and considerable delay.

This can by no means be called *funking*, for every-one belonging to that category has long since been done with; but horses accustomed to a cramped country with high banks cannot be expected, after coming five miles at what corresponds to racing

pace, to stretch themselves out over a swollen brook
with a bad take-off.

'My old horse will never get over this,' says a
veteran member of the hunt, and one of its greatest
ornaments. 'What a fool I was not to turn off as
soon as I saw that our fox was heading for Ardwell
Wood! But I didn't think it would be as bad as
this. Hang me! if the Fordham Brook to-day isn't
as broad as the Whissendine!'

Good Blankshire man he might be, but he wasn't
above taking the Whissendine as a standard of
measurement. Who is, that has ridden over those
enchanted pastures, if only for a season, as was his
case? With a sigh of regret he turned away, but it
was the act of a good sportsman who wanted to see
the finish of this fine run. Would that Evy had
followed his example!

Algy clenches his teeth, saying to himself, 'I
will get over.' Now, there is no doubt in my mind
that the determination of the rider communicates
itself to his horse when there is a brook in front of
them; and Practitioner, though perhaps not absolutely a glutton at water, feels that he has got to do
his best this time, and goes at the brook with his
ears pricked and 'a rush like the Limited Mail,'
landing the other side on his knees, it is true, but
righting himself at once. Indeed, he would be
half across the field in a few seconds, when it
flashes through Algy's mind that Evy's mount is
known to be at least an indifferent water-jumper.

In an instant he pulls Practitioner onto his haunches, and turns in the saddle. What does he see ? The new horse has already refused the brook once, but, urged by Evy's spurs, makes a wild jump, accompanied by a swerve, and falls sideways into the brook with his rider under him. It is a ghastly fall to see, and the danger of it patent to anyone. Algy, hurling himself off his horse, runs to the brook prepared to do what is possible from that side, while the men on the other, alive to the situation, are also off their horses. Stirrup-leathers are unshipped and fastened together, and as the horse's head appears above the surface it is secured, and the struggling animal pulled off his submerged rider.

The few seconds that pass seem an eternity to the half-maddened Algy, who stands helpless upon the other side ; but they *do* pass, and at last a dripping head and an outstretched arm are seen, and Evy, half swimming, struggles somehow to where Algy, now lying flat down and holding out his hunting-crop, is able to reach him and drag him safely to the bank. A cheer goes up from the men across the brook as Evy, shaking himself like a water-spaniel, and gasping for breath, turns to them with a smile, and says :

'Thought I might as well get out on the right side. I felt you fellows pull the horse off me, and, sure enough, you saved my life, for I was jammed right down in two feet of mud at the bottom, and I

know to an ounce how heavy an able-bodied hunter
weighs on your chest under water.   If you had not
been there with your wits about you        Well,
thank you a thousand times—all of you!'

To Algy he said *nothing*, but the brothers looked
into each other's eyes, and words were not necessary.

'By Jove! that *was* a cold bath,' said Evy,
shivering, as he wrung out his coat.   Meanwhile,
there being a farmhouse close by, several labourers,
always on the look-out for hounds in a hunting
country, are soon on the spot, and with the help of
a stout cart mare the luckless 'new horse' is also
rescued from his dilemma, and stands dripping on
the bank under his master's eye.   It is characteristic
of Evy that at this moment he is thinking more of
the gallant manner in which the animal carried him
up to the brook than of his behaviour when he got
there, and he says cheerily, addressing his horse, 'I
was trying to find a name for you, and now I have
got it—C.B.'

'Why C.B.?' they shout across the brook.

'Companion of the Bath, to be sure.'

'Good—very good, for a half-drowned man; but
don't you give him another such chance.   And now
how are you going to get over to your precious C.B.?'

However, a long plank is procured, and Evy trots
across with his arms extended, and using his hunting-
crop like a balancing-pole, he declares that Niagara
and a tight rope is nothing to this, and Blondin not
in it with him.

And Algy? All this time he has hardly spoken a word, while Evy has been able to make a joke of what might have ended in his death. But if the situation had been reversed, *he* would have been the silent one, for both the brothers were naturally courageous, and it was the danger to the other, not his own, that moved either of them.

'Now, Algy, old boy, wake up—I am not done for this time; we'll get home as fast as we can, and, you bet,' he says, turning to the others, 'we will drink your health in something better than muddy water, however well iced.'

Algy raises his cap to the other men, and says, with much emotion, if with little eloquence: 'Perhaps you fellows think I shall forget what you have done to-day. Well, I *shan't*—ever!'

# CHAPTER IV

## CROSS-ROADS.

'ATWISHA! Atwisha!'

'Hang it, Evy!' says Algy, as he lights a cigarette and draws his chair up to the roaring fire, 'that's about the twentieth time you've sneezed since we began dinner.'

'Yes, and there will be about twenty more, you bet, before we turn in. I've got a jolly good cold, and no mistake. No wonder, either! Ugh! that water was cold.'

Algy shudders.

'No cold water,' says he, 'could make me shiver as I shall always shiver when I think of those awful two minutes—I suppose it wasn't more. One doesn't mind an ordinary spill; we have tumbled about too much together not to chance a broken arm, or even a leg, with *comparative* equanimity. But this was different; you might have been drowned, or kicked to death, or smothered in the mud; and I could do nothing from the side where I was. Come, don't let us talk about it, and I will try to think that "All's well that ends well."'

'Quite so,' observes Evy, 'only all hasn't ended well yet. I've twice had inflammation of the lungs, and you can't call it "ending well" if I am to be stopped hunting for the last fortnight we are together. But need it be the last fortnight, Algy, old chap? This is the first time in our lives that we have had a serious difference of opinion ; in smaller matters you have always given in to me; why are you adamant now? Will nothing make you change your mind? I feel beastly seedy—I swear I do. At-at-wis-wish-ha !'

'No,' says Algy, laughing at his brother's abortive sneeze. 'Not the real article, that sneeze ; he's a bagman, and you'll be as right as a trivet in a few days. You needn't try to work on my feelings now you're safe out of that infernal brook, just because you've got a bit of a cold.'

'The first serious difference of opinion.' This was quite true, and must now be explained. The second year the twin brothers were at Oxford, Algy had begun for the first time in his life to think of his future career. The idea of doing nothing but hunt and shoot became intolerable to him, and the fact of his being the younger of the two brothers somewhat intensified this feeling, so that it became clear to him that he ought to enter a profession of some sort.

On the other hand, he realized that his elder brother was cut out for the life of a country gentle-

man, and that in course of time he should represent
his county in Parliament. Now, they could not both
sit for their county, nor were two people required to
manage an estate which only belonged to one of
them. Moreover, Algy felt that he had it in him
to fly at different, possibly higher, game; and he
resolved therefore to try for the Foreign Office, as
being the branch of the Civil Service for which he
was best fitted.

Once his mind was made up—and here his determination of character stood him in good stead, for
many were the temptations to lure him from his
goal—he had set to work to perfect himself in foreign
languages, and to study the other subjects, a knowledge of which Her Majesty's Principal Secretary of
State for Foreign Affairs requires from all candidates
desirous of entering that distinguished office.

In due course he had passed a brilliant examination, and, at the time our story opens, was under
orders to report himself in Downing Street at the
end of the month. With first-rate abilities, great
perseverance, and plenty of interest to back him,
Algy was now looking forward with something like
enthusiasm to the career he had chosen. There was,
however, one drawback to his satisfaction in the fact
that it would entail partial separation from his dearly-
loved brother, from whom he had never been parted
for more than a few days at a time.

'Well, Algy,' answered Evy resignedly, 'if your
mind is really made up, there is nothing more to be

said, for I know what a determined beggar you are, and only wish that I had your steadfastness of purpose. Still, I feel that, once we are separated, I shall make an ass of myself in some way or other. I dread too that, now you elect to pitch your tent in London, and live in a sphere of completely different interests, you won't care any longer for the old home, and hunting, and all that. Why,' he continued, warming up, 'you will perhaps even come to despise your bucolic brother.'

Algy's eyes flashed for a second as he said :

' None of that, Evy ! not even in joke must you say such things to me ; you always have been and always will be my first object in life, and if a cruel fate took you away from me, my next object would be our old home. " If Nature keeps me alive," as Tennyson says, I should throw my career and ambitions to the winds, and my life would be given to the effort to succeed you worthily, and to do the work which should have been yours. Come,' he added, a little ashamed of the emotion he had shown, ' try to take a more cheerful view of things; it is true that I have got to be off in a fortnight, but that brings us to the end of January, and when you have finished up hunting you can join me in London. What you call my new "sphere of interests" will interest you, if at first only because it is mine ; but, bless you ! before long you'll find that you can move and breathe quite comfortably there until I get some leave, when we can go off anywhere you like together.

I tell you, I *couldn't* be happy doing nothing ; but if it hadn't been for you I should have gone into the Diplomatic Service, which might mean Brazil or China to start with, and real separation instead of the three hours between this and Waterloo.'

'You are right, Algy,' replied Evy, after a pause, as he went into the hall. 'I believe you've stuff enough in you to make an Ambassador or a Minister for Foreign Affairs, and you must have your way in this matter. I won't say—at least, I'll try not to say— one more word in opposition to it. But '—taking up his flat candlestick—' I'm going to separate now, though it is only about ten, for I feel very seedy. Hang that iced brook ! Good-night. Atwisha !'

# CHAPTER V

### BROTHERLY LOVE.

CURIOUSLY enough, on being called the next morning by Patterson, Algy had no presentiment of the deadly enemy that was menacing his brother. The shock, the relief of having Evy safe by his side, had made him treat lightly what is always a danger, viz., such a chill as may settle on the lungs at any moment; and—as Evy had truly said—he had already had two attacks of inflammation. The first had been brought on through getting wet one day when running with the beagles at Eton, and the second at Oxford, where he had plunged into the river to save an inexperienced freshman who had ventured out in an outrigger, without the vaguest idea of what that frail craft was capable of in unskilled hands. But what do such trifling ailments mean to boys just beginning life? The attacks had been slight and followed by quick recovery; a weak spot, however, had been left in one lung, destined, alas! to develop serious mischief.

'Well, Patterson, has Mr. Evy done sneezing yet?'

3

'He isn't sneezing now, sir,' replies Patterson, somewhat seriously; 'but he says his chest feels very much oppressed, and he is coughing a bit. Hadn't we better send for Dr. Andrews? You know, Mr. Algy, inflammation of the lungs often comes after a chill, particularly when you've had it before.'

'All right, Patterson; I'll go and see him;' and, jumping out of bed, Algy is in his brother's room in a few seconds.

'Well, C.B. No. 1, how are you?'

'Bad,' replies Evy gloomily. 'I've got an awful pain in my chest. What a bore it is! for I do so want to enjoy the rest of our hunting together, and here's an end of that, if I'm to be laid up. Send for old Andrews, Algy. I dare say he'll be able to patch me up in a day or two.'

The flushed face, the laboured breath, give Algy a fresh shock, and, as he gives orders to have the dogcart got ready immediately, he mutters between his teeth: '*Fool* that I was to have treated his cold so lightly last night! I might have made him do something—I don't quite know what, but *something*—instead of which I only chaffed him about his sneezing.'

'Dr. Andrews is here, Mr. Algy,' announces Patterson; for the doctor, not yet having started on his morning round, had jumped at once into the dogcart sent for him, leaving word for his own carriage to pick him up at Huntingford. Dr. Andrews, though still a comparatively young man, had known the twins for the past fifteen years, and was as devoted to them as were all their neighbours.

'Now, Algy,' says the cheery doctor, as the former runs down the stairs to meet him, 'what is the matter this time? And are you my patient, or is Evy?'

'It's Evy; but I don't think there's much the matter with him,' replies Algy, the wish being father to the thought. 'He got into a brook yesterday out hunting, and has caught a bit of a chill; but I suppose he'll be all right in a day or two, won't he?'

'My dear boy, how can I possibly tell till I've seen him? Let's go upstairs and "vet" him, as you call it. I won't coddle him, or stop his hunting unless it is absolutely necessary, I promise you.'

'Well, Evy,' says the doctor—also a hunting man when he has the time—'so you got into the Fordham Brook? For about the twentieth time, I suppose, but it must have been precious cold yesterday. I hear that you had quite the best of it, you and Algy, until your mishap, and I know you will be glad to hear that your stout old fox got to ground in the B—— country, so will probably give you another good day's sport, when I hope, like John Gilpin's biographer, "I may be there to see." Colonel Miles came to me this morning with a sprained wrist; it was he who told me all about the run, and how you and Algy were in front up to the Fordham Brook, which he declared was almost unjumpable ; any way, he admits that he never thought of attempting it, but made straight towards the point he felt sure the fox was heading for. And now, dear boy, let me see what is wrong with you.'

The usual examination is gone through, stethoscope, tapping on chest and back, etc., after which the harmless-looking temperature thermometer is produced, which has caused many a seemingly light illness to at once assume a serious aspect. Is this modern invention a blessing to mankind, or is it not? Certainly it cannot be disputed that doctors are now made terribly nervous when that tell-tale instrument registers, say, 103 degrees ; with the result that the pulse, which for countless generations has been our unfailing monitor, is almost entirely disregarded nowadays, and the patient's state of health gauged by the thermometer alone.

It was so in this case. Dr. Andrews having carefully inserted the tube under his patient's tongue, he walked away with Algy to talk over sport and the neighbourhood in general while the necessary time elapsed for the thermometer to register its fiat. On withdrawing it from his patient's mouth and examining it at the window, Dr. Andrews gives an ill-concealed start, and says to Evy :

' My dear boy, your temperature is high, very high ; you must stop in bed to-day ; I will send you the necessary medicine, and come and see you again

this evening.  I know that Algy will have my directions carried out, otherwise I should send for a
nurse at once ; but I hope that there won't be any
necessity for that.  I shall tell Patterson to get the
linseed poultices ready ; don't you move or talk
much, for you have got a slight attack of inflammation of the lungs, which I hope will pass off—but it
will only do so if you take care of yourself.'

' I'll see to that,' says Algy, as he opens the door
for the doctor ; 'you don't think there is anything
*seriously* wrong, eh, doctor ?  You *can't;* he was all
right yesterday ; why on earth do you put on that
grave face and frighten me to death ?'

' Oh, my dear Algy,' says the discreet doctor, ' I
don't want to frighten you, and no doubt at your
age a chill and a little fever may seem nothing ; you
must not forget, however, that all sorts of things
may develop if care is not taken.  Above all, don't
let Evy get out of bed ; Patterson will look after
him well, and the medicine I shall send will put
him into a perspiration, which I hope will relieve
the fever.  You had better leave him quiet to-day,
for then he will go to sleep, which he wouldn't do
if you remained in the room with him.'

About an hour afterwards, as Evy was dozing,
the young footman, not having the discretion or
his elder fellow-servant, Patterson, rushed into the
invalid's room and exclaimed excitedly :

' Oh, sir, Mr. Algy has had a bad accident !  He
went to see if the new 'orse was all right, and, as he

was leaving the box, the brute lashed out and kicked him, and *they are now carrying him to his room.*'

Out of bed jumps Evy, the linseed poultice from his chest falling with a thud on the floor.

'Quick! get me my dressing-gown and my fur-lined slippers—they are in the cupboard in the bath-room.'

'But, sir,' replies the frightened footman, 'perhaps, as you have a cold, you had better not get up.'

'Cold be d——d! Don't stand there staring at me, but run and get the things.'

Evy remains shivering in his nightshirt, with bare feet, when the faithful Patterson, fearing that the bad news may reach his young master, enters the room at this moment.

'For God's sake, Mr. Evy, get back into bed! It's nothing at all—not half such a blow as I have often seen Mr. Algy get at football; I happened to be in the stables and saw the whole thing happen.'

Surely the Recording Angel will not put this per-version of the truth to the debit side of the faithful servant's account in the great book? As a matter of fact, Patterson was in his own room, overlooking the stable-yard, when the accident happened, and hearing a commotion, he looked out and saw Algy being carried into the house by the stud-groom and one of the helpers. In a few seconds he was on the spot, crying:

'What has happened? What is it? Is he much hurt?'

'I can't quite tell you,' replied Freeman, 'it was all done so quick: Mr. Algy and I went into the new horse's box to see if he was all right, and Mr. Algy, after he had felt his legs and looked him all over, said to me: "There's nothing amiss with him; I wish my brother was as sound!" I went to open the door of the box, and as I got my hand on the latch, I heard a thud, turned round, and saw Mr. Algy on the ground, and the horse, with his ears laid back, just going to lash out again. I holloa'd at him, and he shrunk up into the corner, so I know the brute didn't kick him a second time; but I don't know where the first kick caught him. Jim was off on Lightning in less than two minutes, so we shall soon have Dr. Andrews here. Oh, Lord! what a bad business—both the young gentlemen laid by the heels at once!'

# CHAPTER VI.

## MARCHING ORDERS.

FORTUNATELY, Patterson proved to be right when he stated that the accident was a slight one; the horse's hoof had caught Algy on the chest and 'winded' him, but beyond a nasty bruise he was none the worse, and was able to come into Evy's room within ten minutes of the alarm. When the doctor arrived, it was a case of 'Mother Hubbard's dog,' but Dr. Andrews was much too fond of his young friends to complain of that.

'A little Elliman's embrocation is all you want,' said he, 'and I shall come round this evening to see how Evy is; I think I had better take up my quarters here—you young monkeys are always coming to grief;' saying which, and truly thankful that it *was* a false alarm, the kindly doctor again took his departure.

The next few days were days of intense anxiety; Evy's temperature kept high, the pulse was quick and weak, and the cough incessant. Thanks to skilful treatment, however, coupled with careful nursing, the patient gradually began to mend, and at length was allowed to sit up for a few hours every day in an armchair.

And now the kind doctor had a difficult task before him ; it was evident that Evy's constitution had been considerably impaired by these repeated attacks, and this time the family practitioner felt it his duty to break to his patient that he must positively give up his hunting—for the present, at any rate—and be off as soon as possible to some warmer climate ; the winter was still young, and in all probability the very first wetting would bring back the mischief.

In vain Evy remonstrated; Dr. Andrews was firm ; he pointed out to his patient the madness of running the risk of either killing himself outright, or becoming a confirmed invalid, rather than give up a few weeks of his favourite amusement.

'But where am I to go, and what am I to do when I get there ?' said poor Evy, who had never been further afield than Paris in his lifetime, and to whom 'abroad' meant all sorts of horrors and discomforts.

'Well,' replied the doctor, 'suppose you go to the Riviera ? Say Cannes or Monte Carlo, where you would meet plenty of nice English people—more of them than foreigners, I'm told—and you can shoot pigeons, or play golf, or yacht, and gamble to your heart's content on wet days. If you decide on Monte Carlo, I can promise you a much better time

than you would have here, for probably the first
day's hunting would knock you up again, and leave
you to spend the rest of the winter in your bedroom.
I have already talked to Algy on the subject, and he
will back me up, grieved as he is at the prospect of
being separated from you.'

'Well, I give in,' said poor Evy with a deep sigh;
'I suppose I *should* be a fool to throw away my
chance of getting all right, and being able to enjoy
life in the future. And if I *am* to leave England,
then the sooner the better; I shall mind it less, as
Algy would not in any case be with me here. How
soon shall I be fit to start?'

'I hope in about a week, if all goes well. If I
were you, I should ask Colonel Erskine to come
over and see you; he has spent several winters on
the Riviera, for his chest used to be very delicate,
and you can see for yourself what that lovely climate
has done for him. He will be able to tell you all
about the different places, and the sort of life one
leads there.'

Colonel Erskine having pronounced favourably on
Monte Carlo, that place was decided upon as Evy's
winter-quarters.

'You see,' said the Colonel, 'it has one great
advantage. Of course, you have a certain amount of
bad days everywhere in the winter, when you can't
go out and are bored to death; but at Monte Carlo
you have always the Casino, where, even if you
do not care to play yourself, you can't help being

amused and interested watching other people. You
will never have seen such a motley crew as they
are. I spent all the wet days there, though I never
put on a five-franc piece.'

'Oh, I dare say I shall play a bit if I go there,'
said Evy; 'in moderation, of course, for I don't
think I'm much of a gambler. I used to play a little
at Oxford, but I hated winning the other fellows'
money, and didn't much like losing my own.'

'Don't be too sure, Evy,' replied the Colonel;
'gambling amongst friends is a very different thing
to playing against a bank with millions of capital.
A young fellow with plenty of money came out while
I was there; he told me he didn't care a bit about
play, and I believe I saw him put on his first stake
of one louis. Soon, however, he got bitten with
player's fever, and, to make a long story short, after
having gone there three years in succession, he
found himself completely ruined, and is now, I
think, sitting on a three-legged stool in a City office.
*You* are not likely to make such an ass of yourself,
I know; but there is a certain French proverb
which is pregnant with truth: "Il ne faut pas dire,
fontaine je ne boirai pas de ton eau;" and if you
*should* feel the gambling fever creeping over you,
remember my warning: pack up your traps *at once*
and be off somewhere else, for it is better to be
bored than "broke."'

In less than a week the doctor pronounced Evy
to be so much better that it would be advisable for

him to start at once, for the weather was cold and
damp, and there was no chance of his leaving the
house except in a close carriage. It was decided
that he should sleep a night in London, and one in
Paris, from which place he could continue his
journey in the *train de luxe* direct to Monte Carlo.

As the brothers drove away together from
Huntingford one dull winter's morning, they craned
their necks out of the carriage window to see the
last of their beautiful old home.

'Imagine,' said Algy, 'if the old place were
burned down whilst we are away! I think it would
break our hearts. Well, that is the only way in
which we can lose it.'

Alas! if Evy's Latinity was not good enough to
reply 'Absit omen,' he should at least, like the
cautious Germans, have added the 'Unberufen'
which has become almost an English word!

# CHAPTER VII.

## 'HARM WATCH, HARM CATCH.'

WE will pass over the sad parting of the twin brothers; whoever has read the foregoing pages can picture to himself the sense of desolation which the parting left with both of them. Algy settled himself in a couple of rooms in St. James's Place, and Evy started off to Monte Carlo, where he was greeted on his arrival by warmth and sunshine instead of the damp and frequent gloom he had left behind him. Remembering his doctor's injunction to be out as much as possible so long as the weather was fine, Evy strolled about the greater part of the first days, returning each time more and more enchanted with the beauty of the place and its surroundings. What a relief, too, when he felt a little tired, to be able to sit down in the open air without fear of catching cold! One of his greatest pleasures was to watch the passers-by and speculate as to their nationality, and, in fact, in a very short time Evy became an accomplished *flâneur*.

One day he caught sight of an unmistakable young

Englishman lounging along with his hands in his pockets, and recognised in him an Oxford friend whom he had not seen since he left the Alma Mater. Evy jumped up from his seat at once, glad to see a familiar face in that crowd of strangers, tempted out by the beauty of the morning.

'Hullo, Dawson!' he cried; 'I'm awfully glad to see you. I was just beginning to get tired of my own company, although this is a ripping place, isn't it?'

'Oh, it's all right when you win,' replied the other gloomily.

'Win? Win what?'

Evy had entirely forgotten that there was such a thing as a gambling-table in the place.

'Win *anything*,' replied Dawson. 'I should be content with a louis, just to say I *had* won; but I've had the most infernal luck ever since I came here: trente et quarante, roulette, baccarat—one is as bad as the other. Still, I'm very glad to see you, Somerville. Which game are you going to start on?'

Evy understood now: here was one of those confirmed gamblers he had heard and read about, but had not yet come across; Dawson had evidently become so completely absorbed in the one occupation of his life that he had no room for other thoughts and ideas.

'Oh, I didn't come here to gamble,' said Evy; 'I got into a half-frozen brook about a month ago, which set up inflammation of the lungs, and the doctor ordered me off here—much against my will, as you can imagine. But you don't look very fit either, old chap ; what's the matter with you ?'

'A run of fifteen on black is what is the matter with me,' replied Dawson ; 'it happened whilst I was at dinner last night, after I had been backing the black unsuccessfully all the afternoon.'

'Oh, Lord!' thought Evy to himself, 'I shall soon have enough of this gambling shop ; can't the fellow talk about anything else ?' Then aloud : 'How long are you going to stop here ? I suppose you'll be going back to your hunting when you get all right, but at present you are the colour of a London shopman in August. Joking apart, what *is* wrong ?'

'Nothing is wrong with me ; but as I spend the best part of twelve hours out of the twenty-four in a bad atmosphere, and never take any exercise, no wonder I look seedy. On a fine day I just stroll about till play begins, and that's all the fresh air and walking I get, except the few hundred yards between my hotel and the Casino.'

'Good heavens, what a life!' Evy could not help exclaiming. 'Do you mean to say that you *like* it ?'

'I'm not sure that I do, but I cannot help it. Well, I must be off now, Somerville, or that black will be turning up again without my being there to back it. I suppose you'll drop in to look at the Rooms some time to-day, for they're well worth seeing ; and once there, who knows but that you may be tempted to try your luck ?'

' Oh, I dare say I shall be,' replied Evy carelessly;
' I'm not above following a bad example.  But as
long as this lovely weather lasts I mean to be out
of doors as much as I can, for I am here to get
sound as soon as possible, and for no other reason.
Sound, my boy, for me, means to be able to hunt
next year from November till March ; and if Monte
Carlo will work that for me, I won't ask whether red
or black is the winning colour.  What do you say
to dining together to-night, and then you can tell
me all about your blessed run of fifteen on black ?'

' Right you are,' answered Dawson ; ' I'll pick
you up about seven o'clock, and show you where we
can dine well and reasonably ; it will give me a little
extra walk, and perhaps a rather better appetite
than I can boast of generally here.'

The next two days being still fine and warm, Evy
was as good as his word, and spent most of his time
out of doors ; he fell in with an English family who
did not gamble, and with whom he had stayed for a
few days when he was at Eton ; but he felt rather
lonely and out of place, and longed unspeakably for
the companionship of Algy.  He had looked in at
the Casino and watched the gamblers with wondering interest, although with no wish to try his own
luck ; indeed, his only preoccupation was to get
back into the sunshine, for he already felt his
strength returning to him.

On the third day, however, down came the rain
in torrents : Evy stood at the window and yawned,

and then sat down and wrote a long letter to Algy—
the second since his arrival. That occupation over,
he again went to the window and looked out, only
to find that it was raining harder than ever.

'What is the good of rain *here*?' he muttered
querulously; 'at home it's all very well, for it gets
the frost out of the ground in winter, and brings on
the grass in spring, but it's awfully out of place in
Monte Carlo. What *am* I going to do with myself
all day?'

He suddenly remembered Colonel Erskine's
words, to the effect that on wet days there was
always the Casino to fall back upon.

'The very thing!' he cried, and, thrusting a few
hundred-franc notes into his pocket, he rang the
bell and ordered a close carriage to be sent for. He
jumped into it at once, and ten minutes later he was
seated at the roulette-table, being initiated by his
friend Dawson into the mysteries of 'impair,'
'manque,' 'à cheval,' 'transversale,' etc. 'Ce n'est
que le premier pas qui coute!'

# CHAPTER VIII.

## TRUTH IN THE GARB OF GOSSIP.

'I WISH Evy would write oftener,' mused Algy. 'Five days without a line! It is intolerable! I shall telegraph, answer paid, "Why don't you write? Are you ill?" And, true to his word, the telegram was despatched as soon as Algy reached the Foreign Office.

In due course the answer came : ' Quite well; am writing '; and two days later the promised letter arrived. Algy tore it open impatiently, but was disappointed to find it very short, and, after reading it through twice, a rather puzzled expression came over his face, as he put the letter into his pocket and went off to his work. Later on, while at lunch with one of his fellow-clerks, he inquired casually :

' Have you ever been to Monte Carlo, Frank ?'

' No, I haven't. Why do you ask ?'

' Because I have a brother out there, as you know; but, although he writes fairly often, he's not much good at descriptions, and I should like to know something about the place.'

'Well, Dawson might tell you about it, for his brother half lives there, and has become a confirmed gambler. He had a lot of money when he came of age, but I believe it's getting beautifully less now.'

'Dawson? I remember of course, now, that Evy did mention him in the two first letters he wrote me, but he has told me nothing about him since. The Monte Carlo Dawson was up at Oxford with us, but I had no idea that our man was his brother. I'll ask him about the place this afternoon, and no doubt he'll be able to tell me what I want to know.'

On returning to the Foreign Office, Algy took the opportunity to have a chat with Dawson about Monte Carlo. After several questions had been put and answered, Algy asked casually :

'Have you heard from your brother lately ?'

'Not me,' said Dawson. 'Arthur hardly ever writes nowadays. He is always in those cursed gambling-rooms, and then sits up half the night working out systems and combinations. That sort of thing leaves him no time for letter-writing. He used to be such a good fellow till he suddenly conceived this passion for play ; but now he seems quite lost to his family and friends. I really don't know how much he has lost, for gamblers never tell, but I'm afraid it must be the best part of his fortune, poor chap! However, that reminds me to write to him again, and have another try at wrenching a letter out of him. We are all awfully sorry for him. It can't be a happy life he is leading, even if he wins, and I hear that he's altered terribly lately.'

In pursuance of his resolve, Dawson wrote to his brother at Monte Carlo, and in due course received the following answer :

' DEAR FRED,

' I was so very glad to hear from you that I feel a brute for not writing oftener myself. But you know what my life is, or, rather, what I have chosen to make it for myself. The morning is the only time I have free, and then I go out for a bit of a walk to get some fresh air, and thus I have got quite out of the way of letter-writing. I am working out some very good systems which I hope will turn out successful, though, of course, one must have a certain amount of luck, and mine has been rather bad lately. However, my bad luck is not to be compared with that of Everard Somerville. Do you know him ? He was at the 'Varsity with me, and has a twin brother in the F O., who is no doubt a friend of yours, if he is as good a fellow as he was up at Oxford. It is very much on my conscience that I encouraged him to play, though I'm bound to say he took to it like a duck to water, and now there is no stopping him. At first he was contented with winning or losing a few louis ; but now he continually goes the maximum, and nearly always loses.

He must have dropped several thousands in the month he has been here, for the weather set in rainy a few days after he arrived, and as he had been warned never to get wet, he was naturally bored to death indoors, with the result that he took to play, and very soon got the needle. To show what there is in luck: there is a German Baron here who *can't lose!* He has no system of any kind, but simply shoves the money on anyhow, and up comes his number in a way that is little short of disgusting. He is supposed to have won 200,000 francs in the last three days. Well, I'll stop now. I find this letter is all about gambling; but, as you know, I have nothing else to write about. Perhaps you had better say nothing to your Somerville as to what his brother is doing, or, at all events, sound him first, and see how much he knows. Good-bye, old chap.

' Your affectionate brother,

' ARTHUR.'

A few days later it fell to Algy's lot at a dinner-party to take in a young lady of the well-known arch and gossiping type, and after the usual common-places she asked him if he had ever been to Monte Carlo. Algy was on the *qui vive* in a moment.

' No,' he answered ; ' but I am interested in the place because I have a brother there now. He has had inflammation of the lungs, and has been sent out there to get all right, you know.'

The gushing young lady looked at her neighbour's card, and saw the name of Somerville.

'Oh, Mr. Somerville! I'm sorry to say I did not catch your name at first. You know how hostesses mumble when they introduce people to one another; and they are often so nervous themselves that they could hardly give their own name at a moment's notice. Of course, I know all about your brother; he is rather a naughty young man, I'm afraid, and a dreadful gambler, isn't he? My friend Miss Elliot, who writes to me about twice a week, tells me that he is one of the highest players at Monte Carlo, and that he looks *so* white and careworn. You must get him home, and well—he! he !— perhaps administer corporal punishment, as I am told he is very young—he! he! he!'

Algy shuddered.

'*Impossible!* Evy talked of as a gambler, and I know nothing about it? Quite impossible. Anyway, I'll make it my business to find out who says so, and cram the lie down his throat. Everybody has got some friend, or at all events some acquaintance, on the Riviera just now, and in a limited space like that everything is more or less public property. I wish I was not so nervous about the matter myself; this infernal story seems to give substance to the doubt which has been floating about in my head as to there being *something* wrong with Evy. He doesn't write so often as he used to, and his letters seems constrained nowadays, and as if written with an effort ; now I come to think of it, the only thing that seems to interest him is the play at the Casino, and who wins or who loses. However, I dare say that in an atmosphere of play everyone writes like that. So I won't convert poor Evy's molehill into a silly girl's mountain. Still, *par acquit de conscience*, I'll draw Brown's later on for someone who can tell me whether there is any foundation for this report.'

'Hulloa, Algy !' cries a voice, as he enters the smoking-room of the above-mentioned club the same night. 'You haven't been here for ages ; we thought you had got too serious to drop in here of an evening.'

'Well, I'm pretty busy,' laughs Algy ; 'got to learn my trade, you know. At the Foreign Office, however, I'm getting on all right and they allow me out now and then. What's the news ?'

'Lots of news,' says a callow youth with more conversation than moustache. 'Poor old Burrowes —who, in parenthesis, is only twenty-five—has broken his leg with the Cottesmore ; Mrs. Reynolds has bolted with Jack Beauchamp ; Alec Smythe has been made a bankrupt, and—oh yes, last but not least, your brother has broken the bank at Monte Carlo ; no, I mean it's broken him. Have a drink ?'

Algy hesitates ; his vague suspicions as to there being something wrong seem about to be confirmed, and he must try to find out what really is the truth.

Like the astute plover, who flies far from her nest
in order to mislead the would-be robbers of her eggs,
Algy commences by feigning intense interest in the
matrimonial and monetary affairs of Mrs. Reynolds
and Alec Smythe, neither of whom he even knows
by name ; and having received as many uninteresting details as his patience will endure, he turns
abruptly to his companion, and says :

' Now, what's this gossip about my brother, and
who told you ?'

' Oh, I often get letters from Monte Carlo from
people of both sexes, and they are always full of
gossip ; I really couldn't tell you who wrote me this
particular item, which I dare say isn't true.   People
get so mixed up in those sort of places, dontcher-
know.'

' Yes, that's it, I expect,' says Algy ; ' they have
probably tacked somebody else's good or bad luck
on to my brother.   Well, I'm off; good-night,
you fellows ;' saying which he strolls leisurely
out of the club, looking as unconcerned as he
can.

Once outside, Algy drove straight home to St.
James's Place, for he felt that he had heard enough
from outsiders, and must now tell Evy of the gossip
that was going about concerning him, and ask him
if there was any truth in the report that he had lost
a lot of money.   But, oh, to think that there should
be any concealment between them, and that comparative strangers should be able to tell him any-

thing concerning his brother that he did not already know !

As Algy sat in his arm-chair before the fire with an unlighted cigarette between his fingers, he began to make excuses for Evy: ' Supposing the thing to be true, poor old boy !' he mused ; ' of course, he is bored to death there on wet days, and if he has lost more money than is wise, he doesn't want to worry me about his troubles, knowing that I can't put my hand on his shoulder and say to him, " Don't chuck away any more money, old boy ; if you do, you'll be riding cab-horses next winter instead of the best hunters in England, as you deserve," or something of that sort.  I know that if I did so he would stop playing immediately ; but Evy has one fault—he is *weak*, and may easily be led into doing things which he himself doesn't approve of.  I must look at his last two letters again, and see if I can read anything between the lines.'

This Algy accordingly did, and although he found nothing in Evy's letters to enlighten him in any way, he felt instinctively that there was a certain amount of restraint about them, whilst he could not help reflecting how few letters had passed between them both.

' I don't know what Evy's epistles ought to be like, for this is almost our first separation, and,' added Algy to himself as he turned into bed, ' I will not imagine evils which probably do not exist. What is more, I won't listen to any further gossip about Evy, but I'll just write to him to-morrow and chaff him about breaking the bank or getting broke, and then see what he says.'

With this wise resolve Algy switched off the electric light, and five minutes later was fast asleep.

# CHAPTER IX.

## TOGETHER AND YET APART.

'MONTE CARLO,
'*February* 18.

'MY DEAR ALGY,

'How could you listen to such rot? Of course, I've played a bit when the weather has been bad, but as to " breaking the bank or getting broke," I've not been near either, and least of all the former. How should people know what one is doing? The players have their own game to attend to, and the lookers-on watch for a short time and then move on to some other table; meanwhile, having seen me or anyone else win a large stake, they immediately jump to the conclusion that we have either won a fortune or lost one.

'I don't see myself riding that cab-horse you speak of in your letter yet; however, I have decided to go home, or, rather, to London, in a fortnight, for I am tired of this place and awfully home-sick. The doctor tells me that I am virtually all right now, and that, if I don't hunt or get wet in England, there is no reason why I should stop on here; so I have decided on London, as that will keep me out of the temptations of Huntingford.  Engage a bedroom for me in your diggings, and we can either stop there altogether or look for something else.  The Grevilles and the Arnolds are here, and we have all been over to Cannes and Nice to play golf,' etc.

'Thank Heaven!' said the unsuspecting Algy, with a sigh of relief.  'I ought to have known that there was nothing to worry about.'

And with a light heart he settled down to his work, which was beginning to interest him more and more every day.

The fortnight soon passed, and Algy might be seen walking up and down the platform of Victoria Station at least half an hour before the Continental train could possibly be expected to arrive.  When it steams into the station only ten minutes late, Algy feels as if he had been waiting for hours.  The meeting, however, between the brothers is of the orthodox British type, and they betray none of the emotion which is in their hearts—just a strong clasp of the hand and a 'How are you, old chap?'  'Here I am again; let's go and look after the luggage.'

This is all that passes between the twins on the platform, but once alone in the hansom, with Patterson and the luggage following, they exclaim simultaneously:

'It *is* good to be together again!'

On arriving at St. James's Place, Algy leads his brother to the light and says :

'Now let's have a good look at you, Evy, and see if you are as fit as you say.'

'That's hardly fair,' retorts Evy, drawing away from the tell-tale glare. 'Remember, I have come straight through from Monte Carlo, and, as I can't sleep much in a train, I'm a bit done up; you shall run me up and down to-morrow, and then I hope you'll be satisfied.'

The wish is father to the thought, for Evy knows full well that his brother's loving eye will detect certain infinitesimal lines in his forehead, caused by the puckering of the brow when anxiety and excitement have held their sway over him during the past few weeks.

Late in the morning following his arrival Evy rings and asks for Algy, but is handed a note from him in which Algy says that, as the Department is short-handed, he has been obliged to go off to the Foreign Office early; that he will be back at about 2 p.m., and begs Evy to remain quietly in bed in order to 'pick up' after his long journey.

Does this come as a relief to Evy? Indeed, it would seem so, for his countenance clears after reading his brother's note, as if an evil moment had been postponed.

'How can I face such a good, honest nature as Algy's with something I am ashamed of to conceal?' groans Evy, as he turns round in bed and tries to

forget his troubles in sleep.  This relief, however, is
denied him, for Algy's simple trust only serves to
accentuate the weakness and folly of his actions
during his sojourn at Monte Carlo.  These have been
very disastrous, and, which makes matters worse, of
the £15,000 which Evy has lost, a little more than half
has been borrowed from a money-lender, Evy being
ashamed to draw such a large sum from his Bank,
whose senior partner had been one of his father's
oldest friends, and as such had given the twins much
friendly advice concerning their investments and the
management of the property.

'Hang it all!' thinks poor Evy, writhing in his
bed, 'I couldn't face old Chalmers with such a lump as
that against my account; I'll own up to the £7,000,
and try to get the rest back before it has to be paid:
luck must turn; it always does—everyone says so—
and I'm not going to be down-hearted.'  Saying
which, Evy rings for Patterson to prepare his bath,
and is soon ready to undergo examination by Algy.

When the latter comes home, he finds Evy sitting
in an armchair near one of the windows, the blind
of which is half drawn down; and as Algy comes
into the room Evy jumps up, seizes his hand, and
says:

'I didn't know how good it was to come home;
I've been watching the clock for the last hour, and
thought you had forgotten your promise.  Why
can't we always be together? and why haven't you
been with me all this time?  Confound that Foreign

Office which separates us! But tell me: do you really like the work, Algy? Does it make up to you for the loss of hunting and my society?' asks Evy wistfully.

'I am quite contented with my life, and I propose next year, if you are fit and well, to take my leave in the winter, so that we can have lots of hunting together. I could not live without an object of some sort, and my present ambition is to be Secretary for Foreign Affairs some day—"how's that for high?" as the Americans say. And now I am going to "vet" you in broad daylight, as per agreement last night.'

Algy proceeds to run his hand down Evy's legs as if he were a horse.

'Hum! plenty of bone, but not much muscle there; arms flabby. I suppose you didn't take much exercise?'

'No, that's just it,' replied Evy, taking advantage of the loophole offered him. 'You see, I was told to stroll about, and not tire myself, so I got into the way of loafing about, and     I don't think the place agreed with me—barring the lungs, of course. You see, I'm used to a lot of fresh air and hard exercise, and I didn't get much of either there, and so     and so     Perhaps you will think I am looking seedy, but really I am all right, and I mean to go in for some mild gymnastics under cover, so as to get back my muscle.'

Algy takes his brother by the shoulders and turns

him to the light, and the dreaded moment—hitherto deferred—has arrived.

'Why, Evy, you've got crow's-feet and a line in the middle of your forehead!' exclaims Algy, aghast at the discovery.

'Of course I have ; you don't expect a fellow to have a serious illness and be sent abroad, and then have nothing to show for it, do you ? I'm rather proud of those lines, though it takes a microscope— or your eyes—to see them. Everybody told me when I left Monte Carlo how fit I was looking. Don't let's talk any more about my health, for I'm sick of it ; let's talk about our plans. What about rooms? These seem very nice, and my bedroom is most com- fortable. Suppose we stop where we are ?'

'Yes, that would be all right,' replied Algy ; 'but, you see, there is no other sitting-room vacant in the house, and of course you must have your own. I do a lot of writing here, so I must have this large table, and there isn't room for another ; the room is altogether too small, and you wouldn't be comfort- able. No, I have heard of some very nice rooms in Bury Street that I think would just suit us : bed- room and sitting - room for me, bed and dressing room, with a sitting-room, for you—you know you can't do without a dressing-room—and a bath-room between us.'

'Yes, but what's the damage ?' asks Evy, turning his back and looking out of the window.

'Goodness me ! I don't know. I only just looked

at the rooms and thought them nice, but I didn't ask the price, and I dare say they are pretty expensive.'

' Well, as I said before, suppose we stop here ; my bedroom is large, and I can have a writing-table put into it if I want one, although I write nearly all my letters at the club ; it will save us half the money.'

' Fancy you thinking about money, Evy ! Why, this is something quite new !'

' Oh, I don't see the use of chucking it away. We may want it some day—who knows ? Anyhow, I have taken a fancy to these rooms, so do let us stop here—for the present, at any rate.'

' Of course we will, as you like 'em, Evy, so that's settled. Now I must be off. Suppose you go across to Bubb's and get two stalls for Wyndham's new piece, which I hear is very good ? We might dine together at Willis's and have a real good talk over all you have been doing since we parted ; for you know, Evy,' he adds, ' your letters after the first week or so did not tell me much about your life out there.'

' Hum, no, I suppose they didn't ; but you know I never was much of a scribe, and what little I had to write about wouldn't have interested you, for the life was so different to what you and I have been accustomed to. Let's begin where we left off, or, rather, let's begin our London life together ; you will keep me straight, and not let me make an ass of myself if I come across any high play ; it is no use denying

5

that I *am* a little bit of a gambler, and, with nothing else to do at Monte Carlo, I dropped a bit more than I meant to. But that's all past and gone.

'Yes, and to think,' says the loyal Algy indignantly, 'that people said you had lost thousands!'

Evy seems to have some difficulty in lighting his cigarette, as he again turns to the window and says:

'I vote we dine quietly at the 'Varsity Club instead of Willis's Rooms, and I'll go to the Criterion and get the tickets; saves three bob,' he adds nervously.

'All right; I hope this economical fit will last, Evy, in which case you and I will soon be millionaires; I expect you are thinking of those cab-horses I prophesied you would have to ride next year.'

'Ye-yes, that's about it,' replied Evy; 'I do want to have none but first-class hunters when I get back to work; that beast C.B. cost me too much.—More, I hope, than you will ever know,' he thinks to himself, adding: 'Well, old chap, we will meet here to-night about dressing-time. I only wish I had such a sensible occupation as you have, for now you are going off I shan't know what to do with myself all day; one feels such a "loafer" without an object in view. To-morrow, for instance, except to see your cheery face, and to feel I am at home again, what am I to do till dinner-time? I shall miss the sunshine and the excitement of the Casino, and you will be at work all day. Can't you suggest any occupation for me?'

'We'll see about that when to-morrow comes,' laughs Algy; 'and meanwhile you *are* at home again, and that's enough to send me off happy—so long.'

# CHAPTER X.

## 'LE JEU EST FAIT'

'WHAT is the matter with Evy?' Algy asks himself, as he sits down to his solitary breakfast a few days after his brother's arrival; 'he used to be the first up in the morning, and to interest himself in everything that was going on around him; but now I can never see him before my time for going out, and Patterson invariably says that he has had a bad night and is asleep. He *is* changed, and I can't tell why.'

'Well, Evy,' says his brother as they meet for the first time at the club, where they are dining, Evy having dressed there, 'what have you been doing with yourself? As for me, I have only just got away from the F O., for the row in the East has kept us ciphering and deciphering all day.'

'I?' replies Evy. 'Oh, I met some fellows who were going to play poker, and joined them, and there I've been all day. It is rather an idiotic game, and to sit in a stuffy room for several hours, when you are supposed to be recruiting your health, is still more idiotic. I think I shall go to Ostend or Spa next week and get some fresh air.'

'Ostend or Spa!' exclaims Algy, surprised. 'I thought you had enough and to spare of foreign parts when you left Monte Carlo; why on earth do you want to go abroad again so soon?'

'Really, I hardly know why,' replied Evy; 'but I certainly feel very restless. You see, I can't hunt, so what am I do, kicking my heels in London, and playing poker with those chaps who know a deuced sight more about the game than I do? I should have a much better chance at Ostend or Spa, and lead a healthier life.'

'A much better chance of what?' asks Evy. 'Ostend is a summer bathing-place, isn't it? And Spa—where is Spa?'

'Poor innocent!' thinks Evy. 'How can I deceive him so? Sometimes I feel as if I *must* tell him the truth; and yet the sacrifice of his good opinion would be too bitter—more bitter to him, perhaps, even than to me. No; I must get back the money first, so as to be able to look him in the face. In a new place the luck often turns, and Ostend may revenge me for Monte Carlo; if it does not, I will go straight on to Spa. Fancy dropping £2,000 more here! My luck is infernal, and no mistake. However, there is no use in thinking about it more than I can help, and I am not going to worry my dear old Algy, for he is full of his work, and will never even suspect that I am going off to gamble. How contemptible I feel! How infinitely superior he is to me in every respect! Yet, if I were to tell him of my growing weakness, how tender and compassionate he would be! But I cannot do it—I cannot! Let me only get back my losses, and then I'll swear off play for ever and ever.'

Alas! how many gamblers have made that vow and broken it! What is this fascination of play that consumes some people and leaves others cold? Any public table will supply the illustration of both styles of player; for here you have a millionaire who, trembling in every limb, puts on a stake that certainly does not represent more than the cost of his dinner every day; whereas the man alongside him—perhaps a young Government clerk—sees half his year's salary disappear upon one coup with an impassibility as complete as that of the croupier who rakes it in.

Having made up his mind, Evy told Patterson to pack his things, and the very next evening saw him at Ostend, sitting at the fatal green table and listening to the click of the roulette ball—arbiter of so many destinies. But luck was worse here, if possible, than at Monte Carlo, and, after fighting for ten days, Evy moved on to Spa, where, to his intense relief, matters improved, and he was, at all events, sometimes a winner. Consequently he wrote in enthusiastic terms to Algy of the beauty of the place, even in winter, of the purity of the air, and of the comfort of the Hôtel d'Orange, and added that, as he already felt so much better, he should stop on a bit.

Algy, rejoicing in the altered tone of his brother's letters, of course urged him to remain where he was; and another week passed, during which luck continued in Evy's favour. One morning, however, Evy received a letter from his brother's greatest friend, Lord Clement Armytage, who, while having a sincere liking for Evy, had been able to discern the exceptional qualities of Algy's character and mind, and had taken him as a model for himself in all things.

'DEAR EVY' (wrote Lord Clement),
'I have bad news for you, though nothing, on my honour, that need alarm you. Algy had a bad spill yesterday out hunting, and has broken his right arm—only a simple fracture, and the arm has been satisfactorily set—so that it is a mere question of time for him to be about again. But the poor old chap frets dreadfully at his work being stopped, so I went down to the Foreign Office, where, as you know, my father is a *persona gratissima*, and told them what had happened and how distressed Algy was at his work being for a time thrown upon the shoulders of some-one else, who might thereby be unable to take his leave when he wanted it.
'You never saw anything so touching as the way the fellows clustered round me, all saying at once: "I'll do his work: blow the leave! Tell him not to bother about that." It was easy to see that he was one of the most popular men in the Office, which will

not surprise you any more than it did me. So that's all right.

'But the first thing Algy said to me, when I went to see him after his accident, was, "Write to Evy, for he will be expecting a letter from me; but tell him that my accident is nothing, and that he is on no account to leave Spa, which is doing him a lot of good,' etc.

Hard as it is for a gambler to turn his back upon good fortune, it never occurred to Evy even to hesitate, and Patterson, that lightning packer, having enabled him to get off by the night boat from Ostend, he arrived in St. James's Place the following morning.

'Well, Algy,' he said, as he grasped his brother's left hand warmly, 'it wasn't C.B., late "the new horse," that put you down; what brute was it?'

'No, not one of our lot,' replied Algy; 'they're none of them fit to go—all laid up—though Freeman begged hard to keep the Steamer and Practitioner fit, in case I could get a day now and then from town. However, I had made up my mind that it was safer not to be tempted, when Georgie Everitt came one day and persuaded me to have a gallop with the Windsor drag. He mounted me on his best horse— a real good one he was too; but the fence that put me down was hardly fair, and I came across an almost unjumpable part of it. Any way, down we came, but I had cut out the work until then, that's one consolation. Indeed, if it wasn't that I ought to be in Downing Street, I should not mind being laid up for a bit,

as it has brought you back to me. But how about
Spa as a "health resort"? You don't look to me
very fit, though your letters were so cheery.'

'It was ever so much better than Monte Carlo—at
least, I *felt* ever so much better,' replied Evy, pulling
himself up short; 'beautiful air, you know, early
hours and just a little mild play at the Cercle des
Étrangers to enliven the evenings.'

Algy gave a little shudder. Was it possible that
Evy had gone there to continue his high play? No,
the thought did his brother injustice; play was only
a slight incident in Evy's life.

'Well,' he asked, 'were you more lucky than at
Monte Carlo? It must be such a bore to play and
always lose.'

'Yes; I had very fair luck, and altogether enjoyed
myself. Spa is a nice quiet little place; and as I
found a few people I knew, and made some acquaintances among the foreigners—notably two Russians
and a Frenchman, awfully good chaps—I had a
pleasant time. I shall go back there as soon as I have
seen you on your legs again. No offence—I mean
arms.'

All details of the day with the drag and the manner
of Algy's accident having been given, Evy began to
fidget.

'Of course,' he said, 'we can dine together here
somehow, and as I suppose you have to turn in early,
I will look in at the club, after you are tucked up,
to hear what is going on. Meanwhile I'll have a

bath and change my clothes. Have you got lots of books?'

'Oh yes, lots ; and Clement Armytage is coming to play piquet with me—an awful excitement for an invalid ! He won seventeen and six from me yesterday, which was taking a mean advantage of a man when he's down.'

'My God !' thought Evy, 'if he only knew ! But he never shall know until I am on my death-bed, for I feel that I shall ruin myself. What gambler can be more helpless, a more certain victim, than I have shown myself? With luck against me, it can only end one way. Not suicide—no ! I should never be coward enough for that, and I'll see this thing out to the bitter end.'

Everything went well with Algy's arm, for his fine constitution, his temperate life, and last, not least, his optimistic view of everything, made his severe accident as light as it could be.

'Oh, I am getting on first-rate !' was his invariable answer to the many friends and acquaintances who came to see him—no one who had been much in Algy's company could help loving him—and they came in shoals.

Cough, cough, cough ! One morning Evy came into his brother's room, saying :

'What a climate ! I have only been here a week, and I feel as if it had undone the good of months. I have a lump of lead on my chest, and cannot breathe when I wake in the morning. I think I shall go back

to Spa, where I felt so well : and, as you are so nearly
all right and can get about with your arm in a sling,
perhaps I ought to look after my own ailments, if we
are ever to have a real good hunting season together.
That's the one thing,' he added, ' that I do honestly
look forward to.'

' Off you go to-morrow, old chap ! Patterson's
used to that sort of thing by this time ; and I will
join you in a week or so, for I shall get a few days'
leave as soon as I am out of the doctor's hands.
That wondrous air you write of from Spa will turn
them to good account for me too.'

' N—o, don't do that,' said Evy nervously ; ' it is a
dull little place at this time of the year, and as soon
as you are fit to move I will come back to you, and
we can go to Brighton or Margate, or any one of
those places where people are sent to recruit. Spa is
a long way off, and I don't quite know what you
would do when you got there.'

' Very much the same as you do, I suppose,'
rejoined Algy, smiling.

' God forbid !' thought Evy ; ' not that there is any
danger of that, unless he changes, as quickly as I
did, from a good sportsman, who loves fresh air and
wholesome amusements, to a confirmed gambler,
living in a fetid atmosphere, moral and physical, and
only just awake to the degradation of it. No ! I
don't see Algy descending so low as that, and, as
long as I can keep it from him, he shall not know the
level to which I have sunk ; and yet, ashamed as I

am of the life, I do look forward to that green table. The magic words "Le jeu est fait" are as music to my ears, and I shall never again be able to rest quiet in any place where they are not heard. Not until,' he added grimly—' not until my own "Rien ne va plus" is spoken.'

# CHAPTER XI.

WE can now pass over several months in the life of the twin brothers. Evy went back to Spa, where his luck was certainly much better than at Monte Carlo, and he became more than ever infatuated with the delight of play. According to promise, however, he returned to London as soon as Algy was able to move, and together they went to Brighton, from which place, after a week of it, they went to stay with a friend of theirs, who had recently accepted the mastership of a subscription pack in a poor but sporting country. The first day on the flags, the inspection of the young entry, the daily visit to the stables, all had a wholesome effect upon Evy, who for the time being almost forgot his preoccupations in the pleasure of finding himself once more in an atmosphere of hunting.

But after a few days given to convalescence Algy had to return to his work, and Evy therefore found himself once more on his beam ends in London, where the illicit baccarat—to say nothing of écarté at a high-play club of which he became a member—claimed him once more for their own, and luck was once more dead against him.

Late in August Algy was able to get a well-earned holiday, and they betook themselves to a grouse moor, which for the last three years they had shared with two college friends, and there they remained until the end of September, by which time Algy's leave was up.

'What am I going to do now with myself?' asked Evy, the morning after their arrival in St. James's Place.

'Why, go home, of course, and see how Freeman and the horses are getting on. No doubt I shall be able to take a day now and then; but in any case you will write to me about your sport, and I shall follow you in spirit over every fence, always excepting the Fordham Brook upon C.B. I draw the line at that,' said Algy, laughing.

But Evy yawns. 'I don't see the fun,' he rejoined, 'of hunting without you; and, moreover, the doctors tell me that I must be very careful at the beginning of the winter, so I think I shall be off South somewhere—anywhere—and come back in February, when perhaps you will be able to get away.'

Still is Algy unsuspecting.

'Not a bad idea,' he said. 'Besides, you can go to Pau or to Rome, for there's hunting of a sort at both places—good enough, at any rate, to condition you for Huntingford and the Vale in February.'

'Well, any place will do where one can see the sun; but I think I shall start with Nice, where the Maxwells go next week, and there I can think about where to go next.'

'Nice? That's all right,' said Algy to himself, forgetting for the moment its proximity to Monte Carlo; for the steady-going Mr. and Mrs. Maxwell were about the last people one could associate with the idea of a pilgrimage to that Mecca of gamblers.

'Eight o'clock, sir, and it's raining, so we shall have a smooth passage after all this wind,' said Patterson, as he called his master two days later in time to catch the morning express to Paris.

'*Eight o'clock, and it's raining,*' thought Evy. 'How well I remember those very words as Patterson called me on the ill-fated day when I was obstinate about riding that new horse who half drowned me, and drove me to Monte Carlo in consequence! Yet why blame the poor brute? It was Kismet, and had to come sooner or later. I wonder whether there are many men who despise themselves as much as I do myself now, when every hour that separates me from the game seems to me as long as a day? Still, this time I will use every rag of resolution I have got left to stop short at Nice, so as not to be led into the daily and hourly temptation which assails one if one lives at Monte Carlo.'

Three days later he wrote announcing his arrival, and his delight at the climate and the beauty of the country round Nice. Alas! the beauty of the sur-

rounding country soon resolved itself for Evy into
the road to Monte Carlo, whither he went regularly
every day, returning at night to Nice, and dating his
letters to Algy from that place. Hogarth's well-
known pictures have shown us what such a life as
this may lead to, and we will pass over the details of
Evy's fall.

His letters to Algy got fewer and the intervals
between them longer, and one day early in February
the latter received a telegram worded :

'Coming home on Tuesday ; meet me Victoria at
4.30.'

What could it mean ?  He had given no previous
intimation that he might return suddenly ; nevertheless, unexpected as it was, Algy was delighted at his
return, and, as was his usual practice when going to
meet Evy, found himself on the station platform long
before the train was due.

But, oh, the difference this time in the appearance
of the beloved brother as he dragged himself out of
the carriage and stretched out a feeble hand to Algy !
Can this be indeed Evy ?  The bent back, the halting
footsteps, are those of an old man !

While Evy was fumbling for his ticket, Algy
managed to take Patterson on one side, and said
to him reproachfully :

' Why did you not write to me ?'

' Mr. Evy made me swear not to let you know,'
answered Patterson, speaking low and very fast,

' upon pain of instant dismissal ; and I could not
leave him alone there. I *had* to swear to be silent.
The truth is that he has ruined himself, and you, sir,
as well ; and it has broken his heart. Don't ask me
any more, Mr. Algy ; he will have to tell you himself.
And he is ill, sir—very ill—but not so much in body
as in mind. Coming, sir! I will see to the luggage.
Here are your rugs ; please put one over you in the
brougham. This is not the South of France, sir,
remember,' he added, as cheerfully as he could, but
with his eyes full of tears, which he brushed hastily
away as he walked up the platform.

Algy was mute, struck dumb by what he heard
and saw ; but he grasped his brother's wasted hand.
In the brougham he said, tentatively :

' I am afraid the long journey has knocked you
up.'

' Yes,' replied Evy, ' and I feel dreadfully seedy.
If you don't mind, I think I would rather not talk
until we get home, and I've pulled myself together a
bit ;' and so they remained until the brougham pulled
up at the door of the St. James's Place rooms. Evy
tottered into the sitting-room, sank into an armchair,
and closed his eyes ; while Algy watched him with
a look of agony upon his face which he felt that he
would presently have to conceal.

After a few minutes, during which Evy's brow con-
tracted painfully, he opened his eyes ; stretching out
his hand and convulsively grasping that of Algy, he
moaned rather than said :

6

'It must come out; let me tell you at once : I am ruined, and Huntingford is gone! I have sold my birthright and, what is worse, yours.'

His head dropped into his feeble white hands, and he burst into tears.

The unexpected shock was so great that it took Algy a few seconds to recover himself, but only a very few. He felt nothing but pity and love for the stricken soul wailing out its anguish before him ; and, kneeling beside his brother, he took Evy's two hands into his own and, bending his bright curly head over them, sobbed out :

'It is all my fault—all mine, dearest Evy! You entreated me not to leave you. Brothers like us cannot live apart from one another, and if we were separated, you said, harm would come of it! If harm has come, it is through my selfishness in obstinately following my own wishes. But never mind,' he continued : 'somehow or other we will get the old house back—Huntingford is not every one's place, and the man who has bought it may be ready to sell it again soon. Don't you see us sitting there again, one on each side of the fire, with a bottle of port between us, and probably our feet in gouty shoes, fighting our battles over again and again ? Cheer up, Evy; "plaie d'argent n'est pas mortelle," and we have got one another.'

Evy looked up with a wan smile, which would have made an angel weep.

'Did Heaven ever create another such good fellow

as you are ?   Not one word of reproach !   D——n it !'
he said, ' not one thought of yourself; there is no one
like you !   But it is too late ; the blow that has fallen
on me is one from which one cannot rise.   My
strength and my health are gone.   I have made a
mess of my life, and even your love cannot keep me
alive much longer.'

The next few days were sad indeed.   The doctor
was called in, examined Evy carefully, but shook his
head and said he would like to have another opinion
—ominous words.   Then the specialist consulted
gave it as his belief that, although both Evy's lungs
were more or less affected, the principal danger lay
in the want of vitality, and in the absence, apparently,
of any wish to recover.   This made the case one of
grave anxiety.

By degrees Evy told Algy of all that had passed
since they first were separated—of his temptations,
his weakness, and his fall, until finally, rendered
desperate by bad luck, and being convinced that it
must turn, he delivered himself over to a foreign
money-lender, taking little or no account of the sums
borrowed, as he became more and more reckless and
bad luck pursued him ever more relentlessly.

Poor Algy !   What can he think of this madness,
which has robbed them of their home and will cost
Evy his life ?   His loyal nature is subjected to a
severe strain ; but he never falters, and his tender
love is ever on the alert to soften, so far as it can be
softened, Evy's passionate remorse.   The doctors,

however, make no secret of their opinion that, short
of a miracle, Evy's time is short upon earth, and, as
the days drag on, ' No improvement ' is their invariable verdict.   The patient gets weaker and weaker.
' No vitality,' say the doctors—' no effort to fight
the disease ;' and so it is : the broken-hearted man is
simply going under.

One morning, however, Evy mustered up his remaining strength, and, calling Algy to his bedside,
he said to him, very solemnly, and in a voice which,
feeble at first, gathered strength as he continued, from
the fervour which supported him :

' You know my life, and this last fatal year—all of
it.   I have played and I have lost, but—remember
this—others have made fortunes at play ; I have seen
them do it.   And I implore you to try your luck as
against mine.   Do not think that this is sentiment
gone mad, and that I want you, like the Corsican
brother, to avenge my memory.   Look at the question practically ; it is the only chance you have of
recovering Huntingford.   How thankful I am now
that I settled that £15,000 upon you, just to give
you pocket-money !   Do you remember how you
jibbed at it, and said that, as I paid all the house
expenses, it was absurd to put down a big lump sum
for you.   Thank Heaven, I insisted on doing it ; for
that money I have not been able to touch.   It is
yours, and you may turn it into millions.   Millions !'
he repeated, sitting upright and his eyes flashing.
' Do you hear, Algy ?—*millions !*   The German

Baron only began with a capital of £4,000, and I
hardly ever saw him lose. Yet he had no system,
any more than I had. It was all luck. And why
should not you have luck? Oh, Algy, *promise* me
you will try; it is the last thing I shall ask of you in
this world—don't refuse me.'

His pleading eyes rested anxiously upon his
brother's face. It was hard for Algy to say 'yes' to
a thing so utterly opposed to his nature and character, but it was still more hard to refuse his dying
brother's last request.

He modified his consent, however, by asking:

'How long must I give to it? What is to end the
trial?'

'Two things,' rejoined Evy promptly. 'I have
thought it all out. Start with Spa, and give that
three months; then go to Monte Carlo, and stay there
three months. Do the same the following year; and
if after that you have not won, well, I should like
you to begin again. But here is the second clause:
Should you, in the meantime, find a good and true
woman whom you love, and who loves you, she will
naturally object to the life for you. If so, *chuck* it.
So far, it is true, we have neither found nor looked
for a woman whom we could wish to marry. Country
life, with its sports, engrossed us both. After that,
for me, came my accursed gambling, and for you the
care of a career so full of promise. But you are
young, and, after the shock of losing me, some woman
may step in to take my place in your affection.'

Algy raised his hand in mute deprecation.

'Yes,' resumed Evy ; 'it is the law of Nature, and I pray that it may be so with you. Therefore, whether or not you have been successful at play, if true love comes to you, hail it with open arms, and with all the pent-up strength of your heart, even if a cottage is the only temple you can raise to it. Ah, Algy ! to think that I should lie here, dictating to you—to you, so much wiser than I am, and who have always been the Mentor ! But promise,' he adds, the fictitious strength which had supported him through this last appeal to his brother rapidly leaving him— '*promise* that you will at once try to avenge my ill luck, and to recover what in my madness I threw away. *Promise !*'

A fit of coughing stopped his further utterance, but he stretched out his hand, which Algy held, while he solemnly repeated after Evy :

' I promise !'

Two days more of growing weakness and the doctor said, on leaving the house at ten o'clock at night :

' Stay with your brother, Mr. Somerville. It will soon be over, and you two must be alone when the end comes. I can do nothing more ; but there will be no suffering, and, although his pulse has nearly stopped, he will be conscious for a few hours longer. God bless you and support you !'

Algy remained sitting by the bedside of his dying brother, hardly even now able to realize that they were soon to be separated for ever in this world. The clock ticked on, the noises in the street continued, but he heard nothing. His head was buried in his hands, except when he raised it to look at the ashen face upon the pillow, with its closed eyes, and listened to the laboured breathing, which fluttered and became more and more feeble. At last—he is but young, and is unaccustomed to grief—he flung himself on the floor and gave way to his terrible anguish in loud sobs. The noise roused Evy, who, only partially conscious, but slightly raising himself in bed, looked at his brother.

'Hullo, Algy!' he said. 'Down again? That's three falls before sandwich-time! I believe I've been in a brook, too, I feel so queer and wet.' The dews of death were gathering on his forehead. 'Ah, I know—the new horse! Mason told me he wouldn't jump water—and then—and then something awful happened. I—forget what.'

Evy sank back on his pillow again unconscious. His brother knelt by his side and held the cold hands. Algy's spirit was in wild revolt against this cruel fate. He felt no resignation, no hope of a future meeting— nothing but blank despair.

Evy's dull eyes opened once more, and this time there was in them a look of complete consciousness.

'Good-bye, Algy dear,' he said. 'I feel that I am about to leave you, and I don't know where I am going; but wherever it is, I shall see no one I have loved as I love you. We have been all in all to one another ; but remember what I have said : the love of a good woman is even better than ours.   And try— try to get back the old home.   Good—bye.'

He gave a slight shiver.   There were a few more laboured breaths, and all was over.

# PART II

# CHAPTER I.

A DOCTOR'S carriage had just driven away from No. —, Upper Grosvenor Street. Entering the house, you would find in the library an elderly man, who, with his arms folded across his broad chest, fixes his eyes expectantly on the door. A young girl enters with an eager look upon her face, as if she had been waiting for news of more than ordinary importance.

As she is the heroine of this story, I ask permission to tell you at once that she is rather above the middle height, and admirably proportioned. Nowhere would you see freshness more complete, for it is the precious bloom of youth that has not known care. A bright, happy face indeed, with clear gray eyes and a laughing mouth. No room there for tragedy, you would say at first sight—hardly even earnestness enough to take life seriously. Wait to judge her until life *is* serious, for then the tender, sensitive lines lurking tremulously about that laughing mouth and on the broad brow will tell you more of her than you have seen now.

'Well, Hilda,' said her father, for such was the relationship between the man and the girl, 'thank God! the doctor takes a very favourable view of your mother's case. He says that, after a bad attack of this d——d—I beg your pardon—this infernal influenza, people are often left prostrate, and that all she wants is a bracing climate, with iron waters and baths. He recommends Spa, and that we should be off at once. I have decided, therefore, to start the day after to-morrow. How do you like the idea of this sudden move?'

If the face had been bright before, it was now brilliant sunshine.

'Oh, father, this is good news! Didn't I say that mother was not so ill as you both thought? I could not—perhaps because I would not—believe in danger for her. To look on her as an invalid would be too dreadful for me, for I don't seem to understand sorrow and sickness in a world that has been for me so full of happiness. Darling mother! won't we take care of her at—where did you say? Spa? In Germany, I suppose; all cures are in Germany, aren't they?'

'My dear child,' replied her father, 'how very ignorant you are in matters of ordinary knowledge!' Ordinary knowledge, however, he reflected, must cover a considerable area if it included the precise situation of a place so well hidden as little Spa.

Slightly shifting his ground, therefore, he continued : 'I suppose that, like most advanced young ladies, you have been so highly educated as not to know many simple things that a village school child is taught—such as the date of the battle of Waterloo or of the Crimean War. Now, tell me——'

'No, I can't, father. I don't know anything about those antiquated things, though no doubt I could puzzle you over plenty of subjects, as we were taught to call them at the High School. But meanwhile tell me where Spa is, and how we get there.'

'Well, Hilda, we shall have to cross the sea ; perhaps your High School condescended to teach you that England is an island ?'

'Father, don't be sarcastic ! Can't you see that I am brimming over with excitement at the idea of going abroad anywhere for the first time in my life ? I repeat, where *is* Spa ? But first I must go and see mother, to tell her how glad I am she isn't really very ill.'

Suiting the action to the word, she jumped up and ran to the door.

'My dear child,' said her father, 'how impetuous you are ! Do sit down again ; your mother is tired after her long interview with the doctor, and has, I hope, gone to sleep. Do remember that you are twenty, that you have had two seasons in London, and that you must not be so impetuous. You don't seem to be able to fix your attention on any one thing for two minutes at a time.'

'Oh yes, I can, father—on Spa at this very moment. Tell me all about it; begin like the guide-book.'

'I will,' replied her father, and in a pedantic voice he declaimed : 'Spa, the well-known watering-place, lies in a high valley of the Belgian Ardennes, and is three hours by rail from Brussels; its iron waters, the curative powers of which have been recognised for five hundred years, are said to have saved the life of Peter the Great, whose memory is still green in the town, as the principal Square bears the name of Pierre le Grand. Ahem! Do you happen to have heard of Peter the Great in the course of your studies ?'

'Oh, father, how you tease me! I believe I know all about What's-his-name. But tell me, what do people do at Spa, when they are not drinking the water ?'

'Well, there is racing and pigeon-shooting; but the public gambling is the principal attraction for a large proportion of the visitors.'

'Public gambling? How do you mean?' asked Hilda; 'do they play whist and bézique in the streets ? In front of the cafés, I suppose.'

'My dear child, you are too naïve! Do you really mean to tell me that you have never heard of gambling at Monte Carlo? Why, probably many of your partners spend a good deal of their time and more

of their money there. What do you talk to them
about in the intervals of dancing ?'

'Oh, they want to talk about all sorts of things,
but I never give them time. Dancing men are
scarce, and when I get hold of a good one I keep
him whirling round till he has not got much breath
left for talking. But I do remember one man saying
to me that he had been beaten twenty times running
on his pet Transvaal ! No, Transversale, it was ; I
thought he was saying something about reversing in
waltzing, and I told him I didn't like it because it
made me giddy. So he never asked me to dance with
him again. Afterwards a friend of his explained to
me that he had been talking about a game they
played at Monte Carlo, and that he said I was one
of the most ignorant girls he had ever met. I
thought that *was* hard, for I fancied I knew such a
lot.'

'Never mind all that now, Hilda,' said her father;
'pack up your trunks, and you will know all about
Spa and roulette in a few days.'

We can pass over the well-known journey from
London to Brussels, where Mrs. Brabazon, with
her husband and her daughter, halted for one
night before continuing the short journey to Spa,
where they arrived at 4.30 on a fine afternoon in
July.

Hilda had been in ecstasies over the lovely scenery
of forest and deep valley which meets the eye immediately after leaving Liége ; but Colonel Brabazon,

who had made that same journey at least a dozen
times, and was much interested in the book he was
reading, confined himself to saying that no doubt the
scenery was very pretty if the frequent tunnels
between Liége and Pepinster gave you a chance
of enjoying it consecutively, and did not cause
you to put down your book every minute and a
half.

' Pepinster !' shouted the Belgian guard as the train
steamed into that junction, and, knowing there was an
English family bound to disembark there from first-
class waggon No. 36, he threw open the door, saying,
' On change ici pour Spa, savez-vous ; le train se
trouve en face ;' and the famille Brabazon were pre-
cipitated on to the platform with their smaller goods
and chattels tumbling after them, for the German
express had no time to waste before the Douane halt
at Herbestahl, a little further on.

' Where is my large bag ?' said a feeble voice, as
Mrs. Brabazon, pale and languid, stepped from
waggon No. 36.

' And where are my rackets and the things I tied
up in my mackintosh ?' chimed in Hilda, as the train
steamed out of the station.

' And where is the luggage, sir ?' almost screamed
the truly English lady's-maid, who had never before
left her native land or her boxes, and could not be
made to understand that once registered, and the
ticket in reliable hands, there was no further respon-
sibility upon her, and that it would be a bad sign,

rather than a good one, if she ever saw her luggage again until she arrived at her destination. 'I saw them put down a ladder on a boat, and at Brussels you said it was all right, and that they were to be left at the station until the next morning, except the small black box with the things for the night; and I had my feet upon that in the omnibus,' she added triumphantly, 'for I have heard that foreign thieves will steal a thing from under your very eyes.'

Notwithstanding all these vicissitudes, our travellers were at last safely landed, luggage and all, at the Hôtel d'Orange, one of the best in Spa, and Hilda, wild with excitement, announced her intention of immediately flying to the gambling-rooms to see the wonderful game her father had told her of, but which, like the heathen Chinee, she did not understand. Her adoring father, who could refuse her nothing, was quite prepared to take her; but it was explained to him by the courteous and well-informed manager of the hotel that the Cercle des Étrangers was a club, and that, under the Belgian law affecting clubs where play takes place, all would-be members must be balloted for, and that this entailed a delay of five days.

To the impetuous Hilda five days seemed an eternity, and she was about to remonstrate with her father, when he said to her, somewhat severely:

'Please remember that you are an English girl abroad for the first time, and that you must not dis-

pute the rule laid down by the authorities of the
country in which you happen to be.'

Hilda burst out laughing, but said :

' All right, father, I will conform ; but don't be so
magisterial ;' and, throwing her arms round his neck,
she kissed him until he begged for mercy.

# CHAPTER II.

## FROM GREEN SWARD TO GREEN CLOTH.

THE first five days having elapsed, father and daughter enter the sacred precincts of the Cercle des Étrangers, and a scene such as Hilda has never dreamt of, greets the young girl's astonished eyes. In the interval of waiting for their admission, Hilda had walked, had ridden and driven over the beautiful country that surrounded Spa. She had also played lawn-tennis on the picturesque ground above the railway-station, with its amphitheatre of wooded hill forming a background of unrivalled beauty.

Everything delighted her, and the day was not long enough for the pleasures which that young and joyous nature could get out of it. She was up at six, and went to bed at ten with a happy smile upon her sweet lips, longing for the morrow which would give her another day of innocent enjoyment. Are there no guardian angels watching over these childlike natures to guard them against the rude awakening?

The cabalistic words monotonously droned out by

7—2

the croupiers at half a dozen tables before every coup, were the first sounds which fell upon Hilda's ear as she entered the spacious *salle de jeu* with her father. Her natural nervousness had been somewhat increased by having their *cartes d'entrée* minutely examined at the door ; but Colonel Brabazon explained to her that this was essential to the inviolability of a club where gambling goes on. Truly a quibble, but withal a useful, and sometimes a pleasant, quibble.

'What did the man say?' asked Hilda. 'What is that little old woman in black gesticulating about? Oh, do look, father!'

Such, amongst others, were Hilda's exclamations when, for the first time in her life, she set foot in a room devoted to play as the business of life, and as she looked upon some of the varied phases of human nature which are common to such resorts.

'Hush!' replied her stolid father, who had frequented Monte Carlo in the days of his somewhat riotous youth. 'Look as much as you like, but please don't talk. I didn't much care about bringing you here, but, as usual, you over-persuaded me, and here we are. Do content yourself with looking on, or, rather, with what you call studying human nature ; and for Heaven's sake don't attempt to give me the benefit of your views out loud.'

Hilda followed her father's advice, and continued to watch with great interest what was going on around her. She was amused, if somewhat shocked, at the little old lady in seedy black, who, with a reticule upon her arm, was ever on the alert to despoil some inexperienced player. There was one just near her, a bride of a few weeks, who furtively and with a blush put one yellow counter upon a transversale, looking and feeling, no doubt, as if she were perilously near committing a crime.

Hilda's attention was next drawn to a gaily-dressed lady, seated on the other side of the bride, whose permanent blush was palpably not due to Nature, and who a moment afterwards stretched out a much-beringed hand to take up the timid bride's winning stake. In this, however, she was forestalled by the black-kid-covered claw of the more experienced 'snatcher,' who put the twenty-five francs into her reticule without lifting her eyes from the table, or moving one muscle of her mummy-like face!

Another type of interest was a young man who, holding a forty-sou piece between his finger and thumb, was debating with himself whether to put this last remaining coin on an even chance, or go out and have a drink in the adjoining room. Here let me say in a parenthesis that at Spa one is allowed to play with forty-sou pieces at the roulette-table, though not at trente et quarante, and that refreshments are obtainable in the room next to the play-room, both of which privileges the model halls of Monte Carlo do not offer to their frequenters.

All these little comedies were closely observed by Hilda with a smile upon her face, as with difficulty she restrained herself from making audible remarks

to her father. He remained standing patiently by
her side, the pearl of chaperons, rather bored, it is
true, but nevertheless deriving a certain enjoyment
from his daughter's naïve appreciation of the scene,
which to him, at least, was by no means a novel
one.

Suddenly the smile faded from her lips and eyes as
a young man seated himself wearily in the vacant
place immediately opposite to her, which had
evidently been reserved for him, for the croupier, on
seeing him, at once took up the card and pencil, with
the one-franc piece, which marked it as engaged, and
handed them to him.

What a face it is, with large, sad, gray eyes, a
Grecian nose, and a small, sensitive mouth, but,
alas! a world of unhappiness and of intense purpose
in the whole expression of that perfect face! Where
had she seen it before? Well might Hilda ask herself that question, for it was under far different, and
for him far happier, circumstances that she had first
seen Algy Somerville.

His name, it is true, was unknown to her, but in a
moment she recognised the young paladin who had
come to her aid in the hunting-field some eighteen
months previously.

From this moment her eyes never left the figure
before her, his own being fixed unceasingly upon the
table. Sometimes he won, sometimes he lost; but
the expression on his face, meanwhile, never varied a
shade. And Hilda watched him with an interest that

made her forget both time and place, until at last her patient father said to her :

'*Really*, Hilda, haven't you seen enough of roulette for one night ?  Suppose we go home, and you shall tell me the rest of your impressions to-morrow.'

Rather to his surprise, Hilda immediately acquiesced, and was absolutely silent as they walked down the broad staircase of the Casino and passed into the Rue Royale.

As they wished each other good-night, Colonel Brabazon could not but notice this unaccustomed silence, and said :

'My darling, I think that for once you really are tired ; and no wonder, after all we have been doing to-day.'

'No, father,' replied Hilda, 'you know I am never tired ; but don't you think'—hesitatingly—'that some of the faces one sees playing at the tables are rather—rather sad ?'

'Of course they are, my child,' answers her father ; 'but I thought you only saw the comic side of the whole thing.'

'So I did, father, at first ; but—I suppose I am tired.  Good-night, dear.'

The next morning was bright and sunny.  Mrs. Brabazon, having consulted the clever English doctor who lives in the Avenue du Marteau, and having ascertained from him how many glasses of the Pouhon spring she was to swallow, and how many douches she was to take, decided to put off commencing the cure till the following day. An excursion to the famous Cascade of Coo was accordingly decided upon, for, as she remarked :

'Once I begin the treatment, my time will be greatly taken up, and I shall not be able to get so far.'

'Is it—is it very far?' inquired Hilda hesitatingly.

'Well,' replied her father, 'it takes pretty well all the afternoon to do it comfortably and have tea ; but, of course, that is just what you have been longing for—new scenery, new scenes, new people to study, and so on. We will have luncheon at one, and start at two. I will go and order the carriage now.'

To Colonel Brabazon's surprise, Hilda did not show the enthusiasm that she was accustomed to display when anything in the way of an expedition was proposed—so much so that he remarked :

'Well, Hilda, you don't seem to be very keen about it. Are you disappointed with your travels already ?'

'Oh no, father!' she replied hastily, and with a vivid blush, which fortunately escaped him, or he would have been still more puzzled; 'I should like the drive very much. But shall we be back in time to see more of those—those funny people at the Casino? They interested me so much.'

'Humph!' replied her father; 'when we left last night you seemed to think them more tragic than comic.'

Again the tell-tale blush rises to Hilda's cheek.

'Well, father, I suppose there are both comic and tragic people to be found at gambling-tables; anyhow, I should like to go and look on again, if you will take me.'

'All right,' replied her father; 'we will look in while your mother is resting after her drive. It doesn't matter at what hour we dine here. It is not like the German baths, where you have to go to bed at ten and get up at six, and are forbidden to eat anything you like.'

The little excursion was a great success; but during the whole time that it lasted there was the wistful look of an absent mind upon Hilda's face, which did not escape the eyes of her doting parents, accustomed as they were to watch every expression of that mobile countenance.

After their return, and as soon as Mrs. Brabazon had been comfortably settled upon the sofa in their sitting-room, with the cushions carefully arranged by her daughter, Hilda turned to her father, saying eagerly:

'Now, father, come and have another look at the people in the Casino.'

'Now, my sweet child,' replied that long-suffering parent, 'it's rather late. I have ordered dinner in an hour, and I want to write a letter. By Jove, though,' he added hastily, 'the *New York Herald* will be in the reading-room, and will have the result of the Scotch election. Come along—quick!'

Hilda was at the door almost before he had time

to finish his sentence, and a few minutes more found them on the scene of action.

'I am going into the reading-room,' he said, 'and will join you in a minute or two.'

A minute or two! One second was enough for Hilda. She went straight to the spot where she had stood the previous evening, her heart beating tumultuously the while. Would he be there? Was he an habitué, or only a passing visitor? Her doubts were soon satisfied, for there was the man whose face had haunted her since she last saw it. To what extent she did not realize until her eyes rested on it again. Love at first sight! May the decadent emotions of the present day never obliterate that almost divine sensation which comes to one woman only in ten thousand, and but once in her life, to influence her whole future—sometimes for its happiness ; sometimes, oftener indeed, for its unending sorrow.

Hilda's eyes were fixed on this face ; but the sad, beautiful gray eyes were, alas! riveted on the table, and on the stake he had in front of him.

'Vingt trois, rouge, impair, et passe,' proclaimed the croupier, and the stake—a large one—was ruthlessly raked in.

That set countenance remained impassive—not a muscle moved ; but Hilda gave a perceptible shudder, which did not escape her father, who came up just at that moment.

'Why, Hilda,' he remarked, ' you are shivering,

and yet these rooms are stifling! You must have caught cold from that long drive. That beast C—— has got in by a majority of over three hundred. I only hope we shall have a good dinner to make me forget the disappointment.'

'A miserable election, a good dinner—how could such things affect anyone?' thought Hilda as she left the room, casting a lingering look behind her at the face—for her already the one face in the whole world.

No matter how interesting the drive, how beautiful the scenery, regularly before dinner Hilda asked her father to take her to the Casino, alleging her great interest in the people playing there. She had forced herself into giving that reason to her father, who would doubtless rather have remained quietly in his arm-chair reading the papers or the last good novel.

On one occasion, some few days later, when Hilda as usual stood glued at her accustomed post by the roulette-table, her father asked her with a certain amount of irritability in his voice:

'Why don't you sometimes come to the trente et quarante table, where they play higher? You might, at all events, see more tragedies than comedies there.'

Alas! the necessity for concealment engendered in that frank and honest nature prompted Hilda at once to reply:

'Oh yes, father! I should like of all things to see the other game.'

Let the Recording Angel veil his face, for this was

probably the only untruth which Hilda had ever uttered to her father.

They therefore moved on to the table at the top of the room, and, although this could hardly be called a case of 'virtue rewarded,' still, Hilda's heart gave a great leap as a few minutes after they had been watching the game the sad, impassible player who preoccupied her stood once more opposite.

As he took his place, the croupier next to whom he was seated, said :

'Eh bien, monsieur, vous nous revenez ?'

'Oui,' replied the new-comer calmly. 'J'ai trop de guigne à la roulette depuis quelques jours.'

We will pass over the next few days, during which the drives and the visits to the Casino continued. One morning, however, at breakfast Colonel Brabazon said to his daughter :

'There is a ball at the Casino to-morrow night ; the Ellises with a large party are going, and the d'Etremonts will be there, so you are sure to get plenty of partners. It will be a pleasant change for you, after looking on for nearly a week at other people cutting their own throats.'

If truth be told, the devoted father was getting somewhat tired of their nightly visits to the Casino.

Again Hilda is untrue to her real nature, for she expresses an enthusiastic wish, which she does not feel, to be present at the ball ; but she asks her father hesitatingly :

'Do you think the gamblers—I mean, the young men among them—go to these balls?'

'Poor devils!' replied her father; 'yes, I should think they also were glad of a change now and again. I dare say I shall see you whirling round the room with that sad-eyed youth, who is certainly a gentleman, if he is a gambler; and it will be any amount better for him to have a good waltz with you than to sit glued to his chair, staring at the board of green cloth all the evening.'

# CHAPTER III.

## FRIENDS INDEED.

THE next evening the beautiful girl and her father entered the Casino ballroom, a fine Louis XVI. room of excellent proportions, which some rather mediocre paintings of a much more recent date are unable to spoil.

Looking round, you can evoke the period when Spa was the most luxurious watering-place on the Continent, and when half the noble and beautiful women of Europe disported themselves in these salons, which provided for its votaries pleasure in many of its most attractive forms.

But they called the salons La Redoute, instead of Le Casino; and when they played it was pharaon or biribi, which were more picturesque games than roulette.

Has Spa improved with the lapse of time ? Bringing places and people 'up to date' is not always a success.

Be that as it may, on this particular night the room was looking its best; and many eyes were at once

directed towards Hilda and her father. The former
soon had no lack of partners, and being passionately
fond of dancing, she for the moment forgot the face
that had haunted her since her *début* in the *salle de
jeu*. At last one of her favourite London partners
came in, who, catching sight of her, at once came over
to her side.

'This is luck, Miss Brabazon,' he said ; 'I have
just come to Spa, and you are certainly one of the
last people I expected to meet here. When can I
have a dance ?'

'I am afraid I have nothing before the third valse.'

'By Jove !' ejaculated her companion, 'this is worse
than London—Miss Brabazon with her hands full
before the orchestra have been at work five minutes !
Never mind,' he said, as she was carried off by the
fortunate proprietor of valse number one, 'the third
valse it is !'

Lord Clement Armytage, to whom we must now
introduce the reader, was one of the best-known young
men in the London world. Though a younger son,
he was fairly well off, and sat in the House for what
might almost be called a family borough, if there were
such an anomaly left. He had a bright, happy nature,
enjoying every moment of his life, and in that respect
was almost the counterpart of Hilda. Accordingly,
although neither was the least in love with the other,
they were the best and truest of friends.

The fact was, however, that within the last few
months Clement Armytage had fixed his affections

upon a serious, rather sombre girl, whose present determination to marry no one he had vainly attempted to combat. This disappointment had brought into his character a certain shade of gravity which hitherto had been wanting there ; and just about the same time the unsullied blue of Hilda's sky was darkened by a threatening cloud.

Thus, these two particularly good-looking young persons, who until now had been content, metaphorically speaking, to valse through life to the strains of Strauss, were destined to learn that they now had something more serious in common than their mutual light-heartedness, and that the bonds of their friendship were to be riveted only the more closely thereby.

As soon as the first bar of the third valse was heard, Lord Clement came up at once to claim Hilda.

' Now, Miss Brabazon, we will have a good turn ;' and off they started. The floor was good, the music excellent, but, to Lord Clement's surprise, before they had been once round the room Hilda stopped short, saying :

' Let us talk a bit ; you must have so much to tell me. Is Miss A. as obdurate as ever ?'

Her partner looked at her in surprise. ' Why, Miss Brabazon,' he said, ' you never would let me talk to you about my unfortunate love affair ; you said it was not at all in your line, and that it was a pity I made myself unhappy about a girl who

evidently didn't like me well enough to give up her
learned pursuits in order to make me happy. I have
told you, over and over again, that I should never
care in that way for any other woman,' he continued,
with a light in his eyes, the ecstasy of which was
shaded by sadness, 'and you only laughed at me.
If you were not *you*, I should say you snubbed me.
But, as you ask, I will tell you that she is just the
same and that I am just the same, and that I shall
wait patiently, hoping that some miracle may open
her eyes. Now let's have another turn ; we are
wasting time, as you always say when you have
danced me quite out of breath.'

'I am out of breath to-night,' said Hilda, 'and—
and tired. I had such a long walk this morning.'
Was this duplicity growing upon her ?

'By all means, then, let's sit down and have a talk,'
replied her partner. 'Now, you begin.'

'Do tell me,' said Hilda abruptly—'do these . .
the people who gamble, I mean, ever come to these
balls ?'

'I wish to God they did !' Lord Clement replied,
with more emphasis than the occasion seemed to
demand ; 'at least, I wish *one* did,' he added under
his breath.

'You don't approve of gambling, then ?'

'I hate it ! I loathe it !'

'What ! do you play and lose, that you hate it
so ?'

'No, I never play myself ; but I have looked on

8

often enough, and what I have seen has sickened me of the thought of gambling.'

'Are you a member of the Cercle des Étrangers?' she asked eagerly.

'Of course I am—I had to be,' he added, with a bitterness in his tone to which she is quite unaccustomed. 'I have got a sad business on my hands that has brought me to Spa, but don't let us talk about it now; have another turn?'

It instantly occurred to Hilda that possibly the sad business to which he referred was connected with the lord of her thoughts, and, as she was determined to ascertain this, she said to her partner as soon as the valse was over:

'Suppose we go and have a look at the gambling; it interests me very much.'

'You can't go so smartly dressed, can you?' he asked.

'I can put my cloak on, if you will kindly fetch it from the vestiaire.'

'But will your father let you go there with me?'

'We will ask him,' replied Hilda. 'I should think he would be only too glad to be let off his almost nightly visit, which I am afraid bores him a good deal.'

Colonel Brabazon's consent having been willingly given, for he knew the sincere friendship that existed between Hilda and Clement Armytage, also the high character of the latter, which made him a fitting chaperon for any young girl, the two adjourned to the play-room, and Hilda drew her companion to the spot where she first met her fate. Yes, he was there, in his old place, his expression exactly the same as it had always been. The two friends watched the game for a few minutes together, and then Clement Armytage said :

'One moment, Miss Brabazon ; I am just going to speak to that man opposite.'

Hilda's heart gave a great bound as she saw her companion pass to the other side of the table, and touch the preoccupied player lightly on the shoulder. The latter looked up with a sweet, but unmirthful, smile ; a few words were whispered in his ear ; he shook his head, whispered something back, and Clement Armytage was again by Hilda's side : her face was deadly pale, and her mouth quivering. Seeing this, he thought, naturally, that the young girl was feeling faint.

'This atmosphere is awful, Miss Brabazon,' he said. 'You look very white; come and sit in the gallery, where it is cool.'

She laid her hand on his arm without a word— indeed, she was incapable of speaking—and they left the room, where the heat certainly was as great as that of the fabled regions to which Lord Clement would willingly have consigned it.

By the time they had seated themselves comfortably in the gallery, Hilda recovered herself sufficiently to be able to say carelessly, while holding her fan before her face :

'Who is that young man you spoke to ? I have

often noticed him; he—he looks as if he had a history.'

'A history! I should think he had,' replied her companion—'one of the saddest, one of the most remarkable, you have ever heard. If you read it in a novel, you would scarcely believe it. I can't tell it you all now, for you look very white and faint still; besides, I want to get back to him; he will leave off play at twelve o'clock, and it is nearly that now,' he said, consulting his watch. 'I will only just tell you that he is my greatest friend—a man of the noblest character, besides being one of the best fellows that ever stepped; and that his present life is too extra-ordinary and too sad for you to be able to take it all in in a few words. I came here on purpose to look after him, and to see what I could do, and we shall have a long talk to-night. Will you come out with me to-morrow morning? We can sit on one of those quaint old carved white seats in the Promenade de Sept Heures, and you shall hear the whole tragedy, for tragedy it is. I am glad to think you are in-terested in my poor friend; and you will be still more so when you hear his history. Shall I come for you about eleven?'

'At eleven?' said Hilda in a low voice. 'Very well, at eleven.'

'And now I will take you back to your father.'

# CHAPTER IV

## 'TÂCHE SANS TACHE.'

PUNCTUALLY at eleven on the following morning
Lord Clement Armytage walked into the courtyard
of the Hôtel d'Orange, and found Hilda Brabazon
sitting on one of the seats with a book in her hand.
Was she really reading? Her eyes, it is true, were
fixed upon the page before her, but the look in them
did not denote any great interest in the work she was
apparently perusing.

'Good - morning, Miss Brabazon. Am I not
punctual? I hope you are none the worse for the
dance last night, and the awful atmosphere that
pretty near did for you?'

How banal these commonplace sentences sounded
to her sensitive ear, tingling with impatience to hear
the promised story! But she answered composedly :

'Oh, thanks, I'm all right this morning. Now let
us go at once to the Promenade de Sept Heures, where
we shall be undisturbed, and you can tell me about
your most sad-looking and interesting friend.'

Nearly two hours have elapsed before the friends rise from the carved white seat. There has been so much to tell on the one side, so many questions to be asked on the other. We know the whole story of the twin brothers, and Clement's closing sentences brought it down to the present time.

'And so you see, Miss Brabazon, there was nothing to be done. Once Algy Somerville has got a fixed purpose, nothing will turn him from it. All his friends—myself foremost of all—tried to dissuade him from this terrible existence, which is almost as hateful to him as would be picking oakum; but he remained obdurate. His brother's last request—although, poor fellow! such an unreasonable one—was sacred to him, and there he is, as you see him, with all the joy and sunshine of living gone out of his life. Ah, if you had only known what he was before this calamity befell! He was the idol of the F O., full of fun and mischief in the intervals of his work, where he was as steady as Old Time, and was looked upon by the head of his Department as the most promising youngster of the lot.

'Few people know how bitter Algy's regret was at the enforced sacrifice of his career ; but I can tell you this, that the regret was shared by his colleagues, which is an uncommonly rare occurrence; for an Office is in the nature of things selfish, and the retirement of one man means the promotion of another.'

'Is there nothing to be done?' says Hilda falteringly, as they walk slowly back to the hotel. 'Could you—could you introduce him to me? I should so like to talk to him.'

'No use, Miss Brabazon. He would make you a polite bow and some remark about the weather, and then turn on his heel. It is *hopeless* at present to do anything with him. But perhaps time may prove to him the futility of trying to win back a large fortune at the gambling-tables ; and, having done his best to fulfil his brother's wish, he may again become a reasonable being. It is almost too much to hope that he can ever be his own bright self again, for he has changed terribly in the last few months. Well, good-bye for the present. I must get some exercise, and I am going to bicycle to Pepinster, which seems to be the only flat road in this neighbourhood. We shall meet about six, and if you come to the Casino we shall see the same sad face that you have been watching with so much interest since you came here. It has made you quite serious—for the first time in your life,' he adds, smiling. 'Anyhow, I will try and get Algy to come and dine with me, for I don't believe he allows himself enough to eat. He has given up smoking, and every penny he can save from the bare necessaries of life he devotes to the purpose of his present pursuit.' Armytage stamps his foot. 'Forgive me, Miss Brabazon, but it maddens me to see such a man as that throwing away his life for a chimera—it can be nothing else. Good-bye again, or, rather, au revoir. It has been a great relief to me to pour this sad story into such sympathetic ears.

If Algy would only fix those long gray eyes upon you instead of on the green cloth, how different life might be for him! Perhaps he will some day, if you give him the chance.'

'*If he gives me the chance!*' says Hilda to herself, as she goes straight up to her bedroom to think over what she has heard of the man who, from the first moment she saw him, has occupied her thoughts. Without being spoilt, she has been made so much of in London drawing-rooms and in country houses, and has so invariably discouraged her would-be suitors, that a sudden idea seizes her.

'Suppose I rather throw myself at this Algy Somerville's head? That might turn him from his terrible life. I shall have a thousand a year when I come of age, and meanwhile my father and mother, so good and loving, will do everything they can to help me, once they realize that I am for the first time in my life seriously and desperately in love. They have reproached me in fun with flirting, and with being frivolous. That is past and gone. Now my fate is on me, and I shall never, never change. I fell in love with him at once, and though, for aught I knew, he might have been an adventurer or anything. Now I know his history, what is he to me but a hero —my ideal of all I had ever dreamt of in man?'

A knock at the door.

'Pardon, mademoiselle, on vous attend pour le déjeuner.'

She follows the waiter mechanically down to the

dining-room, where the excellent repast provided would have tempted the appetite of any ordinary individual ; but you cannot minister to a mind diseased, and Hilda rejects every tempting dish almost with a shudder.

'Now, look here, child,' says her father severely : 'we have come here for your mother's health, and, thank God! she is much better. But I am not going to have *you* on my hands as an invalid just because you choose to stop in hot rooms and get faint, and then lose your appetite and look like a ghost. No! Just you go and bicycle or ride with Clement Armytage and Mdlle. d'Etremont, or with her brother and Mme. de Breville. They all want you to join them in their rides and picnics. Instead of which you drag me to those stifling rooms, where one can hardly breathe, and, hang me!' he says, clenching his fist, 'you don't even want to play. It's always, " I want to look on and study human nature." Are you going to write a book, and to put in that extremely gentlemanlike but melancholy young man you are always watching as the hero ? If so, the book won't be lively. Anyhow, it is evident that Spa does not agree with you ; and, as your mother will have done her cure in another week, we will be off to Switzerland, where, I hope, the mountain air will restore your roses and your energy ; for just now you are like a half-dead fly, and it worries me, and—and,' he adds, 'irritates me. It is so unlike you to be fainting and having no appetite. There, my child,' he says, as he sees the tears coming into poor Hilda's eyes, ' I don't want to be harsh with you ; but I *was* so proud of your health and spirits, and now both seem to have broken down suddenly. We will be off as soon as the doctor thinks your mother has had enough Pouhon and douches. Just you wait till you see the snowy mountains and the lakes of Switzerland ! You won't hanker much after Spa, charming as it is in its way.'

' But, father, meanwhile will you take me to the Casino to-night ? Lord Clement will be there, and he has been telling me so much about that girl he wants to marry, and who is idiot enough not to appreciate him ; and there is dancing every night, so do take me. I'll have a little more filet de bœuf, please,' she says with the instinct of self-preservation, and she gets it down somehow ; but the young girl's awakening to this absorbing love, combined with an exceptionally romantic story, is too much for her.

The bright young creature without a care, who arrived in Spa, ah ! such a short time ago, is now a sorrowing, thinking woman, but with Hope ever holding its outstretched hands before her. She is so young, and he too. Why should she despair ? She is beautiful—she knows that ; well born, and fairly rich. Can she not in time lure him from his desperate career, and prove to him that a woman's love can compensate even for the loss of an idolized twin brother ? She knows not, when uttering these thoughts to herself, that they were those of poor Evy on his death-bed, and that the love of 'the good and true woman' was found. How long will it take Algy to realize it?

'Now, look here, old man,' says Lord Clement to Algy, when they met in the rooms that evening : ' I've had enough of watching you plastering down those red and yellow counters. Come and have a turn in the ballroom. There is such a charming girl there, Miss Brabazon—pretty, bright, and a beautiful dancer. Very much interested in you, too, as she has been watching you for some days—*do* come.'

'Do come and *what? Dance?*' replies Algy indignantly, to poor Lord Clement, who, having dined well, is inclined to cast off melancholy, and wishes to induce his friend to do the same. 'Dance—do you suppose I shall ever dance again?'

'Well, not till you are fifty,' retorts Lord Clement, still under the influence of his excellent dinner, 'and then it will be too late. You will have to hang round some elderly young lady or obese dowager for the chance of a turn. Take my advice now, and have a valse with Miss Brabazon.'

'Thanks,' says Algy coldly; 'I think I'll wait a little longer before I make the acquaintance of any strange young lady. Oh! no doubt you are going to remind me what my poor Evy said to me, "If you find a good and true woman, who loves you and objects to the life you are leading—chuck it;" but I don't think I am likely to find such a paragon in Spa —do you?'

'Quien sabe?' replies Lord Clement, who, having passed one week in Spain, is rather proud of the Spanish sentences he brought away.

'And, besides,' continues Algy, 'I am going to stick to this hateful business for at least another year, and that is why I avoid making the acquaintance of any girl, however nice. My determination is to carry out Evy's wish to the letter, and to try to win back at play the fortune he lost in this manner.'

'But you have never told me if you are lucky or unlucky.'

'I have won a certain amount; but I have only begun this life, if it is life, for two months, and I have got another month of it here, after which I shall take a bit of a rest, and then go to Monte Carlo. If you knew how I hate the idea of going to that cursed place, which took my Evy from me, morally and physically! I shall seem to see his ghost on every garden-seat, where he told me he sat in the mornings before play began, to get a little air. I shall see it again at the trente et quarante and roulette tables. Yet if I don't go there I may see him standing by my bedside, pointing sternly to the door, and saying, "Why don't you fulfil your vow?" Ah, it is horrible! Sometimes I think I shall lose my reason.'

'Algy! Will nothing I can say make you change your mind? I am almost your brother, in the great affection I have for you, and, as I know what your talents are, and what a career you might make for yourself, I do entreat you earnestly to stop this life,

which you admit is hateful to you. I came to Spa to
urge you to give it up. I will follow you to Monte
Carlo, and again use any influence I have over you.
I'm not going to lose sight of you, and am just as
determined as you are. You were the best brother
that ever lived to poor Evy while he was alive ; but
shall the *living* have no thought given to them ? He
is gone, but if we could bring him back to see you as
you are now, do you think he would be happy ? No.
He must have spoken those words when he was in a
half-conscious state, and did not realize what he was
asking you to do. For God's sake leave this place
with me to-morrow. I have nothing to do for a
couple of months, and will go with you to Norway,
Scotland—anywhere you like.'

The usually composed young Englishman is almost
moved to tears by his own entreaties.

' No good, my dear old chap. I have thought it
all out, and you know it is not in me to turn from
a set purpose. Even Evy couldn't turn me when I
made up my mind to go into the F. O. against his
urgent remonstrances. Alas ! if I had listened to
him then, he might have been alive and well, with
all his fortune intact. I *am* listening to him now ;
that is my only consolation for the past, which
I can't undo, and for the odious life I am now
leading.'

' Then, good-bye, Algy ; I shall be off to-morrow.
But as I said before, I am not going to lose sight of
you.'

And after having clasped his friend's hand, as he leaves the room he says to himself:

'His only chance is "the good and true woman," and I believe she is to be found in Hilda Brabazon.'

# CHAPTER V

## 'WILL YOU SAVE HIM?'

LORD CLEMENT had promised to meet Hilda Brabazon at the Casino at six o'clock, but this entailed
seeing Algy again after their unsatisfactory interview,
and, as they had already said good-bye to each other,
he decided not to go there. He felt, however, that he
must see Hilda again before leaving Spa, and after
some reflection he wrote her the following letter:

'DEAR MISS BRABAZON,

'I have had a long and sad talk with my poor
Algy this afternoon, but, alas! with no result. To
all my arguments as to the wicked folly of sacrificing
his career, and the great chances of distinction which
he possesses, to a quest so distasteful to him and so
futile as the retrieving of his fortunes by gambling,
he opposes his brother's dying injunction that he
should attempt it conscientiously, and all my efforts
to shake his determination are fruitless.

'But where I have failed *you* can succeed, if . . . if

I am not wrong in the thought—a thought, is it, or only a hope?—that the attention with which you have watched him, and the interest which you showed in his sad story. are not due solely to curiosity or to the ready sympathy of a kind heart.  If I am presumptuously wrong, forgive me, and tear this letter up unread.

'But if—and Heaven grant that it may be so!—you feel that the greatest blessing I could ask for Algy might in time be vouchsafed to him, then—ah ! then, my sister Hilda, I entreat you to fight for both of you—for your own happiness in his redemption from slavery.

'Perhaps it is too soon yet to begin ; moreover, I know that you are leaving Spa next week, probably with plans for some months.  But next winter Algy will be at Monte Carlo, and there you can cross swords, with all the advantages on your side.  That you are beautiful, you know, and how attractive, the brilliant marriages which you have refused will have told you.  No step, therefore, which you can take to bring you nearer to him will be open to misconstruction.  Will you come to Monte Carlo?  I shall be there to help you.

'CLEMENT ARMYTAGE.'

It was clear to Hilda, after reading the above, that the letter would not have been written if Lord Clement had not fathomed her secret.  Clear, too, that, although the deliverance of Algy from bondage might be first in his mind, he would not have endeavoured to effect it by this means had he not felt convinced that her own happiness—'his sister Hilda' he had called her—was involved in the success of the attempt.

When they met that evening, therefore, she came straight to the point with all the frankness of her nature.

'Your letter has profoundly touched me,' Lord Clement,' she said; 'but am I equal to the task? I understand what you mean when you say that no step I take can be open to misconstruction; but how can I force my acquaintance on a man who has a set purpose before him, in which a woman plays no part? Suppose he absolutely snubbed me, could anything bring us together after that?'

'Algy is too *preux chevalier* ever to subject a woman to humiliation; such an idea could find no place in his mind.'

'But,' Hilda continued, 'however attractive you may think me, is it dignified, is it possible, to force one's acquaintance on a man who doesn't want it? Here are you, Mr. Somerville's dearest friend, and yet you will not introduce him to me!'

'Not at this moment, Miss Brabazon; poor Algy's sorrow is too recent, his experience of the life he is leading too new, for him to realize all that it means; give him a few months, let him see that there is something worth living for, other than the realization of a dying man's chimera. I feel that it is best to let

him give it a fair trial, for he will never be satisfied
till he has done that much ; but his probation may
be shortened by a good influence.   Are not you the
"good and true woman" whose advent his brother
foreshadowed ?'

'Yes,' dubiously, ' I may be ; but, on the other
hand, if he has fixed his ideal on someone quite
different to me?   I have strong individuality—even
in this cause I could not escape from it—and I fear
that at present he would not see the slightest attraction in me, even if he did condescend to make my
acquaintance.'

'Miss   Brabazon,   stop!'   cried   Lord   Clement;
' when you talk like that, I am not with you.   I am a
man, as you know ; my whole heart is given to another
woman ; is not my judgment therefore impartial ?
I tell you that you are perhaps the one woman in the
world who can save Algy Somerville.   Will you try,
or will you not ?'

Lord Clement almost stamped his foot in his
vehemence.

'Ah, Lord Clement, be patient with me. You
have discovered for yourself'—and poor Hilda's head
sank between her hands—'how gladly I would give
my life to the attempt ; but I am afraid — I
doubt——'

'Nonsense, Miss Brabazon !  How could any man
resist you who wasn't in love with somebody else ?
and *that* my poor Algy is most certainly not. He
has told me over and over again that neither he nor

Evy had ever seen the girl they would care to marry; indeed, they never even flirted like other men, popular though they were with all women, young and old. Well, Miss Brabazon, I have had my say—will you think it over? It will be very good of you if you will write sometimes, and tell me where you are and what you are doing; if you are still interested in poor Algy, you know that anything you say or write to me is sacred. You do trust me, Miss Brabazon?'

'Absolutely,' replied Hilda, stretching out her hand; 'but I shall not write for the present. I want to try resolutely to forget this episode in my life, although I am afraid I shan't succeed. Then, if I find that his face haunts me still, to the exclusion of everything else, I will try and persuade my parents to go to Monte Carlo. In that case, and in that case only, I shall write to you; meanwhile we shall all be going our different ways,' she added wearily, 'and who knows if we shall ever meet again! What an unhappy life poor Mr. Somerville's must be! How he must long for a sight of his old home, and yet what exquisite pain it would be to see it in the hands of strangers! By-the-by, Lord Clement, you did not tell me who had bought it.'

'The place was bought by a rich American who wanted to see what the life of an English country gentleman was like; but, from what I hear, I don't fancy it will suit him, and so probably the old place will be in the market again before long. Well, once more good-bye, Miss Brabazon, and God bless you!'

So they part. Hilda went to her room, and, flinging herself into an armchair, buried her face in her hands.

'What am I to do! Oh, what *am* I to do!' she moans. 'I feel that I would gladly give my life to save his and make him happy, and yet the one thing that I *cannot* do is to put my pride in my pocket, as they call it, and force my acquaintance upon him. No, I *cannot* do that; and besides, at present, at any rate, it would be no use—Lord Clement admits that. Shall I make up my mind not to go to the Casino any more whilst I am here? To think only of the snowy mountains and blue lakes of Switzerland? When I arrived in Spa a few weeks ago my one idea was to go about and enjoy everything. Italy and Switzerland! It seemed a possibility too good to be true; and now? Can I be so suddenly changed, and will nothing interest me but that awful green cloth table, and the long gray eyes fixed upon it? Bah! It is too contemptible! I *will* be firm—at all events, for one evening.'

'Hilda! Hilda! where are you?' cries Colonel Brabazon. 'Now is the time for the usual "evening sacrifice," and here I am waiting as patiently as usual; your mother is asleep, and the *New York Herald* will be in the reading-room, so look sharp!'

A pale, tear-stained face is put out of the bedroom, and Hilda replies:

'I think I won't come to-night, father; I've got a headache, and I had better stop quiet till dinner-time. I hope the election news will be good—you must tell us all about it later on.'

'A headache!' grumbles Colonel Brabazon as he goes down the stairs. 'Hilda with a headache! Well, wonders will never cease! What ails the girl? she isn't herself at all. Thank goodness, we shall be off in a week, and change of air may make a difference. Women are "kittle cattle,"' adds the Colonel sapiently. 'I've never known what to make of 'em; but, hang me! I did think Hilda was above head-aches and faintings and that sort of thing! Well, any way, I shall be able to go straight to the reading-room, that's one comfort;' and, as if to shake off painful thoughts, the kind-hearted father says to himself, 'And I'll lay myself three to one that A—— gets in.'

Colonel Brabazon won his bet, and returned to dinner in high good-humour; for the nonce, too, Mrs. Brabazon felt so much better that she forgot almost entirely her own ailments—some of them fancied— and was as cheerful as the Colonel himself.

'And now about plans,' she says, as the coffee is served. 'Let me see: we leave Spa to-morrow week, spend a fortnight in Switzerland, and then go to the Italian lakes for, say, the same time. That is a delightful programme, so far as it goes, but I think we ought to look further ahead; the waters here and clever Dr. C—— have done me so much good between them, that I really see a prospect of becoming as strong as ever I was. However, I do not feel quite equal to a whole winter in England yet, especially after the dry atmosphere and beautiful sunshine we have been living in. Suppose we go to Cairo next November?'

Hilda drops her spoon into the saucer.

'Or the Riviera?'

Hilda picks up the spoon again, dips it into the cup, and sips leisurely.

'Now, what do you two say, and which shall it be, if either? Or can either of you suggest any other place for us next winter? Tunis? But that is rather far. What do you say, Hilda? You have always been dying to travel. Surely you must have an opinion to offer?'

'I agree with you, mother, that Tunis is rather far.'

She says it feebly and without any apparent interest, and this is altogether too much for her irascible father.

'Hang it all, Hilda! what *is* the matter with you? When I first told you we were coming abroad, you were like a mad thing, bouncing up and down like a pea on a drum; but now I come to look at you, you have got much thinner, or else that dress doesn't fit you.'

Poor Hilda! Shall she tell them? Can she tell them? Alas! there is nothing to tell. Her life is one long doubt as to what she is to do. She has but little experience, and yet she can turn to no one for guidance, for her parents, her natural counsellors, could not do otherwise under the circumstances than urge her to turn her thoughts to other scenes and other interests. No! she can take counsel of no one, and must fight it out all by herself; but she makes up her mind to keep away from the Casino, and to try her best to overcome the feeling which she calls her 'weakness,' though she knows that it has enshrined itself in the stronghold of her virgin heart.

She feels rather relieved, therefore, when her father tells her that he has asked the Italian Minister to dine with them that night, and that, in deference to his Excellency's Southern habits, they are to dine at 6.30.

'I met him years ago at Rome,' says the Colonel. 'He is a very good specimen of the travelled Italian, and devoted to whist ; but his travels have not taught him much there, and he is as far behind "modern developments" as the Vatican itself.'

# CHAPTER VI.

## DACHSHUND *v.* FOX.

JULY, August, and September constitute the season of Spa, upon the proceeds of which the Spadois proper lives for the remaining nine months. It also supplies him, or, rather what he invariably regards as its short-comings supply him, with a subject of conversation for the whole twelve. I speak only of the season of waters, for the gambler's season knows no close time there. For one reason or the other, people come to Spa from most parts of the world, and although in a place of this sort the different nationalities generally herd together, this was not the case with the Brabazons.

The Colonel, it is true, was rather the counterpart as regards England of what the French call *un Breton bretonnant ;* but Mrs. Brabazon was fond of foreign society, and a nephew of hers, who was Secretary of Legation in Brussels, made himself useful in bringing his family into contact with the best elements of it that happened to be in Spa.

If, about the time at which we have arrived, you

had referred to the programme of ' Spa Attractions '—
a threatening document which prescribed for you a
severe course of amusement for every day in the week
—you would have seen that a great International Dog
Show was in course of celebration, and this certainly
attracted a good many people.

Among others was a certain Baron von Rumpenheim, a rich Bavarian and a great breeder of dogs,
who was said to be unrivalled as a judge of dachshunds, or Jeckels, as they are called in North
Germany. He was also a great devotee of field
sports of every description ; and, walking one day
with Hilda and her father, he became much interested
in the account they gave of English fox-hunting in
general, and especially of a great run which had
taken place the previous winter in one of the Southern
counties.

' It must indeed be glorious fun,' he said, ' and I
understand the honour in which you hold the fox.
But, after all, you do not get nearly as much out of
him as you might, if you only gallop after him.
Now, we in Germany do several other things with
a fox.'

' Yes,' rejoined the Colonel gravely. ' Shoot him,
don't you ?'

' That of course,' said the Baron ; ' but there is
yet another form of sport in which he plays a principal
part. See !' he interrupted himself, pointing to a dog
which was trotting demurely behind its owner. ' There
is one of the finest races of dogs in the world, and it

would be difficult to find a better specimen than that
one.'

The dog in question was lightish brown in colour,
with patches of a darker brown, very long in the
body and close to the ground, thin in the flank, but
with great power over the loins; a delicate head with
a long, keen face, and ears like a miniature blood-
hound, as soft as silk, and so thin as to be almost
diaphanous.

'That dog,' continued the Baron, 'is quite certain
to take the first prize to-morrow. And yet, if you
think of the care given to the preparation of a dog
for exhibition, what dog but a dachshund could face
the lynx eyes of a professional judge at an important
show like this, after such an experience as hers was?
For, not a week ago, after hunting for five days and
five nights on her own account in the woods about
here, she got home scarred, gaunt, and more than
half starved. Indeed, she had presumed too much
upon her strength, and, unable to crawl a yard further,
she was lying exhausted by the roadside on the out-
skirts of the town. Fortunately, at that moment St.
Antoine, providence of the sorrowing owners of lost
property, guided to the spot an exalted lady, Imperial
in her beauty as in her birth, who, knowing the dog,
and the distress caused by her disappearance,
graciously brought her home.

'My reason,' he said in conclusion, 'for calling
your attention to the dog is that she is eminently
qualified to shine in the sport of which I have told

you.   But, alas! she belongs to an Englishwoman
who has foolish prejudices, and declines to allow the
dog to take part in it.'

'But, pardon me,' said Hilda, 'you have not told
us of any "sport," and you were speaking of a fox,
not a dog.'

'Quite true,' said the German; 'that was what you
call a digression.   But I could talk about that dog
and her qualities and adventures for an hour at a
time.   To resume the thread of what I was saying:
the sport in question is a trial of courage, strength,
and steadiness between a dachshund and a fox.   It
has existed for a long time in Germany, and within
the last few years a society has been formed in
Belgium for the pursuit of it.   As luck would have it,
knowing that there would this week be many good
dachshunds in Spa, the Society have come here and
have made arrangements for a trial to-morrow morning.   If it would interest you to be present,' he said,
turning to Colonel Brabazon, 'I shall be delighted to
meet you and Miss Brabazon there, and to explain
everything to you connected with the trial, in order
that you may understand what is going on.'

'What do you say, Hilda?' asked her father.   'I
thought I knew all about a fox, but I may be wrong,
and would willingly take advantage of Baron von
Rumpenheim's exceedingly kind offer.'

'By all means,' she answered.   'I am as curious as
can be about this sport.   A novelty it certainly will
be; and we English must give up the pretence of

knowing more about a fox than other people, when the Germans have given us Reinecke Fuchs, and America introduces us to a contemptible fox who is made a fool of by Brer Rabbit.'

An appointment therefore was made for the following morning, and punctually at the time fixed Hilda and her father arrived at a vast tumble-down old building situated just outside the town, with a noble room in it, and a neglected garden, which is one of the faded glories of Spa. It was here that 'the meet,' as the Colonel called it, was to take place, and all you saw at first were several men standing round —well, nothing in particular, so far as was apparent ; but from underground a ceaseless yapping could be heard.

Baron von Rumpenheim came forward at once and introduced them to the President of the Belgian Club, and to the judge, a German with a keen, good-natured face and the inevitable spectacles, who sat on a chair, watch in hand, taking notes. The introduction having been accomplished, the Baron took them aside, saying :

'Now that I have made you acquainted with the judge, you must let me explain to you, as shortly as I can, the details of the trials upon which he has to pronounce.'

With the reader's permission, however, I will act as showman in this matter, and perhaps succeed in shortening somewhat the explanation given by Herr von Rumpenheim, who, besides being an enthusiast in the cause, had, as he admitted himself, a certain tendency to digression.

To begin with, you dig a trench about twenty-five feet long, by a foot broad, and then fill in the sides and top with thin squares of wood, thus converting it into a sort of wooden drain. The top is then covered with earth, laid on thinly, but in sufficient quantity to keep the boards steady and the passage dark.

A large hole is dug at each end to contain a box, in which the fox is placed, the top of which is movable, and which is also fitted with a trap-door on the side next the passage, so as to let him in or out.

So much for the dressing of the stage. The object to be attained is that the dachshund should either bolt the fox—that is, drive him to the extreme end of the drain at which he can get out—or else kill him.

The fox, when put in at one end, naturally runs as far as he can, which is into the box at the other end, when the trap-door is at once closed, and the fox carried off. Yet though the fox is gone, the scent, like that of the rose-leaves in the shattered vase, lingers there still; and the competing dachshund, being put in, is expected to run from one end to the other *mute;* to give tongue when the passage is empty disqualifies him at once. Supposing him, however, to pass this ordeal successfully, the serious business begins.

A fox is put in, and a wooden sluice shut down behind him about ten yards from the entrance. Then the dog is introduced, and has to confront two glaring eyes and the fangs, only too well exposed, of the fox, who under these circumstances never turns his back on the foe. A bad or cowardly dog will yap for a minute or two and then back out into safety ; or he will, as it were, " set " the fox, and yap uninterruptedly without attacking him. This, if continued long enough, entitles him to high marks.

But the first-rate dog goes in at once, and either kills the fox or has to be taken out, the judge deciding that the dog is in danger of being badly mauled. In this case a man with a spade, who is always in attendance, shovels off the earth and lifts up one of the boards, the dog is taken out, and the fox runs into the box at the further end.

The first and last of these cases are, however, of rare occurrence, and the usual result is that the dog remains facing the fox and yapping without interruption. If he will do this for ten minutes by the judge's watch, the sluice is pulled up and the fox runs to the end of the drain at which he was put in, this time, however, the sliding door is shut so that he is again stopped, and the same proceedings are enacted over again, with the exception that this time the dog has to yap for twenty minutes.

Five minutes before that time is up the owner is allowed to incite his dog to attack the fox, which the dog does or does not, according to his courage or want of it. But at the expiration of the time the dog is taken out, the fox runs into his box, and is carried off to wait his turn, should he be required to come on again.

Hilda and her father had arrived just before the first sluice was lifted, and had, therefore, plenty of time to listen to the above explanation before the next battle began.

'But what is the man going to do with that sort of round tongs?' she asked of the German.

'That,' he replied, 'is for use in cases where there is a severe fight between the combatants at the last moment, when the dog, encouraged by the voice of his master, flies at the fox, and the latter seizes him by the throat. The judge can tell in a moment, by the noises, when this has happened; the drain is then opened as quickly as possible, and the fox pulled off with the tongs, which go round his neck like a collar. The tongs are also used to take the foxes out of their box, for though they are generally only cubs, barely a year old, there is not a man amongst us would care to pick them up.'

A fresh fox having been put into the drain, a remarkably good-looking black-and-tan dog, named Rosa, is seen straining at her leash, and almost screaming with excitement; for she has been long enough at the game to know that this time the fox is there, and that she may make as much noise as she likes.

'That,' whispers the German, for loud talking is prohibited in order that the judge may have no unnecessary difficulty in hearing the nature of the underground noises, 'is one of the most courageous dogs belonging to the club, and she has killed several foxes.'

The yapping began as usual, but in about four minutes the sounds changed, a growling and snapping was heard, and the excitement of the spectators became intense. Down went the judge on his stomach, and, with his ear glued to the ground, he reported what was going on, in a mixture of German and not the best of French, which, translated into English, was something like this :

'The dog has seized the fox ; she holds him ; now she has let him go ! Ach ! Mon Dieu ! she has got him again ; she holds him fast; she has probably strangled him !'

All this time the owner of the dog was stretched flat at the opening of the drain encouraging Rosa with guttural sounds, when suddenly he was seen to pull sharply at a black tail, and the gallant little Rosa was dragged backwards from the drain hanging tight on to the throat of the dead cub—a small one, be it said.

Still, this was a fine performance, because a fox is, after all, a wild animal, with a strong jaw and sharp teeth, and the contest is rather unequal between the fox who lives underground and the small dog who leaves terra firma to go after him.

Anyhow, Rosa covered herself with glory, and subsequently took the first prize.

The excitement having subsided, the usual pre-

liminaries were gone through, and as Hilda and her
father were debating whether they would care to see
another trial, the former, to her intense astonishment, saw the well-known figure, rarely now out
of her thoughts, advancing slowly to the scene of
action.

Yes, it was indeed Algy; the magic word 'fox'
had attracted him, and he had come, not so much
to see the novel kind of sport as to get a sight of the
'little red rascal,' which might remind him for a short
time of happier days.

The box containing an untried fox was placed at
the mouth of the drain, and slightly tilted up by
one of the employés, who at the same time rapped
with his fingers and suggested to the occupant to
leave his lair. Not a bit of it! The fox knew better
than that. A thin stick was then pushed through one
of the air-holes, and the fox gently stirred up. This
appeared to amuse Algy, for he actually smiled. Never
before had he seen the animal which was the object
of his profound respect and gratitude treated in this
ignominious manner.

But more was to come. The fox—still declining to
leave the four walls, where, at all events, he felt safe,
for the unknown, represented by a wooden drain—
obstinately declined to move; and, as time was
getting on, the judge was appealed to. It was an
emergency which called for his intervention, and he
accordingly ordered the tongs to be given him, and,
blowing rather hard, he proceeded to kneel down and

10

cautiously open the lid of the box with one hand, while he grasped the tongs with the other.

But this was too much for Algy. An elderly gentleman in spectacles, kneeling on the damp earth, and trying to pick a fox out of a box with a pair of tongs, was too much even for his sad gravity, and he laughed long and loud, perhaps for the first time since his bitter sorrow.

As for Hilda and her father, they had to turn away to conceal their amusement, fearing to hurt the feelings of Baron von Rumpenheim, who, in company with the rest of the habitués, naturally saw nothing unusual in what is an incident very common with this form of sport. After many ineffectual dives into the box, the fox was at last caught by the neck with the round tongs, 'made in Germany' for the purpose, lifted gently out, and put into the drain, where an ordinary 'hunt,' resulting in no injury to either belligerent, took place, and the proceedings terminated.

Although, perhaps, I have written of these proceedings rather irreverently, they had not been without interest, for they undoubtedly furnished a high trial for the instinct, the courage, and the training of a dachshund.

'Still,' the Colonel remarked, as he walked away, 'so long as there is a badger left in the country. why draw a fox?'

# CHAPTER VII.

## 'I LEAVE MY HEART BEHIND ME.'

ON returning home after witnessing the 'sport'
described in the last chapter, Hilda, as usual, went to
her room and sat down to think. Were the Fates
against her, or in her favour?

She had almost made up her mind not to risk seeing Algy again, and this meant keeping out of the
Casino, when most unexpectedly she had come
across him at a moment when she was trying to find
some diversion for her mind from the subject that was
always before her, and all her good resolutions were
thrown to the winds.

'I actually saw him laugh,' she says to herself—
'*laugh*, not only smile! That shows there is something left in him of the old leaven, and that his distasteful task has not yet converted him into an absolute automaton; there is hope yet. I am not going
to give it up. If it had not been for this ridiculous
underground fox-hunt, I might have left Spa without
seeing him again, and have avoided Monte Carlo;
as it is, all my ideas are changed. I shall not feel

10—2

that I am alive until we get there. What deceit I could cheerfully have been guilty of if there had been any difficulty as to our going! But, fortunately, my mother proposed the Riviera next winter herself, and as my father will do anything for either of us, I can safely rely upon their settling it without my interference. Heigho! how hideously selfish and egotistical one becomes when one is in love!'

'Coming, father!' she calls out, as Colonel Brabazon summons her to luncheon; and during that meal they talk of little else but the dachsfox hunt, as they call it, which interests Mrs. Brabazon not a little, and she laughs so heartily at the various incidents that Hilda is almost tempted to allude to the fact that the 'sad-faced young man' had also laughed, under the circumstances, and thus bring him into the conversation. But no; her secret was too sacred, and she too shy, so the subject dropped, to be succeeded by the daily question, 'Where shall we drive to?'

'Oh, anywhere you like,' says Hilda, when appealed to for her opinion; 'only don't let it be too far. The *New York Herald* is in about five o'clock, as you know, and I shall have but few more opportunities of "studying human nature" in the Casino.'

'You didn't go there at all yesterday,' retorts her father, 'and I have just discovered that I can buy the *New York Herald* at the kiosk on the something Place opposite the Établissement des Bains. If I had known that before, I am not sure—not *quite* sure,' he added dubiously—'that you would have got

me into the " Tripot," as our French friends call it, as
often as you have done hitherto, and I don't feel at all
inclined to go to-night. I want to go to—to—what's
the name of the place?' he says, pulling out the map
of ' Les Environs de Spa,' ' and that will take us until
at least seven o'clock ; and after dinner I have got to
read the pamphlet that C—— sent me, though
before I have got halfway through it I expect it will
be a case of the " dustman's coming," as your nurse
used to say to you. I think you must give it up for
to-night ; but as we are off the day after to-morrow,
I promise to-morrow to give you all the time you
wish to spend before the green cloth ; and, what is
more, I will give you 100 francs to put on where you
like, trente et quarante or roulette. Come, that's
a bargain. You won't become a confirmed gambler
in forty-eight hours, so I shall not be afraid, and can
look on at you with perfect equanimity as you sit at
the table with a heap of those nickel pieces before
you, and a puzzled face as to where you shall put
them on.'

'With perfect equanimity indeed, father ; for
nothing would induce me even to put a piece of any
sort on that fatal green cloth.'

'Whew ! You have become serious in these last
few weeks. We shall have you preaching at an anti-
gambling league, or temperance meeting, or some
nonsense of that kind next. Your motto—if you
thought about one at all—used to be : " Live, and
let live " ; and when your cousin Arthur got broke

on the Stock Exchange you only said, "Why shouldn't he, if it amused him? He is young, and can begin again." When the same thing happened to Mrs. Wentworth with her milliners' bills, and she had to set up as a milliner herself, *again* you laughed, and said: "Now she will make a fortune, and live happy ever afterwards." You used to be an optimist, and look on the bright side of everything; now you are a pessimist, and look at everything *en noir*, or, rather, *rouge et noir*,' he adds, with a chuckle at his own joke: 'for nothing seems to interest you but this infernal Cercle des Étrangers; and yet you are not bitten with the spirit of gambling! Well, I can't make you out.'

It is really surprising how obtuse one's father can be sometimes, but, nothing doubting, the simple-minded Colonel continued:

' Let's go for our drive, and when we get to Switzerland I hope you will be once more your own bright self. I think you have been bewitched since you came here.'

'I don't think about it,' says poor Hilda to herself, as she goes to her room to get ready for the drive; 'I know I have. And, my God! what am I to do? I must see him once more before I leave. If only he hadn't laughed, if only he had kept that sad look always on his face, I might have given up the idea of winning him as hopeless, have left Spa, and in time have got over my infatuation. As it is, I *cannot*,' she says, wringing her hands, and walking up and down her room—'I *cannot*. I have seen him laugh and look happy for a few moments, and it shall be the one object of my life to make him look happy as long as we are both alive.'

The drive suggested by Colonel Brabazon was a long one, and all three returned to the Hôtel d'Orange rather sleepy. As soon as dinner was over, the Colonel took up his pamphlet, but a quarter of an hour of it finished him. Mrs. Brabazon, who was lying as usual upon the sofa, smelling-salts in hand, also dropped off to sleep, while Hilda remained staring with sightless eyes at the pages of the novel she held in her hand, and thinking that to-morrow was the last day. Once more she hesitated : should she keep away, and say good-bye to her dream ? or should she not, rather, murmur 'Au revoir,' as she withdrew her eyes regretfully from his face.

'To-morrow shall decide,' she said to herself, as, taking up her book, she left her slumbering parents and went to her room, where at last she slept in earnest.

\*     \*     \*     \*     \*

'Well, this is our last day in Spa,' said Colonel Brabazon, as they sat down to breakfast together ; 'how would you like to spend it ? Your mother must rest quietly before our long journey to-morrow, and as for me, I have had enough of drives to last me a long time.'

'First of all, father, I should like to have another look at that curious old place where we saw the dachsfox hunt; I want to measure for myself the length of the "drain," so as to be able to describe it accurately when I give an account of it to the first M.F.H. we meet. How he will laugh!' she adds cheerfully.

'By all means,' says her father; 'we will go and tout that very artificial earth; even if it is filled up, we can find where it was, and take the dimensions. I thought our friend Rumpenheim was a bit sketchy in his measurements. Have you got a yard measure?'

'Of course, I have got my dressmaker's measure—that will do,' said Hilda; and they started off gaily together for the old tumble-down château. The instinct of sport was strong in both of them, and for the moment the political situation in the country was forgotten by the father, and the sentimental one by the daughter, as they trudged off together to the late scene of the action; and, there being nobody there to dispute the right of going over the ground, the Colonel executed a regular military reconnaissance, which resulted, however, as regarded the measurements, in establishing the accuracy of the Baron's figures. The Colonel then turned to the tumble-down old building, of which he had been reading in the Spa guide-book.

'You see, my dear Hilda, this was the old Château of——' he said, imagining that Hilda was close to him and listening to his description. She was not there, however, as he imagined, but standing on the now uninteresting scene of the late contest, her eyes

fixed on—what? Vacancy, as it appeared to her
father; but in reality what held her spell-bound was
the sight of the spot where he last stood before her,
and threw off his dejection to smile, and even to
laugh. The Colonel therefore broke off suddenly,
saying with some irritation, 'Why, Hilda, you look
as if you had seen the ghost of one of the massacred
foxes—there was only one, by-the-by, and you have
seen many before dug out and given to the hounds,
which is nearly as bad. For Heaven's sake don't
look so glum! What is the matter with you? Can't
you be interested in anything now without putting on
the face of a martyr? Hang me if I can understand
what Spa has done to you! Are you homesick?'

'I don't think so, father; but, remember, I have
never been out of England before, and perhaps all
the new impressions have made me more serious;
have made me think, as you and mother have long
impressed upon me, instead of treating life like the
"three little girls from school" in the "Mikado"—as
a joke that has just begun. Now come away, father;
we know all about the measurements now. Shall I
send a description of it to the *Sporting and Dramatic
News*, signed "One who was there"? Saying
which, she took her father by the arm, and they
returned to the Hôtel d'Orange, to find Mrs. Brabazon particularly well, and anxious for a last drive.

'Yes, a short one,' says her husband, much to
Hilda's relief; 'one hour will be quite enough; that
long drive yesterday at a foot's pace uphill has made

me feel sleepy ever since, and as C—— wants his
pamphlet back, I must not go to sleep over it again
to-night.'

'First of all,' said Hilda, almost fiercely, 'you
must take me to the Casino for the last time,
between six and seven o'clock—you promised me
that!'

'Of course I will,' replied the indulgent father;
' but, thank God ! it is the last time you will drag me
there "to study human nature"; in a few days you
will be studying Nature herself, and if the scenes
in Switzerland don't make you forget the green cloth,
with the sad and anxious faces of the Cercle des
Étrangers, I shall be surprised ; and in the meanwhile
you shall have your way, and, as there is your packing to superintend, your mother and I will go for our
drive alone, and I will be ready to escort you at six
o'clock.'

Punctually at that hour Hilda came into the room
with her hat on, ready to start, and found her
father sitting in the armchair he had appropriated to
himself, deeply immersed in a newspaper; he just
looked up and nodded, saying, ' We had a very
pleasant little drive ; have you seen to your packing ?' and, without waiting for a reply, continued
his reading.

Though in most ways the spoilt daughter can do
anything with her father, she knows better than to
interrupt when he is reading seriously; there is
nothing to be done but to wait patiently, so she

takes up a book ; but after every two or three pages have been listlessly glanced at, her eyes wander to the clock : 6.10—6.15—6.20 !   'He will perhaps leave the room at seven ; he does sometimes,' she says to herself, and something must be done to rouse her father.

'Who did you say was going to stand for C——shire ?' she says in a loud voice.

'Eh—eh, what ? C——shire ? Why, Elliott, of course, and he'll get in, too ; we shall know by the time we get to Basle. I wonder if they take in the *New York Herald* there ? It's a capital paper for giving you just the latest news, but there's not much else worth reading in it, unless you are an American.' Saying which he throws the paper on the floor and gives a yawn. 'What time is it, my girlie—nearly dinner-time ? I'm awfully hungry.'

'Oh no, father, it's not half-past six ; we have got an hour yet, and you remember that you promised to take me to the Cercle for the last time. I wonder if we shall find that fat Italian woman still winning ?'

'Well, come along quick ; she amused me more than anyone I have yet seen at the Casino. I hope I shan't laugh out loud, as I did before when she put a certain amount of her winnings into a red velvet bag and *sat on it*.'

How artful of Hilda to have mentioned the funny old woman ! Her father was now all impatience to be off, and they entered the play-room together as the clock struck half-past six. Hilda's quick glance discovered in a moment that Algy was there. Having changed his place several times since he came to Spa, he had now made up his mind that where he had had the best luck was at the table nearest to the chimney-piece and opposite to the entrance door. There Hilda had first seen him, and there she found him again on this her farewell night—the same sad, beautiful face, the gray eyes fixed on the green cloth.

The croupier said his words mechanically; how well she remembered the first time she heard them! A mystery to her then, and now so familiar. It seems a year since she first crossed that threshold, all anxiety to see and to understand a new phase of life, of which she had only vaguely heard, and almost in joke. Now she knows all the hideous threat that may be conveyed in those two sentences.

Suddenly her father puts a red counter into her hand, saying :

' I have just given a louis for it, and, as you have been looking on so patiently all this time, and I too,' he adds with a sigh, ' I want you to put it on the transversale 19-24, which I notice has been coming up very often in the last few rounds. Put it on for me if you like, just for fun ; but meanwhile I must go back to the fat Italian woman at the other table, who is now sitting upon two bags of winnings, and has plastered the whole table with yellow counters. Remember, the transversale 19-24,' he says, as he moves off, hearing the click of the ball at the opposite table.

Hilda grasps the red counter in her hands ; her horror of even putting one piece on that fatal green cloth prompts her to run out of the room ; but yet, as her father has said to her 'for fun,' and as he has been so good in coming night after night for her amusement, it is churlish to refuse.

Down goes the red counter on the transversale in question, and after about thirty seconds the croupier proclaims, 'Vingt-trois rouge, impair et passe,' in the usual monotonous tones, and Algy, who has been backing this transversale for the greater part of the evening, stretches out his hand mechanically to take up the stake. But on this occasion, as is so often the case with him, his thoughts are far away, and he has forgotten to stake at all.

'Pardon, monsieur,' says the polite croupier, who, having seen the beautiful girl looking on at the game for some length of time, is much interested in this her first stake. 'La mise est à madame ;' and he hands her over five red counters. Hilda wishes the whole earth could open to swallow her and the green table up into one unfathomable abyss. Algy Somerville lifts his head, and their eyes meet for the first time.

'Mille pardons, madame,' he says; 'je m'étais trompé ; je n'avais pas du tout de mise.'

Hilda inclines her graceful head in recognition of his courteous apology, and turns from the table, sick at heart; he has never raised his eyes to hers before, and, if he thinks of her at all now, it will be as one of the many gamblers he sees there, and for whom he must have such a contempt. How can he know it is her first and only stake that has been disputed between him and the croupier on her behalf? Oh, agony! and this her last chance of seeing him—for how long?

She controls herself, however, with wonderful self-command, and walks over to the opposite table, where her father, little knowing what his adored child has been going through, is laughing as heartily as is decorous at the fat Italian woman, who, having had a turn of bad luck, is obliged to draw on the resources of the red velvet bags, which causes her to bump up and down on her chair as she extracts a few counters from her well-guarded store and plumps down again, much to the amusement of the on-lookers. Comedy at one table, and at the other tragedy.

'Now let us go home, father,' she says. 'I won on the transversale you told me to put them on. Here are the five louis. Can't we give them in charity?'

'Oh, my dear child!' he answers. 'I should like to give them to that delightful old woman, and see her sit upon them, and then fish them out again. It is the most comic thing I have seen. But, hulloa! you are as white as a sheet. Don't faint, my darling. These rooms are only fit for a salamander. Wait till you get into Switzerland; there we shall soon have your roses back, and meanwhile say good-bye to the

Cercle des Étrangers.    I don't think either it or Spa
has agreed with you.'

Hilda, as she gets to the door, gives one long look
at the face bent, as ever, on the table, and murmurs
to herself:

' Never good-bye—au revoir.'

# CHAPTER VIII.

## 'NATURE'S VAST SONS LIE CRADLED IN THE STORM.'

THE Brabazons travelled by easy stages to Basle, and Hilda, with the complete change of scene and surroundings, had already recovered some of her former spirits and interest in everything around her, which she had undoubtedly lost after the first few days in Spa. Will the great event in her young life which came to her there, with the absolute absorption of her own self into that of another, be to her for good or for evil?

As the train steams out of Basle, Colonel Brabazon tells his daughter that, although it will be some hours before they arrive at Lucerne, she will meanwhile, if the weather is at all clear, get a very good view of the Alps.

'Only,' he added, 'you won't know where to look for them. Read your book a bit longer, but look out of the window from time to time as we go along, and when you see something that looks like a snowy mountain, you can wake me up—I mean, you can take my *Times* and my pamphlet from me, and I will tell you the different names : for one's first view of the Alps is a thing to remember, and mine is still fresh in my memory.'

Hilda therefore continued to read her book, but looked out of the window at every second page. When will those mysterious mountains, whose history she knows so well, reveal themselves to her impatient eyes ?   She is once more all aglow with excitement for this new experience of life ; her youth, her unspoilt nature, are again paramount, and for the moment she is once more her old, impulsive self, eager for the pleasure that awaits her.

The train rumbles on.   Wooded hills and deep valleys appear before her, picturesque, no doubt, but always with a green or violet hue, which is not what she has been led to expect, from her father's description of a snow-clad mountain.   She returns to her book and reads diligently for at least half an hour, determined not to look out of the window again. Youth is so easily disappointed, and she had made up her mind that Switzerland was to be to her mind something so different from anything she had yet seen, that an avalanche falling on the top of the railway-carriage, or the whole train blocked by a glacier, would hardly have surprised her.   Still, the slow train speeds on its way, and as Hilda sees her mother fast asleep in one corner of the carriage, and her father buried in his *Times* opposite to her, she almost loses patience.

'Is it possible,' she says to herself, 'that people can be so indifferent to the beauties of Nature? Even if they have both seen all this twenty times before, it seems to me that the first sight of a "mountain clad with perpetual snow," however well you may know it, should be an interest that never palls.'

She gives a rather withering glance at her unsympathetic parents, and continues her desultory reading.

'Hilda,' says her father suddenly. after consulting his watch, 'look out of the window now, and tell me what you see.'

She puts down her book rather wearily, and, having taken a good look, replies:

'Oh, the same old thing, father—lots of purple and green hills. Ah! now there is a mist and a lot of black clouds, and above them, again, some very white ones, like fleeces. What a curious atmosphere it is!'

Colonel Brabazon takes off his pince-nez, drops his *Times*, and goes to the window; one glance is sufficient to his experienced eye. He puts his arm round Hilda's neck, kisses her on the forehead, and says:

'There is your first sight of the Alps; what you call the very white clouds are the tops of the mountains, seen above the real clouds.'

'Oh, father, how wonderful! I have so longed to see this, and the reality far surpasses all my expectations; but, father dear, you were perhaps imprudent to bring me here, for my ambitions are growing every moment, and I feel that I must at once carry you off to Chamounix so that I may, at all events, *see* Mont Blanc, even if you won't take me to the top, which I half believe you will,' she adds, throwing her arms round her father's neck.

'Come, come, my sweet child, you do ask a lot of your poor down-trodden father! Remember how at Spa you used to parboil me at the Cercle des Étrangers, and then get faint yourself, and have to be half carried out, with smelling-salts, etc. Now you want to freeze me on the top of Mont Blanc, which I carefully avoided when I was sent the Grand Tour with my tutor, *alias* "bear-leader," after I left Eton. He was rather a la-di-da sort of a chap, belonging to an old but impecunious family; and when we decided to start on our tour, *viâ* Switzerland, he said:

'"Now, look here, my dear boy, you will find me very easy to get on with; I shan't preach, nor urge you to do this, that, or the other, to improve your mind. Fond parents, with an only son like you, think that he must have someone about him to see—well, that he doesn't get his feet wet! All right, I'll see to that. But as we start on our tour in the mountainous country of Switzerland, and as I hate exertion of any kind, I may as well tell you beforehand that I'm d——d if we climb any mountains! they look just as well from the valley, and you can say you've been up them if you like; there'll be nobody to contradict you."

'And so you may judge for yourself, miss, that, having avoided the dangers and discomforts of mountain-climbing in the days of my youth, I am not likely to expose myself and you to them now that I am in the sere and yellow leaf. So many people have made the ascension of Mont Blanc since the early fifties, when the immortal Albert Smith drew the whole of London society to listen to the half-lecture, half-entertainment, in which he recounted his own experiences, that I think it is really played out, and that you and I may well be content to contemplate the wonders of the mountains from the base of them ; and,' he adds, again putting his arm round Hilda's shoulders, 'we will go up the Rigi by train and see the sun rise. There, will that content you ?'

'Not at all,' says Hilda rebelliously. 'I want to walk or be dragged up Mont Blanc ; that is my present idea, and perhaps it may help me to forget the hot rooms and the artificial atmosphere of the Cercle des Étrangers at Spa ; already all that seems a long way off, but I want to forget the—sad faces if I can. It didn't seem to me a wholesome or natural life, and the beauties of Nature, if you let me have my fill of them, are far more satisfactory and—but, oh, look !' she exclaims, as her long-suffering parent subsides into his seat, and, with his pince-nez re-adjusted, returns to the *Times*. 'There are some more white clouds, which I suppose you will tell me are more tops of mountains ; but indeed these are not—they are clouds ; come and look.'

Poor Colonel Brabazon goes again to the window and looks out.

'Some are clouds, some are snow-clad tops of mountains; you can hardly tell the difference in this rising mist. Wait till we go up the Lake of Geneva, where you will see all the highest mountains in comfort, and meanwhile let me go to sleep. The beds at the hotel at Basle were abominable—you said so yourself.'

So saying, Colonel Brabazon discarded his newspaper, closed his eyes, and tried to forget his enthusiastic daughter, with her snowy mountains and mists, and, above all, the idea of the ascent of Mont Blanc which threatens him. He almost regrets having fired her imagination, for has not Hilda had her own way hitherto in everything? As his *Times* drops on to his knees, he murmurs to himself, 'Mont Blanc—no, I draw the line at that; Rigi, railway—return ticket;' and in a few minutes the desired oblivion has come to him.

Not so Hilda, who continues to look out of the window. As she gazes at those mysterious snowy heights an idea occurs to her: Very few women have made the ascent of Mont Blanc; if she accomplishes this feat, Algy Somerville will read of it in the newspapers, for, having seen him in the reading-room of the Casino at Spa, she knows that he keeps himself so far in touch with what is going on in the world which he has renounced.

'I know Lord Clement mentioned my name to

him. If he sees I have made the ascent of Mont Blanc, he *must* look at me with some sort of interest when we meet at Monte Carlo; and I mean that we shall meet there this winter,' she says, clenching her teeth. 'But how am I to set about it? Apart from the notoriety which might bring my name before him —before my lord, who has never as yet condescended to notice his handmaiden—I should love the adventure for its own sake. I am very strong, and I believe sound in every way; if any woman can perform this feat, why not I?'

This idea, having taken a firm hold of Hilda, never left her.

# CHAPTER IX.

## MONT BLANC.

THE Brabazons spent a few days at Lucerne and at Lausanne, and eventually found their way to Chamounix, where tourists of every nation were gathered together, all intent on excursions and ascents, modest or ambitious. Amongst others stopping in the comfortable little hotel were two Americans, Mr. and Mrs. Cartwright, the latter of whom at once took an immense fancy to Hilda, and proceeded to ply her with questions as they sat next each other at the *table d'hôte*.

'Say, now, is this the first time you have left England? That's the country I want to see, and we are going there right away, when we get through with Switzerland. Please tell me all about it, everything you can think of, so as I won't appear too ignorant when I am there. I know that London is the largest city in the world, and has about five million inhabitants; but is it true that many of your titled aristocracy ride on omnibuses because they cān't afford cabs? Not but what I would love to ride outside an omnibus, but, then, as I am not in the four hundred of New York, I don't have to keep up appearances. My husband, bless him!—that's him opposite; and did you ever see such a handsome man? and he is just as *lovely* as he looks.'

Hilda is somewhat puzzled by the two adjectives, 'handsome' and 'lovely.' She raises her eyes shyly, and sees that her opposite neighbour has a beautifully cut face of almost classic outline, also that he has broad shoulders, a weather-beaten complexion, and is altogether a type of splendid manhood; so she cannot understand how the term 'lovely' can apply to him, but has hardly time to think it out, when her voluble neighbour continues:

'Now, say, is that sweet, delicate-looking woman you came in with your mother? I know the aristocratic-looking man is your poppa, because I heard you say, "Father, must we sit at the table with all those people?" and I felt badly when you sat down by me, because I thought *you* wouldn't like it. I know some of you English are a bit stiff, but I do hope we'll be friends. I took a liking to you the moment I saw you sitting in the garden before dinner, and taking notice of that ugly little mongrel of a dog that seemed to have lost its master. And I said to William James Cartwright—that's my husband— " I'm sure that pretty, proud-looking English girl has a warm heart." I could see you were English because American girls don't look so quiet and reserved. And now, say, what have you come to Chamounix

for ? Do you mean mountaineering, or is it to pass
the time till Parliament opens ? I am sure your
poppa is an M.P.—he looks it. Or have you come
here for your delicate māmma's health ?'

Hilda is rather taken aback. Never before has
she been 'interviewed' in like fashion ; and yet, as
she looks at the sweet, smiling face of her garrulous
little neighbour, she feels drawn towards her, and she
answers brightly, and without a shadow of the British
hauteur :

'Well, to tell you the truth, I have a very great
wish to go up Mont Blanc, or, at all events, to get
as far as the Grands-Mulets. I am afraid I should
never be able to persuade my father to go any higher,
and my mother is too delicate to attempt the mildest
form of Alpine climbing ; but,' she adds, her enthusiasm getting the better of her, 'I would like above
everything I can think of at this moment to make the
complete ascent of Mont Blanc.'

'What ? You want to get right on top of that
huge mountain ? Well, so do I ; and that's what I
mean to try to do. My husband, William James
Cartwright, has engaged the most expērienced guide
in all Chamounix to take us up. He says he has
never lost but one climber in the twenty years he has
been at his trade, and that man died of a long-stand-
ing disease that had troubled him for hâlf his life, but
which took him a little bit sudden about an hour after
he left Chamounix. That guide's all right, you see,
and he has got five others who he says are the best

anywhere about the Alps, so I feel quite confident;
and to-morrow two young men, friends of William
James, are going to join us. They are in fine training, as they have been running round Switzerland for
the last month; but, as I want to do a bit of walking
—say ten miles a day—before I attempt that big
climb, I guess we shān't start till—let me see, this is
Thursday; well, about Tuesday. Oh! I would love
to have you come with us, Miss——I have no idea
what your name is.'

'Hilda Brabazon,' says our heroine, smiling, and
trying not to be stiff; but she is so utterly unaccustomed to this sort of conversation and cross-
examination that she feels, to say the least of it,
awkward and rather ill at ease.

But a few more sentences from the warm-hearted
and genuine little woman beside her dissipate all her
doubts as to the guilelessness of her new-found
acquaintance.

'Well, to tell you the truth, I didn't know if you
were a Miss or a Mrs. But you are real sweet, and
as soon as you find a husband like my William James
—just look at him: isn't he *lovely?*—you say *Yes*.
But I believe you English girls want to be in-
dependent when you are married, and never dine
out together, because it isn't smart. Say, is that
so?'

Hilda has not gone through two London seasons
without being aware that there is some slight foundation for the unsophisticated little American woman's

doubts upon this subject, but before she has time to collect her thoughts and frame an answer, her neighbour bursts out with :

'Now, Miss Bramson, how about Mont Blanc ; do you seriously wish to get to the *summit ?*'

'I do indeed,' says Hilda quietly. Is there not much at stake, according to the idea which has entered her head as to the probability that the notoriety attaching to an ascent of Mont Blanc by a woman might bring her name to Algy's notice ?

'Well, it is to be done, and I am going to try it ; but I am not going to subject myself to any acute discomfort, and so we are going to start as far as the Grand Mulets, and then see how it pans out, and if we want to go any farther. I think, Miss Bramson, your father and mother, as you say in England·—we say poppa and māmma—are looking tired and bored, and so I can only thank you for having made my dinner so pleasant, and I do hope you will come for a walk with us to-morrow, because if we are going up that very laarge mountain together we must kinder train for it. So now good-night, Miss Bramson ; no, that ain't right, I know ; I saw you *smile*,' says the quick-witted little woman : 'tell me once more, and I won't forget.'

'Hilda Brabazon.'

'Well, it's a sweet name, and just fits you ; and now tell me, are you related to any of the aristocracy of England ? I have been married two years, and my great grief is that I have no dear little child ; I want a little gurl, and I would love to have her marry an English duke ; say, have you any coming on ?'

This is too much for Hilda's gravity.

' I must answer one question at a time,' she answers, laughing. 'Yes, I am related to some people whom you will find in our peerage ; but they are not very particular friends of mine, so I don't think more of them than of many of my other relations ; personally I put friendship far above ties of blood. As to eligible dukes in the future, there is time enough to think about them when your little daughter has come into the world, and if she is as good-looking as her father and mother, she ought to " annex " —isn't that one of your American expressions ?—an English duke, or at least a marquis. Now, really, I must go ; I see my father and mother are getting impatient, and are already half-way up the stairs ; good-night : I know I shall dream of Mont Blanc ;' saying which she runs off as fast as she can before her little American friend has time to begin another sentence.

The latter part of this conversation has taken place in the corridor outside the *salle-à-manger*, and the moment Hilda's parents see that she is released and prepared to follow them, they continue their way up the steep, narrow staircase to the third floor, no other rooms having been available on the short notice which was all they could give, owing to Hilda's determination to get as near Mont Blanc as she could, which forced them to hurry over all intermediate stages. On reaching the comparatively large bedroom apportioned to her mother, the latter, who is seated in an armchair, being somewhat exhausted with her climb, greets her with :

'Well, Hilda, I thought you would never get away from that little chatterbox.'

'Oh, mother! you have no idea how charming she is ; she is *just sweet*,' says Hilda, imitating her new friend's accent to the life.

Mrs. Brabazon stretches out her hand for the inevitable smelling bottle, and says rather severely :

'When we started to come abroad, I warned you against making casual acquaintances, knowing your impulsive nature. What can you know about this American woman, who you say is "just sweet"? Good heavens! what an expression!' says Mrs. Brabazon.

Hilda, with a great effort, suppresses the retort she is about to make, kisses her parents, and says :

'Well, good-night; I am going to get up very early and go for a long, long walk, so as to be in training for the Grands-Mulets—because you know, father,' she says, kissing him once more, 'you have promised to take me as far as that : now, haven't you ?'

'Did I promise ?' says the unfortunate Colonel. 'I don't remember; but if I did in a moment of weakness, I know you will hold me to it. Meanwhile, what did I do with my pamphlet? Oh, there it is ; now be off to bed, and get up at four o'clock if you

like; but do try and get rid of some of your super-
fluous energy before reasonable people breakfast.'

Hilda gives a warm hug to both father and mother
and leaves the room. Hardly has the door closed
behind her, than Mrs. Brabazon sits bolt upright
in her chair, no sign of weariness apparent, and
says:

'Now, George, thank Heaven Hilda has got something to interest her at last. I know my bad health
and my natural indolence have made me more
inattentive than I should have been to the poor
child's state of mind, though I *have* seen that she is
much changed since we left England. She turned
from gay to grave at Spa; did she have a *caprice de
jeune fille?* You were with her so much more than I
was that you ought to be able to tell me this. *Did*
she fall in love with anyone there? It seems impossible, but yet a woman's instinct is rarely wrong, and
I cannot otherwise account for the great change that
I have noticed. She is always sweet and affectionate
to me, and, though we have done our best to spoil
her, you *cannot* spoil a nature like hers; and she is
naturally so unselfish that, no doubt, if she has any
trouble or preoccupation, she has tried to conceal it
from me. Often, however, when she thought I was
asleep, I watched her, and saw her with her book on
her knees and a wistful look in her eyes. From the
moment, however, she left Spa she has seemed
different and more like herself, so now let us try to
indulge her in any whim that is reasonable.'

'Yes, but it is *not* reasonable for a young girl to wish to climb to the top of Mont Blanc, and, of course, to drag me up with her ; but that is the idea she has got into her head at this moment—"you bet," as I heard her new American friend say a dozen times to-night at the *table d'hôte*. As to her having fallen in love at Spa, she was always watching a very good-looking, sad-faced young man, a friend of Clement Armytage's, who told me that he had a most melancholy history ; but I didn't ask him what it was, and he did not volunteer to tell me. All I know is that Hilda never spoke to him, because, when we saw him at the dachsfox hunt, I told her, seeing that for the first time he seemed interested in something besides the green cloth on which I had noticed his eyes were always fixed, that I would ask him, as from one Englishman to another, what he thought of it. But she exclaimed, " Oh no, please don't ! he doesn't care to know any strangers ; Lord Clement told me so," and changed the conversation. So, you see, there could have been no love-making, could there ? And I never saw her,' continued the Colonel, eager to talk about Hilda, 'take the slightest interest in any other man all the time we were in Spa. Of course, Clement Armytage doesn't count ; they are the best of friends, and she knows all about the girl he wants to marry, and who can't make up her mind to say " Yes." What a fool she must be,' he adds, 'to refuse such a real good fellow, and such an attractive man as that ! Well, that is no business of ours ; she will probably marry a man who will treat her badly, and serve the minx right!' says the Colonel, who is easily started on the war-path in defence of his friends, and who has a genuine liking for the straightforward, manly young fellow he has known for several years.

Hilda, after she has retired to her room, sits on a very uncomfortable stool which calls itself an arm-chair, and *thinks* and *thinks*.

'I want to go up Mont Blanc partly because I want him to know I have done it, and partly—well, because I *want* to. That dear little American woman is bent on it, too. We will do it together, come what may. Meanwhile, I must go into training, and seven o'clock to-morrow shall see me start for a walk.'

'Say, Miss Brabazon, are you awake? It's just a heavenly morning, and it's haalf aafter six; now, do hurry up, and let us go for a walk.'

Hilda is out of bed in a moment, all her fresh young nature aroused at the prospect of something in the shape of adventure. Gone for the moment are the memories of the hot rooms of the Casino at Spa, and the exultant or despondent faces she saw there. She puts on her dressing-gown and runs to the door. Mrs. Cartwright is also in dressing-gown, but with little bare pink feet, as she explains she had no time to find her slippers.

'Wait not to find thy slippers, but come with thy naked feet,' carolled Hilda.

'I just peeped out of the window,' said the other,

and saw how beautiful it all looked; because, you know, there was a naasty mist last night; so I thought I would just see if you would like to come out with me and William James. *My!* he *was* cross when first I woke him up; but I put a wet sponge on his face, and told him his bike had been stolen from the lobby, and you should have seen him scooting round the room trying to find his pants. I wiped his face, and kissed him, and told him his bike was safe in the proprietor's hotel parlour, where I had persuaded him to put it myself, and he sat down in a chair and just laaughed, and said I was an angel; but there I chipped in. "Now, William James," I said, "I can see from your agitation that you value your bike above your wife;" and I drew myself up—way up—as high as I could. "Supposing someone had said to you, ' Your *wife* is lost or dead,' what would you have done?"

' "Well," he said, " I shouldn't have waited to look for anything. I should have run out, bare-headed, bare-footed, and never stopped till I found you, dead or alive."

' And, if you believe me, the great silly had tears in his eyes. I guess, though, I won't make any more jokes about his bike. Now, say, how soon can you be ready, Miss—I know—Brabazon?—I wrote it down last night, and I won't forget it again.'

' In half an hour,' replies Hilda, having at last got in a word, laughing heartily. ' I shan't do my hair, or attempt to be tidy, till we come back, but will just have a bath, huddle on my clothes, and meet you in

12

the *salle-à-manger*, as we must have some coffee before we start.'

' That's *so*,' says little Mrs. Cartwright, running off. ' Then, in haalf an hour we will meet again, and then I guess I'll have *something* on my feet. Now, did you *ever?* Here have I been talking all this time without even a stocking on! I do hope William James has found his clothes by this time. Well, then, in haalf an hour.'

Hilda shuts the door, and smiles to herself merrily as she thinks of the absolute stranger of the night before, with whom she now feels herself on terms of perfect intimacy, owing to the bare feet and ' William James's ' search for his ' pants.' Then she proceeds to ' hurry up ' with her dressing, eager to make a start with that training which is to take her up Mont Blanc.

The next three days are devoted to similar excursions, in which Colonel Brabazon joins, the party being added to by the two young Americans, friends of the Cartwrights, already alluded to, and who, being in real mountaineering training, are inclined to be patronizing as to the capabilities of the rest of the party to make the total, or even the partial, ascent of Mont Blanc. But they are mercilessly brought on to their marrow-bones by little Mrs. Cartwright, who suggests to them that if they want to ' walk round and show their muscle,' which metaphorically they have been hitherto rather too ready to do, they had better ' hire a hall.'

'For,' she says, laughing, 'we are not acrobats. We just want to go to the top of Mont Blanc, or as near as we can get, and when we can't walk any more we are going to be dragged up by the guides. That's their *biz*. But where will you be? You'll be too proud to be helped, and so you will be left behind, while Miss Brabazon and me are taking sketches of the surrounding country.'

All laugh at the little American's badinage, but meanwhile the subject is seriously discussed amongst the parties concerned, and Colonel Brabazon has got to be made to promise that he and Hilda will go as far as the Grands-Mulets, and then 'see about it.'

The experienced guide, who has already been mentioned, knocks at Colonel Brabazon's door the next morning, and asks in excellent English if he can speak to him. Colonel Brabazon invites him into his room, and begs him to be seated.

'Sir, I understand from the American family Cartwright that you will like to join them in the ascent of Mont Blanc, which I have made successfully sixty-three times, so monsieur will see I have experience. The weather is most favourable for the ascent just now, and I would like the party to start to-morrow; but I must know beforehand how many will take part in the ascension, so that I may get the requisite number of guides to accompany us. I understand that there are to be two ladies who will attempt the ascent, and they must have two guides each, the gentlemen one. Mr. Cartwright has been most generous, and has given me *carte-blanche* as to the expenses, which he wishes to pay entirely himself. He desired me only to ask if monsieur and mademoiselle would be ready to start at eight o'clock tomorrow morning.'

'Good heavens!' thinks the Colonel to himself, before he can frame an answer. 'Here is this man, who talks like a guide-book, ready to send us all to kingdom come, and takes it for granted that I am going to say "Yes" at once. This is the doing of Hilda and that enthusiastic little American woman.'

'Really,' he says politely, 'I must think it over. I have never been up a mountain in my life, and I think I am rather old to begin. My daughter, on the other hand, is rather young, and may lose her head and tumble over a precipice into a crevasse.'

'That is impossible, monsieur,' replies the guide. 'Both ladies will be tied with ropes to four of my most experienced comrades, and, as the ascent under favourable circumstances is a question of endurance, and not of danger, monsieur need be under no apprehension. Many other of our mountains, though not so high, are far more difficult and dangerous to attempt. If the ladies become tired, or the weather is threatening, they can return with their guides, and the gentlemen continue the ascent. I wait monsieur's commands.'

'God bless my soul! what am I to say to this dictatorial Alpine Prime Minister ?—Well, Monsieur le Guide, I really must think it over, and consult my daughter; but I will give you the answer at one o'clock. Will that be time enough for you to engage your guides, supposing we determine to make the ascent?'

'Perfectly, monsieur; they are all awaiting my orders;' saying which he bows himself out of the room, leaving the poor Colonel gasping in his chair. As soon as he has recovered himself a little, he goes into the corridor and knocks at Hilda's door.

'Come in—oh, it's you, father! I was just coming down to breakfast.' She looks rather guilty, as indeed she feels, knowing what has probably taken place.

'Hilda, a man who looks like a cross between a Spanish hidalgo and a brigand has just been *interviewing* me, as you would now call it, and he seems to take it for granted that we are prepared to start to-morrow morning for the whole ascent of Mont Blanc, and to be tied with ropes and run the risk of avalanches, precipices, crevasses, and God knows what besides! Of course, he says there is no danger, and that the weather is most favourable; but I have read enough about Alpine climbing to know that all the guides say that. Now, do you seriously want to risk your neck and mine, and leave your poor invalid mother a widow and orphan—I mean childless—for the sake of this mad freak?'

Hilda throws her arms round her father's neck and laughs her old silvery laugh, which somehow rejoices his heart.

'I have squared the widow and the orphan, and she gives her consent—*there!* what do you think of that?' she adds triumphantly. 'And now listen to me: how many times do you think this Constant Bertier has made the ascent successfully—that is, without an accident happening to anyone under his charge?'

'Oh, I heard sixty-three times,' says the Colonel with a groan; 'at least, so he says.'

'And I know it is true,' cuts in Hilda, 'because the Cartwrights and I have seen his book, signed by the people who made the ascents with him, and the signatures witnessed by the curé and the former and present proprietors of this hotel; so now, father, that's all right, isn't it? and we start to-morrow? Mrs. Cartwright isn't particularly robust, and doesn't expect to get to the top of Mont Blanc, and when she turns back I give you my word of honour that I will turn back too. Talk to her about it to-night at dinner; you must see what a little trump she is, and you do like what you have seen of her, don't you?'

'Indeed I do, my dear, and I think she is a genuine warm-hearted woman. Her affection and admiration for "William James" would melt a heart of stone. How very *unfashionable* she would be in a London or New York drawing-room, wouldn't she?'

'Of course she would; she would just "get left," to use her own expression,' replied Hilda. 'And now we will all meet at dinner at half-past six, and settle finally about to-morrow. I am going for an hour's walk *uphill*, to finish my training ; and then I want to do some dumb-bell exercise, in order to be able to hold on to the ropes with plenty of developed muscle ; so au revoir till dinner-time.'

'Oh, these *fin - de - siècle* girls !' says Colonel Brabazon to himself as Hilda leaves the room. 'If it isn't bicycling, it's—well, running an equal danger of meeting with sudden death or being maimed for life ascending a mountain. Is it worse to be run over by an omnibus in Piccadilly, when your bicycle "skids," and you fall off and break an arm or a leg, or are killed outright, or to chance going up a historical mountain with a guide of sixty-three years' experience ? No, I mean a guide of sixty-three. He can't be that, though ; he looks about forty-five. I have it—a guide who has made sixty-three ascents of Mont Blanc. That's it; I was always good at statistics ! Dear me, how sleepy this mountain air makes one feel ! Where is that pamphlet about— what was it about ? I think I will take forty winks, and then think it over——' Rap, rap, rap at the door. 'Come in,' says Colonel Brabazon, reaching out his hand for the pamphlet, which is at the other end of the room, on the top of his chest of drawers, but which he fancied he had been reading. 'Come in ; *entrez.*'

'May I really come in ?' and a bright little face is thrust through the half-open door, and Mrs. Cartwright stands hesitatingly on the threshold. Colonel Brabazon, courteous and well-bred, though still rather sleepy, is on his feet in a moment, his hand up the handle of the door, which he pulls wide open.

'Pray come in, Mrs. Cartwright. I wish I could offer you a more comfortable apartment; but in this crowded little hotel it was impossible to get a sitting-room. Please take this armchair, which I know is comfortable, as I am afraid I go to sleep in it several times a day, for I find this air makes me terribly sleepy.'

'Why, you don't say!' says the little American woman, sinking into the chair that has been offered her, while Colonel Brabazon remains standing before her, his head bent in a polite bow; '*I* never seem to have any time for sleep; I'm just that mad to go right *on top* of Mont Blanc that, what with exercising my legs and my arms, I never seem to have any time for sleep. Now, see here, Colonel: I'm an Amurrican woman, this is the first time I have been in Europe, and so I shouldn't wonder if you think me a bit of a savage! Well, let that slide. Anyhow, I was happy in my home till I married my husband, William James; now I'm happier still, and I only want to make everybody happy round me. I have seen a lot of your daughter, Miss Hilda, since we have been here, and I think she is just the sweetest, loveliest girl I have ever met; but she has had some trouble lately. I don't know what it is; I wouldn't for any-thing try to force her confidence, but, anyhow, she seemed to brighten up so when I suggested that we should go up Mont Blanc together, that I just do want you to give your consent : that's what I've come for. If I caan't get to the top, Miss Hilda and I will come down together—that's agreed. Now, what do you say : will you come, too? Why,' she says, looking at him critically, ' you caan't be a boy, as you are Miss Hilda's father, but you look just as fit for mountaineering as William James; but, then, he is lazy and fat, which you are not. Any way, we have engaged guides enough to pull us all up when we get tired ; so now it only rests with you to say " Yes," for I have set my heart on gratifying that sweet Miss Hilda's wish, and I don't think there is scarcely any risk, do you ?'

This is the first moment that the still sleepy and partially bewildered Englishman has had an opportunity of getting in a word, but, as he knows from experience of the voluble little lady before him that an opportunity must not be lost, he also proceeds to ' speak a piece.'

' Well, you see, Mrs. Cartwright, I must tell you honestly that I have a rooted objection to seeing any woman, of whatever nation, overtaxing her strength, and taking part in amusements or occupations that I consider are only fitted for men. Of course, you will say I am old-fashioned—I am prepared for that ; but one must take the bitter with the sweet. My idea is that a man should be chivalrous, and a woman womanly, but that is, I know, not up to date. A lady gets up to leave the room, and the young men remain seated while she opens the door. I, with my rheumatic old limbs, jump up—no, I don't *jump*,

because I *can't*'—they both laugh—'the young men
continue smoking their cigarettes, and don't attempt
to move.  I don't blame them, really I don't.  The
women of the present day have made themselves so
much the equals of men in all their manly pursuits, that
I think they are the most to blame.  For instance,
take bicycling.  When you get on your bike—as I
believe it is called—your husband——'

He gets no further, for Mrs. Cartwright jumps off
her chair, puts her tiny hands over his mouth, and
says :

'Hold on, there !  My husband objects to me
bicycling.  I would *love* to, if he *didn't* object ; but
he does, and not to see my only brother President of
the United States—he is now clerk in a dry-goods
store—would I put my leg—I mean my divided skirt
—over a bicycle.  But, as William James doesn't
object to my trying to go up Mont Blanc, say, why
caan't you let Miss Hilda try, too ?'

'My dear Mrs. Cartwright, you have broken down
all my stern resolves.  We will start to-morrow, and,
as you say, get as far as we can.'

'Didn't I know you were just a lovely man, and
only had to be talked to the right way ?' said little
Mrs. Cartwright as she rose and prepared to leave the
room.

'No, my dear lady,' said the chivalrous Colonel, as
he took both her hands in his and led her to the
door ; 'but I know how to appreciate a good woman
and a loving wife ; and so now we will discuss all

details to-night at dinner, and make our wills before-hand. You have fairly conquered me, in so far that I consent to myself and Hilda attempting the ascent of Mont Blanc. But, mind, if any obstacles arise, and that extremely plausible and experienced guide is not satisfied that all the "conditions are favour-able," we turn back. Is that a bargain?'

'Yes, yes, I promise,' says the little American joyously, as she runs down the stairs. "'Hail Columbia!"—I mean, "Britannia rules the waves."'

Colonel Brabazon sinks back in his chair as soon as he has shut the door, and laughs heartily.

'Well, of all the wonderful women I have ever met in my life, this is the most wonderful! But *what* a trump! what a little dear!' he finds himself saying, as he looks quite sentimentally at the chair she has just vacated. 'She takes one's breath away with the pace at which she talks, but she also takes away doubts as to the possibility that any modern woman can be a good wife and yet be cheery and jolly and go-ahead. Just imagine any young married woman in these days giving up bicycling to please her husband! I hope "William James" appreciates the sacrifice. I must cultivate his acquaintance more than I have yet done, and see if he is worthy of the treasure he has got as a wife. She is "just sweet," as Hilda would now say, But, good Lord! fancy an old fogey like me taking to these American expres-sions, and—and—— Well, I can't help it; she *is* "just sweet," and Hilda was quite right.'

Clang! clang! clang! goes the *table d'hôte* bell,
and the Brabazons are half-way down the stairs
before it has done ringing, so eager are they to meet
their new friends and arrange everything for the
great event of the morrow. Mrs. Brabazon, though
naturally she is to take no part in the expedition,
shows as much interest as anyone in the arrangements, which are duly discussed by the whole party
with much laughter and chaff, the two young
American men coming in for a large share of the
latter, and being told by Mrs. Cartwright that they
'will certainly be hung out to dry about haalf way
between the Grands-Mulets and the top glacier, so as
we can see where to make for when we start to come
down.'

'I'm not going to be proud, like you,' she says.
'We've only got one pair of legs each, and I guess
the guides have six at least. They've been at it all
their lives; and as for ropes—how many yards did
that boss guide say he had got? Any way, Miss
Brabazon and I are going to be pulled and hauled to
the top somehow; and, Colonel'—turning to him with
a sweet smile—'don't you be too proud. Just you
hang on to the guides, too; I wouldn't haalf enjoy it
if you didn't get right away on top. These two
young men make me tired with all they say they can
do in the way of climbing, but I know they'll be more
tired than me if they don't climb down—how's that
for a pun?—and let themselves be given a friendly
haul, at least, now and then.'

Shortly after this, the ' boss guide,' as she calls him, is admitted to the presence in order that all final arrangements may be made and duly understood, and at nine o'clock the whole party retire to bed to fit themselves, if possible, by a long night's sleep, for the exertions of the following day.

# CHAPTER X.

## 'ALTIORA PETO.'

THE ascent of Mont Blanc has been so ably described by many writers, and it has now become a so comparatively common achievement, that I ask permission to pass over all details of this one. It suffices to say that, the circumstances being altogether favourable, the whole party *did* reach the summit of that great mountain, though all were in a more or less dilapidated condition. We have now to deal with their various impressions on returning to their comfortable quarters at Chamounix.

Let us begin with Colonel Brabazon, who, on entering his wife's room, says :

'God bless you, my dear! You might have dissuaded me from attempting this feat, but you were very sensible, and I shall always be grateful to you. It was a stupendous thing—a thing that I can never forget. Everything was perfectly arranged ; I only wish you had been able to go with us.'

Mrs. Brabazon throws her arms round her husband's neck, saying :

'My dear George, you don't know how glad I am
that all has turned out so well, and that you have so
thoroughly enjoyed yourself. I was a *little* anxious,
but, still, I had great confidence in your chief guide,
and, unbeknown to you and Hilda, I had a private
interview with him, and made him *swear* that, if everything was not absolutely what he called "favourable"
to the ascent, he would send you and Hilda back
with his most trusted men. I also promised him a
thousand francs if he brought you back safely, and
here it is in an envelope,' she adds, smiling through
her tears of pleasure and emotion.

Colonel Brabazon is deeply touched ; he kisses her
tenderly, and says :

'It was good and unselfish of you to let us go, and
even to encourage us ; for, of course, there must
always be a certain amount of risk in making the
ascent of Mont Blanc,' he says, drawing himself up
proudly. 'Ay, ay, how stiff I am ! I think I will
go to bed, dear, and stop there for twenty-four hours.'

'Here is your *Times*, George, that came this
morning.'

'Oh, bother the *Times* ! Have you got any Elliman's embrocation ? That's much more to the purpose. Oh, if you knew how my legs, ankles, and
feet ache ! I think to be amputated at the waist
would be my greatest comfort at this moment.'

But he laughs cheerily, and hobbles off to bed
armed with a bottle of Elliman's embrocation, that
vade-mecum of sportsman and athlete.

We will now turn to the Cartwrights, who have thrown themselves into armchairs in their bed-room, declaring themselves too tired to eat, or even to undress. William James lights a cigarette and is silent. Not so his better half; her tongue is about the only part of her person that has any energy left in it, and she starts off at a tangent.

'Well, did ever you know anything so puffectly successful as this expedition? And it was all my doing; you must admit that.'

'Oh, I'll admit anything, my dear, if you or some-body will undo my boots, for I am so stiff I couldn't stoop to pick up a million-dollar note if it was lying on the floor in front of me. Remember, you ladies had two guides each to pull and push you up; we men had only one, and as I am no light weight, I often found the rope slack and had to do the climbing myself. Well, dear,' he says, as he sees his plucky little wife's eyes heavy with slumber and fatigue, 'we've *done* it, and I'm very proud both of you and of myself. We will swagger about it no end when we get back to New York, but meanwhile I am going to tumble into bed, boots and all probably, and you do the same.'

'I'm going to,' says a feeble little voice, 'for I just caan't undress, and that's all about it. My! what a big mountain that is! It's ever—ever—ever so much higher than I thought; but I *am* glad we got up to—to—— Did we get to the top, dear? I seem to forget. I *am so* tired ;' her pretty little head falls back, and she is asleep.

But Cartwright is on his feet in a moment, all his own aches and pains forgotten. He lifts the fragile little figure in his arms, places her inside her bed, only taking off her boots, and, kissing her on the forehead, says to himself :

' There is nothing like a woman for pluck ; she must be more dead beat than I am, and that's saying a good deal. Well, here goes ;' and he tumbles into his own bed, boots and all.

We now turn to the two young American men, who, proud of their mountaineering experience and fine training, are both loath to admit that they have had about enough of it.

' Well, Reggie, it was not so very difficult, after all, to ascend that much-talked-of mountain,' says the younger of the two, aged twenty-three.

' No, no,' replies the other, whose limbs ache to such a degree that he would gladly tumble into bed and leave the discussion of the expedition till the next day ; but both are too young and too proud and enthusiastic to own themselves dead beat. ' No, it was not much, except for the ladies and Colonel Brabazon ; but, of course, they could never have got to the top if they had not been dragged up. With you and me it was different, for we had very little help, had we ? except when Constant said we were to be tied on to one guide. I kept the rope quite slack —did you ? I felt ashamed of letting a fellow not half so strong or active as I am drag me after him, but of course we had to obey orders. How did you get on with your guide? We had so few opportunities of comparing notes.'

'Oh, I did much the same as you. I left the rope slack to save the poor devil the trouble of hauling up a younger and stronger man than he was. Would you like your revenge at bézique before we turn in?'

'No—no, thank you. I've got some letters to write, and I want to be up early to-morrow to arrange about the ascent of Monte Rosa, which I believe is much harder work than that of Mont Blanc. Mere child's play, isn't it?'

'Oh, nothing at all! But I feel as if I could sleep a bit,' says the other, leaving the room.

'Yes, mountain air does make one drowsy,' replies his friend, as he prepares to wrench himself out of the armchair, in which he devoutly wishes he might pass the night, did not his pride come to his rescue.

As it is, the two young men retire to their rooms, only too thankful to bolt their doors, as is advised by the printed regulations in almost every Continental hotel, as a precaution against thieves; but in this case the precaution is far more necessary between the two young athletes, who each wishes to conceal from the other that the ascent of Mont Blanc has been too much for him, and that his only idea is rest, and

as much of it as he can decently get without attract-
ing attention.

And Hilda?   We must now penetrate into the
privacy of her cosy little bedroom, where her mother,
having been up to see that she has everything she
wants, leaves her in the hands of their mutual maid,
who, having known Hilda from a child, proceeds
to undress her and tuck her up in bed as she has
done many times before, saying as she leaves the
room :

' There, Miss Hilda, you look as white as a sheet,
and so you have ever since we came to foreign parts.
Only a week after we got to Spa you seemed quite
different.   Shan't I be glad when we get back to
England !   This place is bad enough, but, oh, that
Spa !   Well, good-night, my dear, and as we start for
home in a few days, I hope I shall soon see the roses
come back to your cheeks.'

Hilda lies back on her pillows wellnigh exhausted
with the physical strain she has undergone; but
her large eyes are wide open—she is thinking.   Very
few Englishwomen have made the ascent of Mont
Blanc.   He reads the papers; the account of the
ascent of Mont Blanc must attract his attention :
that is all she asks for.   As she gradually falls asleep,
quite worn out with the fatigue she has undergone,
her one thought is : He will know about it.   He, who
is such a sportsman, will appreciate her pluck, and be
proud of his countrywoman.   The deep snow, the
crevasses, the glaciers, where their footsteps were cut

with ice-axes, seem to fade from her mind as she falls into the deep sleep of physical exhaustion, her last waking thought being : ' He will hear of it. He has such sporting instincts still that it may interest him to hear about Clement Armytage's friend. I wonder—I wish——' deep sleep—oblivion.

It seemed to Hilda that she had only been asleep a few minutes, when a loud knocking at her door aroused her from her deep slumber ; in reality she had been asleep since eight o'clock the night before, and it was now ten the next morning. The persistent knocking caused her to put on her dressing-gown and hasten to open the door. On the threshold stood poor little Mrs. Cartwright in travelling costume, with tears streaming down her cheeks, and a little woe-begone face, who greeted her thus :

'Oh, my dear Hilda—say, I can call you Hilda just this once—we have had such terrible news ! William James has had a cable to say that his mother, whom he adores, and so do I, has had a bad accident in New York, and been run over by a tram and her thigh broken ; and we are to start immediately, as she has a good deal of fever, and is in a critical state. So we are off just as quick as we can catch a train to take us anywhere where we can get a mail-boat. We have not had time to fix up our route yet, but I couldn't leave without wishing you good-bye, and as I guess the quickest way will be by Paris and Havre, and the train starts in haalf an hour, I haven't much time. I would like to have said good-bye to your father and mother. They were both so good to me, and yet I know at first they didn't take to me. You English think that Americans who come to England only care about society and fine clothes, but that is not so when you are fond of your husband, as I am of William James; and just now his sorrow is mine, and I can think of nothing else. So now, my dear, kiss me good-bye. I will write you from New York how things go, and meanwhile I will never forget the happy days we have passed together, and will try in future not to be so scared when I meet an "English family of distinction," for you have all been so good to the little American nobody. Now I must go.'

She throws her arms around Hilda's neck, and kisses her warmly on both cheeks. The usually reserved girl, whose whole soul has latterly been filled by one individual, is fairly overcome by the sweet, unselfish nature now before her. She returns her new-found friend's embraces as warmly as they are given, and thus they part.

The last entry in Hilda's diary before leaving Chamounix is: 'Said good-bye to dear little Mrs. Cartwright; I am not much given to making new friends, but saw enough of her to be convinced that she was one in a thousand, and I only hope that we shall meet again some day.'

The great event of the ascent of Mont Blanc once past and gone, anything else would be an anti-climax; Colonel Brabazon therefore suggests to

Hilda that they shall start for England without delay, the weather having broken up within the last twenty-four hours, and mists and snow-storms having set in. So the Brabazon family, bag and baggage, are soon once more *en route*, and this time for their native land, where they arrived in due course of time at Victoria Station, without more than the usual amount of the difficulties and annoyances to which travellers are still subjected, who have much luggage, suspicious-looking parcels, etc., all of which have to go through the 'ordeal by touch' at the hands of the Custom House officials.

However, Mrs. Brabazon and Hilda are spared these tiresome details of a return from the Continent, as their carriage is waiting for them, and they drive home at once, Colonel Brabazon having gallantly volunteered to see the luggage cleared himself. The lady's-maid is truly grateful for this, as, having once reached her native land, she is inclined to hold forth as to the superiority of foreign manners, and Colonel Brabazon finds her at daggers drawn with a stolid official to whom she has declared that a parcel, well tied up with string, is only odds and ends of bits of lace.

'Lace,' exclaims the official, 'that's just one of them things we've got to look after.'

'Well, it isn't lace, then,' says the lady's-maid, now thoroughly roused ; for, able to use her own language, she is prepared to show fight.

'Well, p'raps it's tea,' says the polite official, 'and

that is contraband—that is, you have to pay duty for it, miss.'

'Miss !' exclaims the lady's-maid; 'in foreign parts they always called me *maddarm*—they were polite, they were; and why should I bring bad tea home from abroad when I can get it good and cheap at home ?"

In a few minutes Colonel Brabazon, having seen his wife and daughter off, returns to the Customs office, and the knotty question of tea or lace is soon amicably settled, a four-wheeler called, and luggage, lady's-maid, and long-suffering Colonel comfortably transferred to Upper Grosvenor Street, where we will leave them for the present, all glad to be once more 'at home,' and at liberty to think over the varied experiences of their prolonged trip.

# CHAPTER XI.

## THE MOTHER'S VICTORY

THE Brabazons, having no country-house of their own, have been for some years in the habit of spending the autumn months in country visits, but always with a *pied-à-terre* at some seaside place, such as Brighton, Eastbourne, St. Leonards, or one of the other places of that sort which attract Londoners at that season of the year, and which render them the double service of amusing them and setting them up for the life of cosy dinners, supper-parties after the theatre, and the usual routine of town life before the ' season ' proper begins.

Two days after the arrival of the ' family,' as the elderly housekeeper in Upper Grosvenor Street terms them, Colonel Brabazon calls a *conseil de famille.*

' Now, then, here we are settled down—at least, I have nearly got over my stiffness, after what that sweet American woman called " walking up the big mountain." It will be long before we do such another tramp as that.'

Hilda's eyes are moist in affectionate remembrance of her warm-hearted little friend.

'But what are we going to do now?  The Elliots have told us to propose ourselves whenever we like—the Gervases also; then there are duty visits to relations, who will expect us as soon as they know we have not yet settled down in town; now, where shall we begin?  My dear,' he says, turning to Mrs. Brabazon, who is beginning to yawn, 'first of all I vote we take our usual house at the seaside, as a base of operations.  You have only to tell me the place, therefore, and I will at once have a house found for you where you can be comfortable and as quiet as you like, until it is time to settle in London for the winter.'

'For the winter?' says Hilda to herself.  'No; that must be at Monte Carlo: *he will be there*—Clement Armytage will be there—and there the campaign shall open which is to make or mar me.'

'Father,' she says abruptly, 'don't let us make any plans beforehand.  London in the winter is dismal with the fogs, and—and, well, you have spoilt me by taking me abroad.  Suppose we go to Brighton for a few weeks, and after that to the—the Riviera; anywhere in the Riviera, for it is all beautiful, I am told, and that lovely climate would be good for mother, who is never quite herself in London in the winter—are you, mother?'

Mrs. Brabazon is fast falling asleep, her smelling-

bottle clasped in her right hand; but she has heard
the conversation, and hastens to say:

' Yes, by all means let us spend the winter somewhere away from the fogs and dreariness of London.'

Hilda's heart gives a great bound. Hitherto her
mother has adhered to the usual routine of her life—
so many country-house visits, so many duty visits,
varied by retirement to the seaside or to London
when she did not feel equal to the strain laid upon
her as a brilliant woman of the world. Failing health
had made this more of an effort to her as the years
sped on, and so she willingly agreed to the sug-
gestion, and Eastbourne was selected for the autumn
programme. Colonel Brabazon, starting next evening to get a suitable house there, was able in the
course of the day to telegraph that it was found, but
was somewhat disappointed on his return to London
to notice that his enumeration of the manifold
advantages he offered was not met with an outburst
of enthusiasm on the part of his wife and daughter.

This is what had happened. Hilda, all intent on
going to Monte Carlo as soon as she thinks that the
season has commenced and that Algy is likely to be
there, says to her mother, her father being absent
and unable to contradict her:

' Now, mother, you know you can't stand an
English winter—no more can I; I cough, cough.
All last winter I was never free from bronchitis,
or something of the sort—now, was I?' she asks,
rather hesitatingly.

Mrs. Brabazon, who is no fool, begins to smell a rat, so she answers at once:

'Yet, my dear Hilda, you remember, when you did have a bad attack of bronchitis last winter at the Elliots', where you thought of nothing but hunting, and the doctor told you if you did not take care you would have to spend your next few winters abroad, how angry you were! and how you said you would rather die in England trying to hunt—if only on wheels—than go to the finest climate in the world; and now'—Mrs. Brabazon breaks off her harangue, and, putting down her smelling-bottle, sits upright in her chair—'my child, you have changed very much in the last two months: something has come over you that I don't understand. Can't you tell me what it is? I know I am a more or less selfish invalid, and thus far your life has been so bright and happy that I confess I have given more thought to myself than I have to you. You are so young, you could have married so well, as the world would say, that I supposed you were perfectly happy with us. I always told you to wait till you were quite certain you had found a man with whom you could be really happy before leaving home, where, at any rate, you have been shown that there is such a thing as domestic happiness after the twenty years that your father and I have spent together. Have you come across anyone unknown to me that has influenced your life? I saw so little of you at Spa, and you were so much with your father at the Casino, that

I could not follow all the acquaintances you made. Did you fall in love with anyone there ?—that would account to me for the change in you from gay to grave. Tell me, my child !'

Hilda shivers ; she loves her mother tenderly, and is deeply touched by her solicitude. It is rather true, as Mrs. Brabazon herself says, that she was then taken up too much by her various ailments to be able to give her whole mind to Hilda, much as she loved the child ; moreover, and with justice hitherto, she had looked upon her as a bright, rather spoilt child, without a care. But now the mother in her is awake and alert, if she cannot help her to happiness, to defend her only child against sorrow.

' Hilda '—Mrs. Brabazon holds out her arms— ' come and tell me if there is anything that is worrying or troubling you, and that it will be a relief to you to tell me about. You know, my darling, that I shall sympathize with you, and give you my best advice, for that *something* has come into your life since we went abroad I am convinced, and that it is occupying, if not troubling, you every day.'

Hilda hesitates ; she looks at the fragile, sweet face upon the sofa, and makes up her mind. Oh, the relief, after all her pent-up feelings of the last two months, to confide in someone, and that someone her own mother, who implores her confidence ! She drops on her knees, crawls over to her mother's sofa, hides her head in her lap, and tells her everything.

How wicked it is to laugh, nay, to jeer, at women who have what is popularly called 'a good cry'! and how rarely such a thing occurs in real life—at all events, amongst such women as are depicted in this story! But on this occasion tears were admissible when Hilda's feelings, so long repressed, burst through the restraint she had put upon herself. If she had stopped to think, she might not have confided the whole story to her mother, and if her mother had been too much taken up with her own ailments to show the real sympathy she felt for her child, as soon as she realized the change in her, this confidence might never have been invited. Life is made up of such chances.

Happily, on this occasion the mother and daughter were one with each other, and when Colonel Brabazon returned from Eastbourne, having found just the little house that would suit them, he was surprised to find his wife lying on her sofa, as usual, but without her smelling-bottle, and Hilda sitting on a footstool at her mother's feet, her head buried in her mother's lap. If the truth must be told, Colonel Brabazon had announced his arrival by a later train, saying he would dine in Eastbourne and require no supper.

That the power is not given to all to understand 'Bradshaw,' anyone will admit who is old enough to remember Frank Burnand's 'Bradshaw' pages in 'Out of Town,' where there are trains that start but do not arrive, and trains that arrive but do not start; and that yet more weird category of trains that neither start nor arrive, but stop at intermediate stations ; and I think it cannot be denied that to ordinary individuals this standard work is a little bit puzzling. Still, Colonel Brabazon, being extremely old-fashioned in some ways, had always pinned his faith to 'Bradshaw,' and set his face against the 'A B C,' which is a useful and simple guide, provided you are content always to go to London in order to make use of it. The day was Saturday, and the Colonel, having naturally overlooked 'Saturday facilities,' made a mistake on the right side, and arrived by an earlier train than that by which he had announced himself ; thus he came upon the touching scene just described.

The self-contained Hilda had no courage, no inclination, indeed, at that moment, to make a second confidence, and she clung to her mother for one moment as her father came into the room.

'Not one word of this at present, mother,' she said hurriedly. A pressure of the hand was all that was necessary in answer.

'Well,' said the jovial Colonel on entering the room, 'you two don't look very lively. What's the matter, Hilda ?'

'Nothing is the matter with Hilda,' replied her mother promptly ; 'but she has very nearly gone to sleep, and so have I, just as if we were anticipating the first effect of the sea-air. Now, tell us how you caught an earlier train than you expected, and what house you have taken for us, as we are all eagerness to be off; London is odious at this time of year. But don't you want some supper? The Elliots sent us two brace of grouse this morning, and there is a whole one left from dinner, Hilda and I having been greedy enough to think that one would not be enough, but it was; now, just ring, and have the other one up.'

And the Colonel, nothing loath, rang the bell.

He supped very well, what with cold grouse, a pâté de fois gras en croûte, and a bottle of excellent claret.

'And now, my dear,' he said, as he lighted his cigar and dropped a lump of sugar into his coffee, 'what was the matter with Hilda, who left the room as soon as I came into it?'

'Oh, nothing,' said Mrs. Brabazon, proud of her daughter's confidence, and brimming over with maternal feeling—she had always been a little bit jealous of the great affection and sympathy that existed between the father and daughter, from which, mainly by her own fault, she had been more or less excluded. But now that was over; henceforth there should be no more preoccupation about herself, no morbid thoughts of ill-health; Hilda's loving trust in her had swept away those barriers, and she understood now that they had before them the crisis of Hilda's life. But the revulsion of feeling was too sudden, and she burst into tears.

'My dear,' said Colonel Brabazon, much alarmed, 'what is the matter? Tears?'

'Oh yes, George—tears of joy! I was so nervous and over-excited that being at home and having a quiet talk with Hilda just upset me—that's all. No, I don't want my smelling-bottle. Hilda is one in a thousand : so good, so sensible, so—well, everything that parents could expect or hope for from an only child! Isn't she ?'

'My dear, I always told you so; but you seemed to differ from me, so I let it alone. You said I spoilt her, and that her refusals of the many brilliant offers of marriage she has had were the result of my spoiling her and making her home so happy, though what the void will be when she *does* leave us God only knows! She is like a sunbeam in the house, and you will miss her as much as I do, my dear; for though she may be more of a companion to me out of doors, on account of her youth and vitality, she loves you tenderly, and never comes into the house after one of our long expeditions without saying : " Can I go to mother? Do you think she is asleep?" She has a heart of gold, that girl, and she will never marry a man she does not thoroughly love and trust; but when will that man appear? Once her mind is made up,' he continued, 'I think she will tell me all about it ; if she does, you must not be jealous : for, really, Hilda and I are more like brother and sister than father and daughter, and she may be a little bit shy of giving you her confidence—not that she has any to give at present, I know. But when the time does come, as I said before, my dear, don't be jealous, nor disappointed should she happen to fall in love with a poor man, who really loves her for herself. Thank Heaven, we can afford to make her and her husband comfortable, so far as money goes ; and she shall marry whom she chooses. Then if she comes to me, saying, " Father, I want to marry So-and-so ; he is poor, but he is a gentleman, and I love him," I promise to break it to you gently; and, though I know you have always expected her to make a great marriage, I think that she and I between us will be able to reconcile you to " love in a (comparative) cottage " for her.'

If a portrait-painter could have seen Mrs. Bra-bazon's face at that moment, it would have been a study to tax his best powers, for in the space of a minute or two amusement, triumph, preoccupation, and affection were all depicted there.

' Yes, George, all you say is perfectly true ; Hilda can and shall marry a man she likes. She has only to make up her mind that she really loves a man, and we will make up ours that he is worthy of her ; you will find that I shall put no obstacles in the way.'

' That's right, my dear ; I am glad you take such a sensible view of matters. Meanwhile there is no hurry ; Hilda is young and heart-whole at present, isn't she ?'

' I think I will have my smelling-bottle now,' says Mrs. Brabazon, putting it to her nose to conceal a smile as her husband handed it to her. ' And now, you know, I have made up my mind to spend the winter at Monte Carlo.  We will start as soon as we have had enough of Eastbourne ; do you agree?'

'Oh yes, my dear; I shall be only too pleased to revisit the scenes of my youth, and I am *sure* it will be good for you.  But how about Hilda ? won't she miss her hunting, and country-house visits, and Christmas balls and festivities ?'

'I think Hilda will be reconciled to pass a winter in the South of France ; however, you can talk to her to-morrow and see what she says.  I am thankful to say I feel so much better that you really need not consult my health ; besides, I am always just as well in London as anywhere else : let Hilda decide.  But now I really must go to bed ; just see how late it is !'

# CHAPTER XII.

## 'WHERE THOU GOEST I WILL GO.'

EASTBOURNE is a delightful place during the autumn months, and the Brabazons enjoyed themselves thoroughly during their few weeks' residence there. As for Mrs. Brabazon, she has taken a new lease of life, for she has learnt the beauty and charm of unselfishness, and that to interest yourself in the welfare of others is far more satisfactory than to remain perpetually engrossed with the contemplation of your own personal ailments, personal grievances, personal fads. In short, from the moment that Hilda confided to her mother the brief history of her one romance, Mrs. Brabazon became a changed woman. Hitherto her only child had appeared to prefer her father's society to that of her mother. Was it not natural? Their two strong constitutions, their out-of-door life spent together, brought them into constant companionship. The hypochondriacal state into which she had fallen had forcibly drawn the father and daughter closer together as companions and confidants. But now everything was changed,

14—2

and Mrs. Brabazon, who until then had been one of the most admired and distinguished women of her day, gave up the invalid's fads and fancies which, to the great regret of all her numerous friends and acquaintances, had latterly taken such a hold on her.

Hilda's confidence, Hilda's romantic story, now occupies all her thoughts, and she lives again in her daughter's youth.

'When shall we start for Monte Carlo?' she asked, shivering, one evening in their house at Eastbourne. 'I feel the cold here terribly, George; you and Hilda have been paying visits and amusing yourselves—it is *my* turn now, and I want to see the sun and flowers. I was alone all last week when you were at the Elliots'  On Monday you go to the Scotts' for a week, and I cannot stand that bleak house, without a bath-room, electric light, or even gas, so after you have done that visit let us be off to the sunny South. Hilda darling, you won't mind, will you, leaving this country life for—for—well, what is not exactly a town life?  You can walk and bicycle and yacht as much as you like at Monte Carlo; try and persuade your father that we shall all three appreciate a winter in the Riviera; it will be such a pleasant change from London smoke and fogs.'

The impulsive Hilda was on the point of again throwing herself at her mother's feet, and thanking her for thus diplomatically paving the way for the realization of her cherished project, but a warning look restrained her. Why are all women artful, and prone to conceal their real thoughts and feelings? That they are so there is no disputing, and although Mrs. Brabazon and Hilda loved and respected the husband and father—although without him life would indeed have been a blank—yet the moment they had a mutual secret they took a delight in keeping him in the dark.

'Well, my dears,' said Colonel Brabazon, 'I am ready to do anything that pleases you both; by all means let us spend a couple of months or so on the Riviera, or anywhere you think will be pleasant for you. I shall be happy as long as you two are: what else have I got to live for? So now talk it over together while I smoke a cigar.'

Mrs. Brabazon's eyes grew moist as she watched the retreating figure of her husband, and the door shut between them.

'Hilda, if marriage is a lottery, I drew a prize! Do you think "the face," as you call him, will prove a prize, supposing you come together, "for better or for worse"?'

'I do think so, mother. See what he was to his brother, when both were alive; see what he is sacrificing to his memory and to his mistaken, almost insane, injunction. If—but, oh, what an "if"!—I can succeed in winning his affection, his confidence, his whole heart, I have no fear. Such a true, steadfast nature, young as he is, shows what he would be capable of for a woman of the right sort—and I mean

to be *that*,' she said, smiling, 'if he gives me the chance ;
but if he should not, ah me !'

' My darling child, could any man in creation,
knowing you cared for him, look upon you with indifference ?   It is impossible.'

' Ah, mother, that is what Lord Clement said; but
there, you see, " the face " never *has* looked upon me
at all, and sometimes I doubt if he ever will !'

And here the poor girl rather broke down in the
contemplation of a life in which he would play no
part—when, perhaps, in time, her parents would
press another marriage upon her !   No ! from that
too terrible fate she would be saved by their love for
her.   And then she derived a little, frail consolation
from the thought that she might devote her life to the
care of others—the sick, the poor, the bereaved—and
keep herself unspotted from the world.

But Mrs. Brabazon smiled as she held out her arms
to Hilda, saying :

' Come here, child ; you are far too young, and of
too bright a nature, to talk like that ; all life is before
you, and I hope all happiness.   You have made up
your mind—and I believe wisely, from what you tell
me, or, rather, from what Clement Armytage has told
you—that this Mr. Somerville is the one man you
really care for as a husband.   If it seems at present
a rather vague prospect, I am with you to help you
all I can to convert your romance into a still more
tender reality, for am I not a woman, and therefore
in sympathy with what, to your rather matter-of-fact

father, might seem an impossible idyl? Once, however, he is convinced that the affair is serious, and
this horrible gambling life is given up, "for your
dear sake," as I know it will be, all will come right.
Kiss me, my child, and God bless you!'

# CHAPTER XIII.

## MONTE CARLO.

'AND now, my dear, when shall we start?' asks Colonel Brabazon towards the end of October, as he and Mrs. Brabazon were sitting at luncheon in London, having just arrived from Eastbourne, and Hilda having gone to spend a couple of days with some friends at Windsor.

'We will be off as soon as you please. If Monte Carlo is a success, we can stay there until, say, next March or April. This house can be shut up, and the servants put upon board wages. Or we could let the house, if you like?'

'Oh no, that is not necessary,' replies Colonel Brabazon hastily. 'I don't understand this sudden bit of economy on your part—you, who think so much of your own furniture, *bibelots*, and so on; how could you endure to have strangers treating them perhaps disrespectfully?'

'Well, I don't know, George. You see, Hilda *might* fall in love with a poor man, and then we should have to save up all we could to enable her to marry him.'

Colonel Brabazon takes off his pince-nez, walks twice up and down the room, and then stops opposite his wife.

'Hilda want to marry a poor man ? Hilda want to marry *any man ?* My dear, you don't know her. I don't say in *time* she may not want to have a home of her own ; but remember how young she is, how heart-whole, how perfectly happy she is with us. And *why* should she fix her affections on a *poor* man ? She has had plenty of opportunities of what you call making a *good* marriage, and rejected them all. No, let us keep her with us as long as she is satisfied with her home. We can talk about poor men when she has fixed her affections on one, and in that case let us hope he will be worthy of her.'

'Yes, yes, that above all,' replied Mrs. Brabazon ; 'for when she gives her heart, there it will remain, and nothing will change it.'

'Good heavens, my dear ! you are becoming senti-mental on Hilda's behalf. All this comes of your wanderings abroad. You used to be as anxious as I was that Hilda should stop with us as long as was reasonable, and then — well, I won't say make a *mariage de convenance*, but, at all events, not be too much led away by sentimental considerations, unless she could exchange one good home for another.'

'Well, I only said Hilda *might* fall in love with a

poor man, perhaps, for the very reason that she has rejected so many rich ones that have wanted to marry her. But, really, I am so much better now, and can appreciate Hilda's sweet nature so thoroughly, that I have learnt to forget myself a little, and am really anxious to make some sacrifice of things that cost unnecessary money, in case it should be wanted.'

'All right, we will put some bank-notes into an old stocking, and hide it away as an extra dowry for Hilda. But I am not going to have strangers come and make hay in your pretty home, so don't talk any more about letting this house. And now let me see : this is Saturday—do you think you would be ready to start by next Thursday ? I suppose you are quite sure that it is to Monte Carlo you would like to go ?'

'Well,' replied Mrs. Brabazon, ' we have talked it over, and we both think we should like that best, if you don't object.'

'Whew !' said the Colonel, 'you have chosen a pretty lively place. Monte Carlo means a lot of dressing up, and visits without end to pay and to receive. How will you like that ?'

'We are not obliged to do more in that way than we like, and—and I understand it has the best climate of all the neighbourhood ; so, if it really is the same to you, write for rooms to the Hôtel de ——, which is not a very dear one ; and if they wire that they can take us in, we will start on Thursday.'

A favourable answer having been received from the hotel, and most of the trunks being already packed, Thursday sees the Brabazon family once more *en route* for the 'foreign parts' held in such contempt and dislike by the worthy, but somewhat narrow-minded, Jones.

The journey in the *train de luxe* was without incident ; and Mrs. Brabazon, true to her new-made resolution, never once grumbled at the arrangements, or complained about her ailments. The Colonel, who was used to be pretty hardly worked on these long journeys, could hardly believe his senses when he found he was allowed to eat, sleep, read, and smoke just when he liked. Hilda seemed to anticipate any little things her mother required ; but they were not many, and the two often exchanged looks of sympathy, and silently pressed each other's hands occasionally as they drew near their destination.

The morning after their arrival at Monte Carlo was brilliantly fine ; but Mrs. Brabazon, who really was tired after her long journey, though she could hardly be got to admit it, consented to stop in bed till dinner, so that, as at Spa, Hilda and her father started off to inspect their new surroundings.

It was not long before they came to the Casino, and Hilda was loud in her praises of its magnificent proportions, but did not express the slightest wish to inspect the inside of it. Had not her mother promised to take her there after dinner, so that they might look upon 'the face' for the first time together ?

After strolling about for two hours, during which time they met several people they knew, Colonel Brabazon and Hilda returned to the hotel, and were surprised to find Mrs. Brabazon sitting in her arm-chair, wrapped in a most becoming peignoir, and looking as bright and cheerful as possible.

'My dear, wonders will never cease; but why did you get up so soon?'

'I told you I was much better, and was not going to think about my health any more. I mean to go about and enjoy myself, and while you are in the reading-room at the Casino to-night, Hilda shall take me into the gambling-rooms and initiate me into the mysteries of play.'

Colonel Brabazon still had his hat, his cane, and a small parcel in his hands, which he threw up in speech-less astonishment, dropping the above-named articles on the floor.

'Are you—pray, are you going to—to gamble—play, I mean, at roulette or trente et quarante?'

'N—n—no, I don't think so; but I won't answer for myself. My present idea is only to look on and be interested in the people who *are* playing, for I want to know something of what seems to interest five out of every six persons I meet. You don't object, dear, do you?' and she lays her hand on her husband's arm, looking up in his face with the winning smile that had so attracted him some twenty years before, but which had been more or less absent from her face for the latter half of that time.

'No, no! Object? Of course I don't. Everybody goes to the Casino, but it is very crowded, and the rooms are sometimes stifling. Give me your strongest salts to put in my pocket, and the moment you feel faint I will take you away. Meanwhile, as you are up, we may as well go for a short drive; the air will do you good. So, if you and Hilda will be ready by three o'clock, I will order a carriage to come round at that time.'

'Yes, I should like a drive; but don't you come— *you* like a long walk; and Hilda and I have a lot to talk about, so order a two-placed carriage of some sort, and come back with a fine appetite for what seems to me an admirable cuisine.'

Colonel Brabazon, who during this last sentence has been picking up the things he had dropped after his first astonishment at his wife's determination to go to the Casino, now nearly drops them again on hearing her declare the cuisine of the hotel to be 'admirable.' Hitherto, no matter how much trouble had been taken in ordering a repast, no matter what costly dainties had been put before her, the poor peevish hypochondriac, after tasting the various dishes, had pushed away her plate, thrown herself back in her chair, and asked feebly that her fan and smelling-salts might be given her. Very different this from the woman who is now eating her first dinner in Monte Carlo, and finds nothing but praise for it, because it has been ordered by her husband, though the chef is not a *cordon bleu*.

As the father, mother, and daughter seat themselves at the little table reserved for them, they become the *point de mire* of many eyes, for, to say the least of it, they are an interesting trio. Two young men are dining together at the table next to theirs, one facing them, and the other with his back turned. The former, addressing his companion, exclaims :

' By Jove, Clem, what a lovely girl ! And she must be well bred, too, if those are her parents. No hair about the heels of any of that lot ; Derby form, all of them. Do look round ! Perhaps you know them, and can introduce me. I haven't come across any nice English people yet, and, as this is my first bit of abroad, and I don't know a word of any foreign language, I can't get on with the *parlez-vous.*'

' Shut up, Jack, or for Heaven's sake don't talk so loud ! If you want me to look round, you must stop chattering, for at the present moment the parties concerned, whoever they are, must be aware you are talking about them. Besides, as if to set at rest any lingering doubt they might have on the subject, you haven't taken your eyes off them since they came in. What it is to be a boy like you, fresh from Eton, and everything rose-coloured round you ! Should you be very much surprised to learn that your charming trio are a retired grocer and his family dressed up to the nines, and so like the real thing that they can pass muster with a neophyte, my boy ? However, I'll have a look at them presently, and report ; meanwhile

pay attention to this " Sole au vin blanc "; it is time
you learnt to dine !'

' Oh, I can't understand these foreign kickshaws !
But that girl has the loveliest eyes I ever saw,
and her father must have been a distinguished
soldier. And as for the mother, she looks like a
duchess.'

' Which of them ?' queries Clem cynically.

However, the voluble youth, having dropped his
voice to a whisper, and the excellent 'Sole au vin
blanc' being disposed of, 'Clem,' or, to call him by
his name, Lord Clement Armytage, turns leisurely
round and surveys the occupants of the table behind
him. The napkin falls from his lap as he springs to
his feet.

' Why, Mrs. Brabazon, Miss Hilda, and you,
Colonel, all here ! This *is* indeed good ! But you
promised to let me know if you came to Monte Carlo '
—and he looks inquiringly at Hilda—' because I
might have been of use in getting you rooms, as I come
here so much. However, you couldn't do better
than this hotel, which is very comfortable, and not
ruinous.'

And he continues a desultory conversation with
Colonel and Mrs. Brabazon, during which time Hilda
is busily engaged in feeding the hotel dog, who, as
he rarely leaves the *salle-à-manger*, and has a jaded
appetite that can only be tempted by the richest
entrées, or possibly by a fresh pâté, or a cheese rather
the reverse of fresh, has now a little rejected heap

before him, consisting of bread, toast, and a piece of the plain boiled potato that invariably accompanies the fish at a foreign restaurant, and the greater part of which is equally invariably left on the plate of the English visitor. But Hilda, whose heart is beating like a sledge-hammer, feels she must gain time before she can ask even with her eyes the momentous question, 'Is he here?' For, if she dreads the 'No,' she fears the 'Yes,' which would bring the tell-tale colour surging over her cheek, at present so ashen pale.

Lord Clement Armytage has watched her all the time he has been talking to her parents, while she mechanically fed, or tried to feed, the dog ; and now this pampered little animal, with an indignant sniff, walks off to an adjoining table, where he smells truffles, and fancies he may be safe from having his feelings and his appetite outraged by a love-sick girl.

The dog gone, Hilda *has* to raise her eyes, and they encounter those of Lord Clement, who bows his head slowly, but with a reassuring smile more eloquent than words ; and then, seeing her emotion, he exclaims at once :

'Miss Hilda, do get up and look into the room *behind you*. That is the syndicate who mean to break the bank to-night.'

Hilda turns round abruptly, and sees entering the room a fat woman, with a nurse carrying a two-year-old child, while behind them comes the evidently down-trodden and impecunious husband, who is laden with a large bag and innumerable parcels.

Hilda laughs merrily, but as Lord Clement pases to his table to rejoin his youthful companion, she contrivs to press his hand, and her eyes fill with unshed tears of gratitude.

# CHAPTER XIV

## 'JOURNEYS END IN LOVERS MEETING.'

ABOUT an hour later, during which the English boy was duly introduced to the Brabazons, they all entered the splendid Casino together, and Lord Clement, having volunteered to show them the way, took them straight to the table where Algy Somerville was generally to be found playing. Hilda put her hand to her heart as if to stop its beating, for in a moment she had caught sight of the face, unseen by her for so many months.

Algy was a shade paler, a little thinner, perhaps, but otherwise unchanged, his expression exactly the same as when she last saw him. But suddenly he looked up; seeing Lord Clement, he smiled, and his eyes turned for a moment to the girl standing by the latter's side. Their eyes met, and Hilda gave a little shiver, which did not escape her mother, who was standing on the other side of her.

Hilda asked her in a whisper :

'You see him, don't you? You recognise him from my description ?'

'Of course. What a beautiful, sad face it is!'

After this they watched the game silently for a short time, until Hilda, fearing her mother would be tired of standing, suggested a move to the reading-room, where Colonel Brabazon was certain to be found with his head buried in some newspaper. This time it was the *Figaro*, with a long and interesting account of a stormy debate in the French Chambers.

Mrs. Brabazon took a chair by her husband's side, and picked up the *Illustrated London News*, while Lord Clement, profiting by the opportunity offered them, proposed to Hilda to come into the next room and see their rash young friend through his first venture.

'He has brought 200 francs with him,' he said : 'how much of it do you think he will take back? Now, Charlie, don't look as if you were going to be hung. Be a man, and chuck down a louis on red. Your face is a good tip for that colour. I never saw you blush before. What's the matter ?'

'I don't want you and Miss Brabazon to watch me put on the money ; it's all so new that I feel as if everyone was staring at me. I know I shall get my stake snatched, or pick up someone else's by mistake, and then what an ass I shall look !'

'All right, old chap,' laughed Armytage, 'we shall leave you to your fate. Come and report yourself when you are broke. If you break the bank we shall hear it fast enough. Meanwhile, Miss Brabazon and I will watch the more hardened gamblers. You will find us in this room or the next;' saying which, they moved away from the table where the innocent was going to make his first step in crime.

'How lucky your friend did not want you to stop and see him through his début!' said Hilda.   'Now we can have a quiet talk, and you know how much I have got to ask and to hear since we last met.'

'Yes ; but, first of all, why did you not keep your promise to let me know you were coming here?'

'I couldn't write.   You remember I told you that I should try to forget this episode in my life, for I felt it was weak and undignified to apparently pursue a man who did not wish to make my acquaintance.'

'Don't put it in that way,' breaks in Lord Clement abruptly.   'I told you Algy Somerville would not make any new acquaintances in his then frame of mind—more particularly that of an attractive girl ; but I feel sure he did notice you, seeing you so often with me, and was afraid.   He did not tell me so, for he is so chivalrous about women that he would never admit the possibility of any woman being sufficiently interested in his appearance, or even in his sad history, to take any trouble to see more of him.   But he looked at you to-night as we stood opposite to him, and, unless I am very much mistaken, he would have given worlds to be able to turn his back on the green cloth, and to stand with us as a spectator. I shall not mention your name to him to-night when we meet after play is over.   Now, here is a com-

fortable sofa where we can talk without being scowled
at for interfering with the labours of the poor people
who are wasting their hours in the pursuit of that
impossible good—a winning system.  Now begin.
Where have you been all this time?'

'First of all,' answered Hilda, 'tell me how you
have progressed as regards that charming, but rather
perverse Miss A——.  I feel so horribly selfish in
talking always and only of myself; but indeed I am
truly interested in what concerns your happiness,
and I cannot understand any girl wilfully throwing
away the chance of winning a good and loyal
husband, such as you would be, unless she had fallen
desperately in love with a man whom for some reason
or other she cannot marry.'

'Congratulate me, then, dear Miss Hilda: for I
know how true your interest is in the fortunes of my
poor heart.  I am rather confident that all is, or will
be, right, and that when I get back to England I
shall find her no longer obdurate.  This is enough
to reassure you, but the manner in which she has
been "hoist with her own petard" is so funny that,
as there is nothing particular to occupy you just now,
it may amuse you to listen to the story of it.

'The man who had taken her fancy is an extremely
clever journalist; he has written articles that *did*
almost set the Thames on fire; and, though she told
me she was not the least in love with him, she
thought they might collaborate in literary work, and
cement this union of their two minds by a purely

platonic friendship, each making a vow to abstain
from matrimony—as that might possibly interfere
with their work—until they had achieved a signal
success.   Their project was to write either a play or
a novel, which should throw all others into the shade
by treating the sensation element from the stand-
point of pure reason.

'They decided upon the former, but unfortunately
one of the incidents of their *fin-de-siècle* piece took
place in a music-hall.   Now, pure reason requires
accuracy, and, as neither of them had ever set foot in
a music-hall, it became necessary for one of them to
repair this omission; naturally, it was for the mascu-
line coadjutor to make that sacrifice, and he braced
himself to make it.

'We must not say which "variety entertainment"
was selected, nor must I mention the name of the
heroic victim; believe me, indeed, when I say that
you are the only person in the whole world to whom
I would confide what happened.   Remember also
that my dear little love is very young.   She has no
mother to guide her, and therefore tried to be her
own guide in what she conceived to be "serious
woman's work," as she called it.   I saw that what
she was really intended for was to be a happy, cheery
young wife, with a loving husband and little children
round her—all life smiling before her.   She can
never be *blasée*.   Her serious turn of mind has even
prevented her from ever seeing a comic piece at a
theatre since she was quite a child; and I am bound

to admit that her literary ally, being equally un-
acquainted with the unreality of fun of that sort, was
certain to take it, if ever brought before him, *au
grand sérieux!* Let me now return to my account
of the visit to the music-hall.

'The serious young man, having duly taken a stall,
seated himself in it about 7.30, determined not to
miss a single phase of the human comedy which was
to be presented to him; but he felt, nevertheless,
that he was indeed making a martyr of himself in
the cause of truth, or, rather, truthful delineation.
He took up the programme and read listlessly through
it, but he knew nothing of the performers: "Little
Tich" sounded to him like a performing dog—such is
fame—until he read that he was a comedian. "Dan
Leno"? Yes, he has seen that name written on the
ceiling of his bus; but, if he thought about it at all,
he had imagined it to be a sort of Pears' Soap or
Bovril advertisement.

'No. 10 goes up on each side of the stage, the
curtain rises, and a dainty little figure appears,
dressed as a child, with short frock, socks, and a
pinafore. He refers to his programme with a yawn:
"Miss Z——, variety artist." The orchestra strikes
up a lively tune, and Miss Z——, with an extremely
pretty, well-trained voice, sings a harmless little ditty
about her dog, which she had taken out in a badly-
fastened muzzle, so that he lost it, and was promptly
seized by a policeman. A little admirable patter
follows, in which the girl explains that the constable

was "very fine and large," while she and her dog
were "very small." "There," she says, "I'll just show
you, for this is a true story." At this moment a huge
bobby walked across the back of the stage, leading
with a rope, that would have held a refractory mastiff,
a diminutive black-and-tan King Charles, with long
silky ears, and a nose so flat that no muzzle which
ever was invented could possibly have fitted it. Roars
of laughter from the audience.

'The little girl pulls out her handkerchief, applies
it to her pretty blue eyes, and, advancing to the foot-
lights, says between her sobs, "*You* may laugh, but I
cried, for my poor little dog was taken off to the
police-station, and I had to go home without him.
Now," she says, clasping her hands and appealing to
her audience, " I believe if any of my kind friends in
front had been present, they would have softened the
heart of that stern bobby, and got him to let me take
my little dog home with me ; wouldn't you, now—
wouldn't you ?" Renewed laughter and fresh ap-
plause.

'The serious youth begins to fidget, and looks
round the vast building to see if any sympathetic
champion is forthcoming ; he is very young, and this
mock scene of beauty in distress appears to him as a
real appeal to his chivalry ; with difficulty he contains
himself on the occasion, but he finds it necessary to
repeat his visit to that music-hall several times in
order, as he explains to his serious fellow-worker, to
gain a greater insight into the mysteries of that form

of entertainment.  On the occasion of his fourth visit, by which time the hapless little maiden and her pet have taken a great hold on his imagination, he meets an old friend, for whom, notwithstanding the latter's frivolous life, he has a great liking, for they were at school together before the serious mania took hold of him.

'" Hallo, old fellow ! *you* here ?  Well, wonders will never cease !  Come and have a drink, or come behind the scenes ; you *shall* do one or the other, to celebrate this extraordinary freak on your part.  I know a lot of these people—awful good sort they are, too, some of them.  The next turn isn't interest- ing ; which is it to be — a drink, or a look at the artists as they appear *au naturel ?*"

'" I—I think I should rather like to go behind the scenes ; you see, I have never been there, and I am collecting material for a melodrama, in which I have to introduce a music-hall scene.  One has to try and suit all tastes to make a piece successful," he adds apologetically.

'" Come along, then, I'm your man ; but do you want to be introduced to any of the ' artists '— ' turns,' we call them—or only to take notes about them when they ain't looking ?"

'" I think I should like to talk to some of them ; not Mr. Dan Leno nor Mr. Little Tich, for I feel as if they would laugh at me, and, of course, I am rather a fish out of water in this sort of place ; but that— that—little Miss Z—— seems a nice simple sort of

girl, who wouldn't either snub one nor play a practical
joke. Do you know her?"

' "Of course I do—a real good girl, clever, funny,
and as well behaved as any girl I know; but look out
for her mother: she is a dragon of propriety, and
never leaves her daughter behind the scenes. She
herself is only a poor work-woman—a widow with
heaps of young children to support; but she knows
that it is quite possible to be a music-hall artist and
yet remain perfectly respectable; and as her Polly
has shown decided talent, and gets £5 a week
for singing this one song and dancing, she lets
her do it, though, as I said before, she never leaves
her daughter, who is only sixteen, and too inexperienced to know the dangers to which a pretty girl
may be exposed if left quite unprotected."

'Well, Miss Hilda, to cut a long story short, the
serious young man made the acquaintance of the
poor seamstress's daughter; next day he went to
see them in their humble little home, where Polly,
when not studying a new song or dance-step, is
generally seated at her sewing machine, making
clothes for her brothers and sisters, all younger than
herself. He fell honestly and truly in love with the
little bread-winner, and, indeed, with the whole of her
family, and *is now engaged to be married to her*, and
declares that he was never so happy in his life.

'Amongst her other accomplishments, she is a
first-rate typewriter, so she is to typewrite her
husband's writings, which we hope will now be a

little more lively and human than they have hitherto
been ; and then the pair—these two extremes come
together—will probably "live happy ever afterwards."

'Of course, the surprise and the shock to my dear
little friend were great; but I have taken care on
seeing her since to point no moral, and I have little
doubt that she will now realize that, though I am not
of a particularly serious turn of mind, I can make
her a devoted husband and give her a happy home.
The last time I saw her she suggested we should go
to the Gaiety, which she thoroughly enjoyed, and as
we said good-bye she pressed my hand, and said,
"Do come and see me directly you come back to
England," which, you know, was great encouragement.
So now I am letting matters rest, and feel convinced
that all will come right in the end. Now let us talk
about Algy, though there is nothing new to tell you,
or I would not have talked all this time about my
own affairs.'

# CHAPTER XV

## MRS. CARTWRIGHT KNOWS.

THE conversation that then ensued between the friends did not reveal that any material change had taken place in Algy Somerville's condition of mind or body. He looked, perhaps, a little more weary each night as play ceased, and he walked listlessly away from the table he had last been playing at. Still, he admitted having won a good deal, but without mentioning the amount, saying, with the ghost of a smile, that it was supposed to bring bad luck, and, as he had to play, naturally he wished to win ; though the hope of getting the large sum necessary for the repurchase of Huntingford was, as yet, far from realization.

As Hilda walked away from the *salle de jeu*, accompanied by Lord Clement, she asked him :

' Has Mr. Somerville made no new acquaintances since he came here ?'

' He just speaks to a few people he has met at the tables, but you will never see him walking about or dining with anyone except myself. However, I do believe, poor fellow! if I rather keep out of his way for a few days, that he will feel lonely, and perhaps his reserve will break down.'

The above programme was duly carried out, and for several consecutive days poor Algy was to be seen dining alone, or sauntering in the morning on the very spot where his unfortunate brother used to wander, also generally alone and brooding over his weakness and his losses. Algy's wistful look, as he occasionally passed the only friend he had in Monte Carlo, and saw him so pleasantly engaged in conversation with a beautiful girl, went to Hilda's heart.

'I cannot stand this any longer,' she said one day; 'go back to him, do all you can for him, and don't think about me. Our experiment is a failure, for, lonely as he feels, his reserve has not broken down, and I believe that nothing short of a miracle can bring us together. Why, there is my dear Mrs. Cartwright!' she broke off suddenly, her whole expression changing, and her face lit up with pleasure, as the sweet little American came running towards her, with both hands outstretched.

'Why, Hilda!—Miss Brabazon I should say—no, I shouldn't—Hilda! I have thought of you so much, and I am so truly glad to see you, that now I don't seem to know where to begin nor what to say! You are going to ask me a heap of questions, too, but you English people take so long getting under way that I'm going to tell you right away all you want to know in haalf a minute. It was a false alarm about

my mother-in-law, God bless her! The accident was
not nearly so bad as reported, and as soon as ever
they told her that only time was wanted to set her
completely right, she said to me and William James :
" Now, just you be off back to Europe, where you
were enjoying yourselves so much, and finish up your
trip ; then come back and tell me all about it." It
was sweet of the old lady, wasn't it ? because we had
decided not to leave her before she was quite out of
the doctor's hands, but, oh ! I did want to come back
and have another good time over here. What's the
matter with mothers-in-law, and why are novelists
and comic papers always making jokes about them ?
I think they are just sweet : I know I love mine ;
and I love my husband, and I love you, Hilda, and
this lovely place, and the bright sun ; say, where
does the melancholy come in that I have heard so
much about, and the suicides ?'

'Oh, you little optimist !' says Hilda. 'Of course,
you look at the bright side of things—that is your
nature. But have you ever been into a gambling-
room and seen the sad, anxious faces of the losers ?
or, worse still, have you watched habitual gamblers,
who, win or lose, have a preoccupied look which
follows the turn of the cards at trente et quarante, or
the fall of the ball at roulette ? Have you ever
watched the faces of these unhappy people and tried
to realize what such absorption means ?' says Hilda,
almost fiercely, and clutching her friend by the
arm.

'Lord sakes, no!' replies little Mrs. Cartwright, smiling serenely. 'That's just what William James and I have come to see. We have read a heap about it, but I don't want to see any tragedies. The first young man or woman I see—I caan't tackle the older ones—I am going to say, "Now, look here, this is folly! Buck up, and use your brains for something better than risking what most of you haven't got on that green cloth." I have got a sort of reforming fit on me, so I tell you; but at present I don't know a soul here to work it off upon.

'How are your good father and mother?' she continues. 'Now, say, how long have you been here? But, indeed, I haven't yet told you how glad I am to see you; and now that that smart young friend of yours has marched off, I am going to give you a good hug.'

Saying which, she throws her arms round Hilda's neck, and kisses her on both cheeks, which embrace Hilda warmly returns.

'How stolid your countrymen are, Hilda! Your friend, whoever he is, just waited to see if I was going to pick your pocket, or do you a personal injury, and then walked away without waiting to be introduced to me.'

Hilda smiles rather sadly, and replies:

'Englishmen are a little bit *farouche*, as the French say; but this particular man is a great friend of mine, and perfectly charming. Only, my dear Mrs. Cartwright, I want you to understand that it is merely a question of sincere friendship between us.   He is very much in love with a girl who does not yet appreciate him, though I hope in time she may ; and he confides to me all his hopes and his fears, as he would to his sister.'

'Hum, well, that's interesting !   And do you con-fide your love affairs—if you have any—to him?'

Hilda is nonplussed.   Her astute and voluble little friend is too much for her.   She has to say rather feebly :

'Well, perhaps I should return his confidence even to that extent ; but, you see, I have nothing to return. I—I have not got any love affair   I am very happy at home, and——'

'And,' breaks in Mrs. Cartwright, 'can you really suppose that, fond as I am of you, I didn't see at Chamounix, when often you were so sad and so pre-occupied, that there was a *something* in your life which, at any rate, could not be confided to me ? But, see ! that unfortunate young man is beginning to think I had better have picked your pocket, after all, and given him the excitement of having me arrested.   Introduce him to me, please.'

'Mrs. Cartwright—Lord Clement Armytage.'

'I am so truly glad to make the acquaintance of any friend of Miss Hilda Brabazon's,' says Mrs. Cartwright, extending her hand to him ; 'but I failed to grasp your name.'

'Lord Clement Armytage,' repeats Hilda.

He bows, and Mrs. Cartwright continues :

'Have you been long here, and are you going to remain some time ?'

Lord Clement has heard of the Mont Blanc episode, and, as is natural, he is favourably inclined towards the little American woman, and he replies with much cordiality.

'I have been here about a fortnight; but as I don't gamble, and the weather is very bad, I think I shall probably leave in a few days.'

'Oh, my dear sir!' says Mrs. Cartwright, 'do not leave us like that. I have had a kind of revelation —do you believe in dreams?—that something will occur that will be interesting to all of us. Do stay.'

Lord Clement again bows, but is hardly ready with an answer, so Hilda speaks for him :

'Lord Clement has promised not to be in a hurry, unless he gets letters calling him home; so I hope we shall keep him some little time. And now, Mrs. Cartwright, will you and your husband join us at dinner ? You will find my mother so much better that you will hardly know her again. But you haven't told me where you are staying.'

'At the Hôtel de ——, where we arrived late last night.'

'That's capital, for we are staying there also. And now, Lord Clement, as Mrs. Cartwright and I have a lot to talk about, will you please go back to the hotel and order a table for six, or we may not get one ? Our usual table will be too small.'

'I will see to that,' replies Lord Clement ; 'but I

must dine with poor Algy to-night. I met him just now, looking sadder than ever, and he says he feels very seedy, so I won't leave him all alone any more.'

Saying which, he lifted his hat to the two ladies and walked away.

' Algy ? Who is Algy ?' exclaims little Mrs. Cartwright.

Hilda's face betrays the secret she has so carefully guarded, and one look is enough for the astute and sympathetic woman by her side. She sees confusion on the sensitive face, and, before Hilda has time to think of her answer, she continues :

' Never mind that now ; I am sure to meet Algy, whoever he is, if he is a friend of Lord Clement Armytage. And now tell me, dear, where you went after you left Chamounix. I am so glad to hear that Mrs. Brabazon is so much better. Then, I suppose, she doesn't carry around that salts bottle any more. I shall hardly know her without it.'

These ready words having given Hilda time to recover herself, they continue their walk and their conversation. But the little American woman *knows*.

# CHAPTER XVI.

## COLUMBIA SETS LANCE IN REST.

THE dinner at the hotel was most cheery and pleasant, although the absence of Lord Clement Armytage was much deplored. Colonel Brabazon especially regretted it, for, as he explained to Mrs. Cartwright, he was far from proud of all his fellow-countrymen abroad ; but Lord Clement was quite another matter, and he was always glad to introduce him to a foreigner as a good specimen of the right sort of Englishman.

'And now, Hilda,' he says, as they are half-way through dinner, 'why did Clement desert us to-night, just when I wanted to show him off ? We have dined together for the last four days ; I'll be bound he is with that sad-looking gambling friend of his—trying to stop him from blowing his brains out, perhaps.'

C-r-a-s-h ! Mrs. Cartwright, in fanning herself, has swept the wineglass by her side right off the table, and Hilda, bending down, is wiping the wine-stains off Mrs. Cartwright's delicate silk dress with her napkin.

16—2

'Oh, how awkward I am! Thank you so much, my dear ; a little benzine will put this right. You were saying, Colonel Brabazon, that Lord Armytage had deserted you to-night. Now, I think that young man showed great tact, for he saw how pleased your daughter and I were to meet again, and perhaps he rather felt *de trop* with me and all my questions about the family, and so he just made the first excuse that came into his head to leave us alone. But, Colonel, I want to tell you all about the way I was entertained, soon as ever we got to New York, about our ascent of Mont Blanc. I know that some of the English papers said it was an unfeminine thing for ladies to do, but *all* our press were unanimous in cracking us up. Now, William James, don't sit there looking at me and smiling ; just say if I wasn't a heroine when I got back.'

'My dear, I'll say anything if you will only give me a chance,' says the faithful William James, smiling still more. 'But I do know that many people, including pressmen, said it was too hard work for women, though they admired your courage and envied your strength.'

'Well, all I know is that Miss Hilda and I were not haalf so done as those two young men who wouldn't be helped by the guides, for they went to bed in their clothes. I know it, because the waiter who called them next morning told my maid so !'

There was a good deal more talk about Mont Blanc and their other experiences at Chamounix, and then a

move was made to the Casino.    Hilda, mindful of her
own experience on entering a gambling-room for the
first time, had given Mrs. Cartwright strict injunc-
tions to make her remarks in an undertone, so as not
to disturb the players, or attract too much attention
to themselves.    The warning was very necessary, for
the excitable little lady was so surprised and taken
aback at the novelty of the scene, that it was with
difficulty she could contain her feelings, and make her
remarks in a whisper, which sometimes became a stage
whisper, until Hilda's warning ' Hush !' made her drop
her voice.    Needless to say, she had endless questions
to ask and remarks to make about the people as they
watched each table in turn for a few minutes ; but
when they came to that at which Algy was seated,
her quick eyes recognised him in a moment as the
' sad-faced gambling friend ' alluded to at dinner by
Colonel Brabazon.    Was not Lord Clement standing
behind his chair watching him ?

As they stood just opposite the pair, Lord Clement
caught sight of them, and whispered something which
made Algy look up.    Mrs. Cartwright was startled by
the beauty and sadness of those long gray eyes, which
were only fixed on the group opposite to him for a
few seconds, and then dropped once more upon the
green cloth.    For once she remained silent ; but
Hilda felt instinctively that this very silence was more
eloquent than words, and that her warm-hearted little
friend had guessed her secret.

As they moved away from this table, Lord Clement

joined them, and they continued their inspection of the rooms, sitting down to listen to the fine orchestra, until it was time to return to the hotel.

Nothing of any importance occurred for the next two days. Both the Brabazons and the Cartwrights had many friends in Monte Carlo, so that, though they met several times, there was no opportunity for any long conversation between Hilda and Mrs. Cartwright. Moreover, the latter passed a good deal of her time in thinking over and consulting with her husband as to the best means of gaining Hilda's confidence, without appearing to force it.

'Oh, if these people were only Americans, I would have got to the bottom of this long ago,' said the poor, baffled little woman as soon as they reached their own rooms, after returning from their third after-dinner visit to the Casino. 'But these English—much as I like them, and I just love Hilda—are so reserved that you feel somehow it would be impertinent to make them say anything they didn't volunteer ; and I have such heaps of questions I could ask. In the first place, what is the mystery about this "Algy"?—I have never even dared to ask his other name, for fear I should appear too interested. He doesn't look so sad because he loses, that much I have ascertained,' she says rather triumphantly, 'because I did contrive to say to Lord Clement one day—by-the-by, Hilda says it's all wrong to call him Lord Armytage. How English people do puzzle one with their titles! Well, as I was saying,

I remarked to Lord Clement that his friend seemed very lucky, and he said " Yes, I think he is a decidedly lucky player ;" and I did so long to say : " Then, why in thunder does he go on playing if it makes him look so sad to win ?"   But I didn't say any more, and I must just wait till some opportunity enables me to have a talk with Lord Clement alone.   Up till now Hilda has always been with me whenever I have met him, and somehow I caan't do my usual questioning before her about the man I know she is in love with.'

The opportunity so much wished for was not long in presenting itself, for the next morning, about eleven o'clock, a note from Hilda was given to Mrs. Cartwright, in which she said that in walking across the parquet floor of her room in a new pair of shoes, with slippery soles, she had tumbled down ignominiously, and sprained her ankle rather badly.   She begged her friend to come to her, as she could not go for the long walk they had arranged to take together that same morning.

Mrs. Cartwright was soon by Hilda's sofa, it not being thought necessary by the doctor, who had just left, that his patient should remain in bed ; and the two chatted on for about an hour, when Hilda begged Mrs. Cartwright to profit by the lovely summer sun, and take a turn in the gardens before luncheon.   And, seeing the latter's hesitation to leave her, she added :

'I should so like Lord Clement to come and see

me this afternoon, and if you go to the gardens now you will be sure to meet him.'

That decided Mrs. Cartwright, for, as she said to herself :

'Now is my opportunity, and my name is not Janie Cartwright if I don't come back a wiser, though perhaps a sadder, woman ; for I am certain there is something tragic I have got to hear.'

Ten minutes later she is on the sunny walk, which has been more or less deserted for the last few days, owing to the bad weather, but to which the brilliant sunshine has now attracted half the visitors at Monte Carlo.    It is seldom that the devoted little wife goes out of any building in which her 'William James' may happen to be, without telling him of her move-ments.    But  on  this  occasion  she  is  particularly anxious  that  her  hoped-for  interview  with  Lord Clement  should  be  *solitude à deux;*  so  she  slips out  of  her  bedroom,  without  passing  through  the little salon where Mr. Cartwright is sitting, absorbed in  the  American  mails,  which  have  just arrived, but occasionally  looking  at  the  clock,  and  wondering if  his  Janie  will  not  soon  have  done  with  the 'good  Samaritan'  business,  and  come  back  to him.

Mrs. Cartwright seats herself on the first bench she sees, it being easier to watch the passers-by when sitting still than when walking about; and as she has a  direct  message  from  Hilda  to  convey  to  Lord Clement, she feels that she need have no hesitation in going up to him and delivering it, no matter with whom he may be walking.

She has not long to wait, for, amongst the crowds of people of all nations passing backwards and forwards, her quick eye soon detects Lord Clement walking with Algy, both apparently engaged in earnest conversation.

It is no idle curiosity that induces the sympathetic American woman to break into the *tête-à-tête ;* for she feels that the moment has come when, with the assistance of Lord Clement, she may be able to help Hilda by fathoming the mystery which separates her from the beautiful sad-eyed young man who is walking slowly before her. In a moment, therefore, she is by Lord Clement's side, saying :

' Please forgive me for interrupting you ; but I have just come from Miss Hilda Brabazon, and she has begged me to tell you that she has sprained her ankle, which will keep her on her sofa for a few days ; and she hopes you will go and see her this afternoon.'

' I am indeed sorry to hear this,' replies Armytage. ' How did it happen ?'

' She was just in a desperate hurry to get out on this fine day, and slipped up on the parquet floor, with her foot doubled up under her. The doctor says she will be all right in a few days if she keeps her foot up. But meanwhile she is rather dull ; so you will go and see her, won't you ?'

'Of course I will, immediately after luncheon.'

During the above conversation Algy, who under ordinary circumstances, on seeing a stranger, would have walked quietly away, has withdrawn a few steps only, and is within hearing distance, making holes in the ground with his cane, and apparently taking no notice of the speakers. But one glance of Mrs. Cartwright's quick eyes is sufficient to assure her that he has been listening. Without a moment's hesitation, therefore, she walks towards him, and, turning to Lord Clement, says:

'Introduce your friend to me, please.'

There is nothing for it, of course. The simple request is at once complied with, and the introduction, which Hilda for so many months has been unable to nerve herself to ask for, is carried by a *coup de main* in one moment by Mrs. Cartwright, who has no idea that the two young men before her feel themselves rather ill at ease.

'I have noticed you at the roulette-table, Mr Somerville,' bursts forth the little American, 'and you are the first gambler—no, I don't mean that; somehow, it doesn't sound polite: I mean, the first person who plays—that I have ever had the pleasure of talking to, and I want to ask you so many questions. Say, didn't you feel badly last night when you had been backing the middle dozen for ever so long and it never came up, and then, as soon as you left it, it came up seven times running? I know it did, because I counted them, and I felt so sorry for you, for I should have been hopping mad myself at such bad luck. You didn't seem to mind, but went on staking as calmly as ever; and when we came back to your table some time afterwards you had a pile of notes and gold in front of you, so I hope you won at last. Now, did you?'

There is a look of genuine sympathetic interest on the smiling little face that is irresistible, and quite breaks down for the moment the icy barrier that poor Algy has set up between himself and his fellow-creatures. He smiles as sweetly as his lively inter-locutor, and, to tell the truth, is much amused at the speech she has fired off at him, with hardly a pause to take breath.

'It is very good of you, Mrs. Cartwright, to take such an interest in my good or bad luck; but we gamblers—for, of course, everyone who plays *is* a gambler, some more, some less—we are so used to the ups and downs of chance that we learn to take things philosophically. You do not play yourself, then?'

'Why, no; but I would love to. You see, my husband and the Brabazons, with whom I spend a good deal of my time, don't care about it; and as for Lord Clement here, whenever the word " play " is mentioned he says a swear word and stamps his foot. And yet whenever I go to the Casino I see him watching you, and he seems much more interested in what you call your ups and downs than you do yourself. My belief is that he is a sleeping partner in the concern, and while you play for both he walks around and says it's wicked !'

Once more has the little American woman fairly conquered British stolidity, and this time her triumph is a big one, for the men look at each other, and both laugh heartily. Occasionally the comic element is enhanced by the tragic, and the two friends, knowing that Mrs. Cartwright must be absolutely in ignorance of the relation existing between them as regards play, are the more amused at the naïve construction she has improvised to explain it.

Mrs. Cartwright has much more to say upon the subject of gambling, but, as she realizes that she will not be able to see Lord Clement alone this morning. she decides to abandon the field for the present, and takes out her watch, saying that it is time to return to the hotel for luncheon ; and, with a reminder to Lord Clement that he is to go to Hilda, she says ' Au revoir ' to the two friends.

# CHAPTER XVII.

## THE DEAF WON'T HEAR.

MRS. CARTWRIGHT, on reaching the hotel, flies at
once to their sitting-room, where she finds her
husband still absorbed, it is true, in the American
mails, but with a distinct grievance against Janie for
having gone out without announcing the fact or giving
him the chance of going with her. But before he
has time to open his lips a daintily-gloved little hand
is put over them.

'Now, don't you say one word ; I just slipped out
on purpose, for I didn't want you to detain me nor
to come with me ; I went to meet a *young man.*'

William James does not start, nor assume a tragic
attitude ; he just smiles, and says :

'Well, little woman, and did you meet him ?'

'Yes, I *did ;* I met *two.*'

'Oh, Janie, this is serious! One is bad enough,
but two ! Now, tell me about it.'

She perches herself on the arm of his chair, throws
the newspaper on to the floor, draws his head towards
her, kisses it on a spot which Time appears to

have thinned especially for that purpose, and begins her story

'I have seen him, I have spoken to him—the man our dear Hilda loves! I saw at Chamounix that she had something on her mind, and I found out what it was as soon as I got here and saw her look at this man, who was playing roulette, with, oh, such a beautiful sad face! His name is Algernon Somerville. I told you about it directly we came back, you remember. No, don't try to pick up that paper; I'm going to tell you what I want to do.'

William James puts the newspaper on the table, lights a cigarette, and, with another smile, says:

'Go ahead, Janie! it's two to one on you. When you take something in hand, you are bound to carry it through; but now tell me about it.'

'I haven't much to tell yet, because there is some mystery about this man, who plays high and wins, but looks so sad. He is a friend of Lord Clement Armytage, who is much with him, and I can see dislikes his playing, yet he doesn't try to stop him; I must find out why that is. Now that poor Hilda is laid up with this sprained ankle, I can more easily get hold of Lord Clement alone, who I can see is a sort of brother to her—no love-making there: I found that out the moment I saw them together.'

William James draws the sweet little face on to his shoulder, and, patting her head, says:

'"Found out"—"found out"! you have used that

expression twice in half a minute, and anyone who
didn't know you would think you were a conspirator,
or at least a "busybody"; but, as I *do* know you, I
conclude you are trying to make two young people
happy against their will; that's the sort of work that
pleases you, eh?'

'Now, do stop; this is serious: I love Hilda Brabazon. She is the first English girl I have met, it's
true; but I can trust my instinct when it tells me
that I shall never come across a sweeter nor a better,
no matter what her nationality may be. But, oh,
this British reserve! I caan't understand it. I saw
Hilda's face when she stood opposite Mr. Somerville,
and I saw him look at her; yet I know they have
never spoken to each other, and that the mystery
which keeps them apart lies with *him*. Lord Clement
can tell me the nature of it, and I shall ask him the
first moment I get him alone. Do you think he will
confide in me?'

'Heaven help him if he doesn't, my dear!' says
William James, as he kisses the shining little head
still reposing on his shoulder; 'I don't pretend to
know anything about this new venture of yours, but
I wish you all success; and, as I took rather a fancy
to the good-looking young Englishman you pointed
out to me at the Casino, and as I am greatly
interested in Miss Hilda, I can only hope, little
woman, if these two people really are in love with
each other, and there is only the British barrier of
reserve between them, that you may be the means of

removing it, and making them as happy in their marrie l life as you and I have been in ours.'

'Amen,' says little Mrs. Cartwright, as she drops off the arm of the chair on to her knees, folding her hands together and looking devoutly upwards.

The following morning is again brilliantly fine, and Mrs. Cartwright, having spent an hour with Hilda, and learnt that the sprained ankle is doing well, sallies forth in great spirits, with the hope that this time she will not be disappointed, but will find Lord Clement alone, and have at last her chance of unravelling the mystery of Hilda's preoccupation in connection with the gray-eyed gambler.

Could the most censorious person accuse Mrs. Cartwright of a wish to pry into her neighbours' secrets, or to collect material for gossip? Surely not; and therefore, when she does have the good luck to meet Lord Clement strolling alone in the sunlit gardens, she at once stretches out her hand, and says:

'Now, Lord Clement, I want to have a long talk with you right away. This is the first opportunity I have had, and I'm going to make the most of it; and as time is short in Monte Carlo, I'll just come to the point at once. Isn't Hilda Brabazon just the sweetest gurl you know, and don't you love her?'

Lord Clement starts; he is not accustomed to American expressions, and takes the question, 'Don't you love her?' literally; so he answers rather stiffly:

'Really, Mrs. Cartwright, you a little startle me.

I have the greatest possible regard and friendship for Miss Brabazon, but, indeed, there has never been any question of love-making between us. In fact, I ought perhaps to tell you that I am almost engaged to be married to a girl I have long loved, and that Miss Brabazon is about my only confidant on the subject.'

'Lord sakes, man! you caan't understand our American-English; we talk of an old man or woman, blind, deaf, and deeply pitted with the small-pox, as a "lovely man" or a "lovely woman," because their natures are good and sweet; and I meant only that you loved Hilda Brabazon same as I do, because *she* is good and sweet—so is your Princess of Wales, so was our Abraham Lincoln, and others—it doesn't mean love-making. How queer you English are! However, don't let us waste time; what I want to know is the history and mystery, because mystery there is, connected with your charming-looking gray-eyed friend; now, will you tell me about it right away? It is not idle curiosity, believe me,' she says, putting her little hand on his arm, 'for *I* know, and I think that *you* know, our peerless Hilda has given her whole great heart to that man, and I want to discover why we cannot, between us, bring them together?'

Lord Clement pauses; his reserve is almost broken down as he encounters the honest blue eyes fixed upon his face expectantly; but still he hesitates, and tries to put her off.

'Please don't be angry, Mrs. Cartwright, but our acquaintance is so short that—that I do not feel

17

justified in boring you with the story of my friend Algy Somerville's sad experience of life; for I should have to tell you a story long enough to weary your kindly interest.'

'Have no fear of that; I wan't to hear *all*, if you don't mind telling it me. Anything you don't wish me to repeat I *won't* repeat, not even to my William James; I caan't say more than that, for I have no secrets of my own that I keep from him. But I must know something of Mr. Somerville's story before I can talk freely to Hilda. I guess, for instance, that his love of gambling is one of the obstacles to his marrying?'

Lord Clement smiles.

'Come to that seat, Mrs. Cartwright,' he says, 'and when I tell you everything about Algy Somerville, you will take back the phrase "love of gambling."'

They seated themselves comfortably, the blue sky above them, the blue waters of the Mediterranean at their feet, and Lord Clement told her the sad story with which my readers are acquainted. Mrs. Cartwright listened in absolute silence, except for an occasional catch in her breath, which showed how absolutely her tender, sympathetic heart was in sympathy with the harrowing tale now being unfolded to her.

When Lord Clement had ceased speaking, she laid her hand upon his, and sobbed out:

'But Hilda *is* the good and true woman; she will save him from this dreadful life. I know it will come right in time,' she says, drying her tears. 'We will manage it between us. Oh, thank you so much for having told me everything! Now, I believe, my task is comparatively easy. I *know* I shall get Hilda's confidence, and you must get Algy's. See how natural it comes to me to couple their first names together. Will you meet me here to-morrow at the same time? Oh, bless that sprained ankle!—it makes our work much easier. Au revoir, then; I feel so happy.' And she looks it, though there are still traces of tears in her eyes.

Scarcely had she walked off in the direction of the hotel, leaving Lord Clement standing by the seat they had just vacated, than Algy Somerville strolled up, a rather brighter expression on his face than was usually to be seen there.

'Well, old chap,' he said quite cheerily, 'I saw you were very busy talking to your little American friend, so I just waited till you had "got through," as probably she would put it. I suppose, by-the-by, she did most of the talking. For the few minutes I saw her yesterday she struck me as being a real good sort, and she has a nice honest face. Am I right?'

'I believe that woman to be more than a good sort. She is one of the very best, for she is full of the milk of human kindness; and not only does she never say an unkind word of anybody, but she seems to forget herself entirely in the intense interest which she takes in those of whom she is fond.'

'Ah! I could see she was a great admirer of your friend Miss Brabazon, and I suppose that is a bond of union between you. Were you '—he hesitated—' talking about Miss Brabazon all that time?'

'A great part of it. And when you have the luck to come across such a girl as that, and find one of the opposite sex whose appreciation of her is equal to your own, it is no great wonder if she becomes an interesting topic of conversation.'

'Really, Clem!' And if Algy Somerville could have put a sneer into his voice it would have been there, but he couldn't. There was, however, rather a bitter tone about it, as he said, 'If Miss Brabazon is such a paragon as you make out—and I am bound to say that from her looks she might be anything good ; only, as you know '—he sighed—' I have never spoken to her—why, as your inamorata is so cruel, don't you agree to take each other for better or worse? You are not in love with her, I know ; but perhaps she is with you, and in any case such a sterling pair as you would be are bound to get along in life happily and peacefully.' Again he sighed.

Armytage stopped short in their walk, threw away his cigarette, and putting his two hands on Algy's shoulders, said impressively :

'Hilda Brabazon has given her whole heart to one man, and she will *never, never* change!'

It was a *coup de théâtre*. Algy started, and gave a slight shiver as he turned away. In a moment, however, he recovered himself, and, confronting his companion, with his usual calm voice still tinged with a little bitterness, he added :

'And pray who is the happy man ?'

'He is *not* a happy man ; he is a very unhappy one.'

There was no mistaking the look in Armytage's eyes as he fixed them upon Algy's. Again the latter turned away, and when he for the second time confronted his friend, his face was ashen white, and his lips quivered.

There was silence between them for a few moments, which seemed more than minutes to both. Then Lord Clement took his friend by the arm, saying :

'It is breakfast-time—ain't you hungry ?' And they adjourned to a neighbouring restaurant, where there were many English, and the tables were placed so close together as to make confidential conversation impossible, which came as a relief to both, for each had to recover from the shock of a secret discovered and disclosed—the latter by the expression of Algy's face, for he had said nothing, and Lord Clement felt that for the present *he* had said enough.

After the excellent *déjeuner à la fourchette*, to which neither of them had done the justice it deserved, they separated, Armytage saying :

'I suppose you are going to your usual task. I am going to play bézique for five-centime points with Miss Brabazon to help while away the time she has to spend on her sofa. Don't you think I have got the best of it ?'

'Indeed I *do*,' fervently replied Algy. 'Do you think—could you tell her—that I hope she will soon be all right? English people abroad are supposed to hang together, and if one of them meets with a mishap, it is only showing a little ordinary sympathy to say one is sorry. Is that all right?'

'Yes, that is all right; I will tell Miss Brabazon. You see, you did her a good turn when you jumped the fence out of the lane after the M.F.H. had been obliged to slam the gate in her face owing to his restive horse. Perhaps you don't remember that little episode? *She* does. She told me about it when she first saw you at Spa, and recognised you at once, though she said to me pathetically in the intervals of a valse, for we were dancing in the ball-room at the Casino, "Why is he so changed? Why does he look so sad?"'

'Then, she knows all about me, for, of course, you told her?'

'Of course I did.'

'And she knows all?'

'All. Indeed, she knows more than you do,' continued Lord Clement, 'for she knows she is the "good and true woman" that our poor Evy spoke of; but she is much too modest and reserved to let *you* know it, unless something unforeseen brings you together. She will never betray herself, for she is proud and you are reserved, and my only hope is in that sweet little American woman, who may hit upon a some-thing—God knows what. Her active brain is so

subtle that she may find a means of breaking down
what she calls the " British barrier of reserve." You
won't believe this peerless girl loves you, knowing all
your history! You will not make any advances to
her, though, of course, I know how much you admire
her personally ; and you may take my word for it
that she is even more perfect morally than she is
physically, which is saying a great deal. A devoted
daughter to her parents, a firm friend, a good " pal "
—what more can you ask of any woman ?'

' I don't ask anything of any woman at present.
My duty is to carry out my poor Evy's strange
bequest, so that, if what you tell me is true, I had
better fly from temptation and leave Monte Carlo.
Spa will do just as well for this hateful life, except
that I have certainly been lucky since I came here.
You know I never get excited or lose my head.
Play is odious to me, and therefore I look on it
merely as the means to an end. I have little doubt,'
he continued, ' from what I hear, that the American
who bought Huntingford is not pleased with his
bargain, and does not take kindly to his *rôle* of
English country gentleman. No doubt, therefore, the
old place will again be in the market before long.
As you know, he gave £100,000 for the house and
two thousand acres, which was a fancy price in these
bad times ; but this man is a millionaire, and could
afford to indulge his fancy. As, however, he is also
a business man, he will probably expect to get very
nearly what he gave ; and how am I, at this rate, to

get such a sum? The rest of the land was sold in lots, to different people, and very badly sold, too; but that I don't care about. Evy wouldn't have cared. It was the *house*, the *home*, he wanted me to get back, and I don't feel as if I should succeed before the effort takes every bit of life out of me. I have now won £8,000, and I mean, after a few more months of this slavery, to go for a big *coup*, which I have never yet done. Don't you think I am right?'

'Yes, go for a big *coup*,' replied his friend quickly; 'but don't let it be at the tables. Try to win Hilda Brabazon for your wife—that is as big a *coup* as any man, be he who he may, can hope to land in his lifetime. No, don't interrupt me. I know what you are going to say. But you are *not* a pauper: you have £15,000 of your own, and have won another £8,000, and—what an "and"!—you can either go back to the Foreign Office or try some other career equally congenial to you; for you have plenty of interest and an admirable record. No! wait a bit longer—I haven't done yet. Hilda Brabazon has £1,000 a year left her by her grandfather as soon as she comes of age, which is next week. So you would start in life with an almost equal income, which you would be sure to increase by your brains as soon as you settled down to a profession. This, therefore, disposes of foolish scruples about money, if any exist in your mind. That Hilda is not mercenary she has had the opportunity of proving on several occasions, for I know from their own lips—not hers—the good

matches she has rejected. One of the best fellows I
know, a great friend of mine, of very old family, and
with at least £10,000 a year, persevered as long as he
could with dignity persevere in the attempt to persuade her to marry him. Her only answer was, " I
will only leave my happy home to marry the man to
whom I can give my whole heart." Now, what do
you think of her ?'

'Have you got a cigarette? I have never smoked
one since Evy died. But whenever we had a matter
to think over together, he used to say, " Let us work
it out while we smoke "; and we used to light up and
walk up and down the smoking-room with our hands
in our pockets for a few minutes, and then our minds
were made up. It was generally a question of which
horse we should ride at a particular meet ; and, serious
as this is, I return to my old considering cap. Don't
speak to me until I tell you, for you are opening up
to me a life of paradise, and the one I am leading is
*hell !*'

He walked away, his companion looking after him
in speechless astonishment. Algy had at last shown
signs of life, of emotion, of temper, even, as he had
stamped his foot on delivering his last phrase. How
different from the state of lethargy into which he had
fallen when nothing could rouse him, nothing interest
him ! Lord Clement lighted his own cigarette, put
his hands in his pockets, and walked up and down
the gravel path to try and recall to Algy the
time when he and Evy were debating over some

trivial subject that had to be settled between them. His outward demeanour remained impassible, but his heart—all in sympathy with the friend of his boyhood, whose turning-point in life these few moments of reflection might prove to be—was thumping hard against his side, and caused him to catch his breath more than once.

After a few turns, Algy came back to him, his half-smoked cigarette thrown away, a set look on his face.

'Clem, old man, my best of friends, you have done what you could for me, and it is *just possible* that some day things may come right for me ; but what you wish is premature. In the first place, I cannot make up my mind to give up my task so soon, merely because the life is hateful to me ; and, secondly, how *am* I to be quite sure that Miss Brabazon—such a girl as you describe, and who, indeed, I believe is all you say—would be willing to release me from my unhappy life, and transform it into a happy one ?

'Really, it is too much of a fairy romance,' he continued. 'We have never spoken to each other, except when I held the gate open for her the day we met out hunting, and asked her to pass through, as I should have spoken to any other lady in a similar difficulty. She didn't even answer me, but gave me a sweet smile, which I remember, a little bow, and passed on. Since then I have seen her constantly with you, and as naturally every man must admire a beautiful woman, if he has any remnants of humanity left in him—and I suppose I have just that—of course I have looked at her, and sometimes I have noticed that her eyes were fixed upon me. But there is nothing wonderful in that, for she knows my peculiar history, also that I am a great friend of yours ; but from that to being in love, and ready to give up her life to me, is a far cry. I am not so vain as to believe that. Indeed, if I did, I should just pack up my things, and be off, first to avoid the temptation of falling hopelessly in love myself, and, secondly, to save her from any possible sorrow, supposing what you say to be true. As yet, however, I cannot believe it. So now let us say no more on the subject. I will try and keep my eyes under better control, for I know that I have looked at her sweet face more than is wise, and it haunts me.'

'Very well, Algy, so be it. We will not mention the subject again for the present ; but I doubt if Mrs. Cartwright will be equally reticent.'

Saying which, he strolled on to the Hôtel de Paris, leaving Algy to resume his uncongenial task.

# CHAPTER XVIII.

## BUT THE BLIND SHALL SEE.

HILDA'S sprained ankle proved more troublesome than the doctor at first anticipated, for after four days she was still compelled to keep her foot up, and found the time hang rather heavy on her hands. Mrs. Cartwright during this time was her constant companion, and Hilda said to her one morning :

' I should like to try to do your portrait, if you will sit to me. I used to be rather good at likenesses. but the last one I did was so unsatisfactory that I have never touched a brush since.' She sighed deeply, and then continued. I know my maid has brought my paint-box; and if you will kindly ring, I will tell her to bring it.'

' Can't I find it ?'

' I am afraid not, for Jones has a knack of hiding things away, and nobody else ever finds anything that is in her charge ; as for me, I *never* know where she has hidden my treasures, such as they are.'

The bell having been rung, after considerable delay the waiter appeared, and was despatched to summon the lady's-maid; but he returned in a few minutes with the information that she was not in her room.

'I dare say she has gone for a walk,' said Hilda. 'I told her I never wanted her at this time. Never mind, I feel too sleepy to do anything except sleep. It is very odd how I stop awake at night now; it must be the want of air and exercise. Anyhow, it makes me desperately sleepy in the daytime.' Her eyes closed; she opened them in a few seconds, and said: 'I should like to show you a sketch I did of my mother last year, and then you can tell me if you think it worth while to let me have a try at you. It is in a leather box in the salon; you needn't bring the box. Where *are* my keys? On my toilet-table, I think.'

Mrs. Cartwright looked everywhere for them; when she returned to Hilda's sofa empty-handed, the latter's eyes were again closed; but she opened them and, being told her keys were not where she thought, exclaimed:

'How stupid I am! Here they are under my cushion. I had one of the boxes in just now to look at something, and didn't put the keys back.' She took one of several off a large ring, and gave it to Mrs. Cartwright, saying: 'There are two leather boxes on my writing-table; it is the one on the left— no, the right. How sleepy I am!' and her eyes closed.

Mrs. Cartwright takes the key and goes into the salon, leaving the door open. She tries the key in the box on the right; it does not fit. 'Poor Hilda is too sleepy to know her right hand from her left,' she thinks, as she tries the box to the left, and finds that it opens immediately

There, sure enough, is a sketch, a double one; but it is of a young man, not of a middle-aged woman. The first sketch represents him in a red coat, mounted on a splendid horse, and with a bright smile upon his face, holding a gate open for a girl, who is riding through.

The second sketch is of the same face, but, alas! the smile is no longer there. The man is seated at a gambling-table, with his eyes fixed upon it, and oppo- site to him stands the same young girl, watching him. Underneath are written, in Hilda's handwriting, the following lines :

> 'Since first I saw your face, I resolved
> To honour and renown you ;
> If now I be disdained, I wish
> My heart had never known you.'

Mrs. Cartwright puts her hand to her lips to stifle a little scream ; she goes to the open door and looks in. Hilda is sound asleep, and Mrs. Cartwright, closing the door, softly returns to the sketch. The likenesses are admirable; there is no mistaking them. Oh, if only Algy Somerville could see this, all would be right—he must be convinced! She wrings her hands, and the tears spring to her eyes; but in a few moments her quick brain begins to work. 'He *shall* see it,' she thinks, as she remembers that Lord

Clement is in the reading-room of the hotel writing letters, and has begged her to send for him if Hilda should feel inclined for a game of bézique. Hastily snatching up pen and paper, she writes, 'Come up here directly—good news,' and rings for the waiter to take the note to Lord Clement.

She has but a very few moments to wait before he appears at the door, when she puts her finger to her lips and, pointing to Hilda's room, whispers, 'She is asleep,' and hands him the sketch.

He looks at it long and earnestly, then says:

'My God, if Algy could only see this!'

She puts her hand on his arm, and says:

'It is right that he should see it, and he *shall* see it. It is our only chance of making them happy, and that end justifies us. I came upon this quite by accident, and Hilda must know nothing about it—at any rate, for the present. She is certain to sleep for at least an hour, and her parents, who have gone for a long drive, will not return till five. Go at once to the Casino, and bring Algy Somerville here; say what you like, do what you like, only bring him. He will see no one but you and me, and I will explain how I came upon this sketch when you come back. Only you must let him know that it did not come to me as a revelation, for I discovered Hilda's secret the moment I saw her watching him in the Casino. Now fly! How shall I live till you come back?'

'You are right,' replies Lord Clement. 'It is a bold stroke, but I will do it.'

Mrs. Cartwright says she will never know how she lived through the twelve minutes that elapse before Lord Clement returns, with Algy Somerville by his side.   She paces the room, watch in hand.   Will the fifteen minutes she has allowed them never pass? And will it be 'they' who return, or only Lord Clement?   But in twelve minutes, instead of the fifteen, both enter the salon, and by this time Mrs. Cartwright is too agitated to speak.   She puts her finger to her lips, points to Hilda's shut door, and hands Algy Somerville the sketch, without uttering a word.   He looks at it earnestly, and turns white to the very lips.   There is dead silence for at least a minute; then Algy turns to Clement, and says in a husky voice :

'Is this her writing ?'

'It is.'

'You swear it ?'

'I swear it.'

Algy then turns to Mrs. Cartwright :

'How did you get this sketch ?'

'In a very simple manner.   Hilda wished to show me a portrait she had done of her mother; but she was already half asleep, and gave me the wrong key, describing the box in which was the portrait as being on the right hand instead of the left.   Of course, when I found the key wouldn't open one box, I tried the other, and this is what I saw right at the top. Hilda meanwhile had gone to sleep ; and then I sent for Lord Clement.'

'You are certain,' asked Algy, 'that she is asleep now, and knows nothing of this ?'

Mrs. Cartwright goes on tip-toe to the door, which she opens softly, and then beckons to Algy to come and see for himself.

A lovely vision meets his eyes, for Hilda's beautiful head, with its wealth of bright hair, is pillowed on a blue silk cushion, and her long dark eyelashes rest on her delicate cheek. He stands for a few seconds watching her, his head sunk on his chest, and his hands clasped together. Then he turns away, and Mrs. Cartwright gently closes the door.

'Poor Evy!' are the first words he utters. Even at that supreme moment his thoughts are with his dead brother.

'Don't say "Poor Evy!"' says Clement Armytage, putting his hand on his friend's shoulder. 'If he could see you now—and sometimes I believe those that have gone before *can* see those they have left— he would be "happy Evy." This is what he wished for you.'

Algy looks at his two companions, a strange light shining in his eyes.

'Thank you,' he says, 'for what you have done. I can hardly realize it all. I must get away from this place at once, and think it out by myself. I will take the next train to Nice—Cannes—any-where.'

'What!' says Mrs. Cartwright, 'you will go away and make no sign, leave no message ?'

18

He takes up the sketch, and again looks at it earnestly; then he hands it back to Mrs. Cartwright, who locks it up in the box.

'Yes, I *will* leave a sort of message, for I know that beautiful old song well. There is a second verse to it.'

He goes to the writing-table, takes a plain sheet of writing-paper, and writes the following lines :

'The sun, whose beams most glorious are,
    Rejecteth no beholder ;
And your sweet beauty past compare
    Makes my poor eyes the bolder.
Where beauty moves and wit delights,
    And signs of kindness bind me,
There, oh, there ! where'er I go,
    I leave my heart behind me.'

He hands the paper to Mrs. Cartwright, and Lord Clement reads it over her shoulder. When they have finished, both have tears in their eyes, and not a word is said.

At last Algy breaks the silence.

'I am going straight to the hotel,' he says, 'to pack up my things and look out trains. In this state of mind I couldn't stop here. I shall take the first train I can catch either to Nice or Cannes, and will write to you to-night, giving you my address.' He gives a long look at the closed door of Hilda's room, and says : 'I leave it to you both who have been so good to me, to say what you think best for her ; and if, after she knows all, she writes me the one word "Come," I shall be here as fast as the train can bring me.   Then, please God, I will never leave her again !'

# CHAPTER XIX.

## AN IMPROMPTU CAREFULLY REHEARSED.

As soon as Algy left the room, Lord Clement and
Mrs. Cartwright turned and confronted one another.

'And now what is to be done?' said the latter.
'Hilda must not know—at least, not at present—that
Algy has seen her sketch of him; but, then, how can
we convince her that he loves her with all his heart,
though he has never spoken to her? Don't you see
in what a peculiar position they are placed? Don't
you see how terribly difficult it is even now to bring
them together?'

'Indeed I do see it,' replied Lord Clement, shaking
his head slowly; 'but we have got over by far the
most difficult part, in persuading Algy that he really
is the only man for whom Hilda has ever cared.
The rest is comparatively easy. Think it over, dear
Mrs. Cartwright; think with all your might and
main.'

Mrs. Cartwright remained for at least five minutes
without speaking, which was a long time for her, and
then exclaimed :

'I have it! We *must* exercise a little duplicity; there is no way but that out of our difficulty, and with such an end in view as this we must not stop at trifles. Moreover, time is short; picture to yourself Algy's state of mind alone at a hotel at Nice, or where-ever he is.

'This is my idea: Very soon Hilda will wake up; I shall tell her you are in the salon waiting to play bézique with her, and she will hobble in, leaning on my arm; you are to have your head buried in your hands, with your back to the door of her room. Of course, she will say, "What is the matter?" I shall then leave you together, saying that I am going for a walk in the gardens, and you will answer, "What is the matter? Algy Somerville has gone away—he wouldn't even tell me where; but I saw him off at the station, and, as the train was leaving, he put this envelope into my hand." Now, wait a bit; that envelope contains the second verse of "Since first I saw your face."'

'Of course,' said Lord Clement. 'How clever you are!'

'Wait a bit,' said Mrs. Cartwright; 'that is not enough. He also put into it a slip of paper (which you must have destroyed, as he didn't write it), saying:

'"The temptation is too strong for me. I feel that I have met the good and true woman whose coming Evy anticipated; but how can I ask the peerless Hilda Brabazon to share my broken life and fortunes?

It is a glimpse of paradise, and I must fly from it as from a thing too good for realization. Still, as you have assured me that she is interested in my sad story, I would like her to know that all the heart I have left is given to her, and that I have gone away humbly hoping she will continue to think kindly of me. Please let her have these beautiful lines of a very old song that I think must be well known even to this generation. Evy and I used to sing it at Eton in the choir, and I have never forgotten the impression the words made on me, though I little thought that they would be applicable to my own case."

' There,' said Mrs. Cartwright, almost out of breath, ' I think I've reeled that off pretty smart, though I know I have put it crudely and in my own rough language,' saying which she burst into tears ; ' but that is what I want you to say to Hilda, directly you see her. Now write it down *quickly*. There is no time to be lost, for she may wake at any moment, and you must have this little speech ready, and show her the verse in Algy's own handwriting.'

' Mrs. Cartwright,' said Armytage, delighted, ' you have indeed the " woman's wit " necessary for an emergency of this sort ; it would have taken me hours to arrive at this solution of our problem, even if I got there at all, and you have solved it in a few minutes. Thanks to you, I quite understand what I have to say to Miss Hilda, and now, for the first time, I am sanguine that all will come right.'

Mrs. Cartwright took out her handkerchief and

wiped her tearful eyes. She remained silent for a few moments, but then she asked him :

'How are you going to persuade her to write the word "Come" that will bring back Algy? I shall always call him Algy now.'

'That you must leave to me. So far, dear Mrs. Cartwright, it is you that have done everything to bring together these two dear people who have fought so obstinately against their own happiness ; but now it is my turn, and I feel that, the way having been paved for me by you, I shall be able, say within an hour, to put the finishing touch to your work.'

'I know you will do it, and do it well,' she said, 'for when it comes to real business, a man——'

Tinkle, tinkle !

'That is Hilda's bell ; she is awake. Sit down as I told you, with your head buried in your hands—you know the rest.'

And Mrs. Cartwright ran to the door of Hilda's room.

'Have you had a good sleep, dear?' she said on entering.

'Yes, but part of the time I was only dozing, and I fancied I heard several voices in the next room.'

'Lord Clement came in just as I was looking for that sketch of your mother ; but you gave me the wrong key, for it wouldn't open the box. You must show it me another time, as I have a headache now, and must have a little fresh air, or William James

will say I look pale and begin to fuss. Lord Clement
is waiting to play bézique with you. Poor man! he
is so depressed; you must try to cheer him up.'

And before Hilda has time to ask the cause of this
depression, she has gone to the door of the salon and
opened it wide, so as to give Lord Clement time to
assume the attitude agreed upon ; she then returns to
Hilda's sofa and offers her an arm, which enables
Hilda to hobble to the next room.   But when she
gets to the door, and catches sight of Clement
Armytage, she stops short and whispers :

'Why, what is the matter with him ?'

'Hush! I dare say he will tell you,' she whispers
back ; then, aloud, 'Now, Lord Clement, here is the
poor cripple come to do battle with you, while I go
for a turn in the gardens.'

Lord Clement has risen from his chair by this time,
and is facing them.

'How are you to-day, Miss Hilda ?' he asked, as
Mrs. Cartwright left the room.

Without answering the question, she fixed her eyes
inquiringly on his face, and said :

'What is the matter with you, my dear friend ?'

He returned her gaze sadly, and said :

'Algy Somerville has gone.'

Hilda turned deathly pale, and gasped out :

'Gone ?'—a terrible dread coming into her mind—
'gone ?  Gone where ?'

'I am not quite sure; but he has left Monte Carlo.'

'Is that all ?' Hilda replied with a sigh of relief,

the colour returning to her cheeks. 'But why has he left so suddenly?'

'Can't you guess? Don't you know the fate of the moth?'

'Yes; but—where is the candle?'

'I don't think *you* ought to ask that question, after all I have told you,' said Lord Clement, assuming an air of severity.

'Do you mean to tell me he left because—because—— I don't believe it.'

'I saw him off at the station, and have no doubt he will stop at Nice, for he said he should be somewhere in the neighbourhood, just for the change he felt he must have. But just as the train steamed off he put an envelope into my hand. Would you care to know what it contained, or is it a matter of indifference to you?'

'I would like to know very much,' said Hilda falteringly, her eyes cast down.

Lord Clement then rehearsed almost word for word the imaginary note suggested to him by Mrs. Cartwright. Hilda's beautiful face flushed and paled alternately, and her breath came in little sobs. As soon as he had finished speaking, she stretched out her hand. He understood, gave her the verse, and turned away. No eyes must see her at that solemn moment.

When she had read the verse, she went up to Lord Clement, and touched him, that he might turn to her. One look at her face was sufficient to satisfy him, for there was a light in her eyes he had never seen there before.

'Now do you believe?' he asked triumphantly.

'Yes, I believe,' replied Hilda slowly and solemnly.

'Then, will you write the one word "Come"?'

'No, I will not write "Come."'

'Ah! How cruel women are, even the best of you!' exclaimed Lord Clement, positively wringing his hands. '*Why—why* won't you write "Come"?'

'Because I shall telegraph it.'

# CHAPTER XX.

## JOY BELLS.

ALGY returned at once, and was met by Lord Clement.

'Where is she?' were the former's only words of greeting.

'Waiting for you on the seat where Evy first sat on arriving here,' replied his friend. 'You know it?'

'I do. Leave me, now, for I can hardly yet realize the situation. God knows I love her. I cannot but believe she loves me—yet we have never spoken to each other! No one must be present at our first *real* meeting. Clem, you understand—leave me. So much happiness bewilders me.'

And, as he spoke, he passed his handkerchief over his damp forehead, and there was a look of terrible doubt and anxiety on his sensitive face.

Lord Clement, however, anxious to relieve the tension of this supreme moment, thought it best to be very human, and, merely grasping his friend's hand, said simply :

'It's all right, old man. Go in and win, and—God bless you!'

Half an hour elapsed, during which time Lord Clement walked up and down the same spot, not covering more than a few yards. Then, as he turned, for perhaps the hundredth time, he saw approaching him the two persons he had so long wished to unite. They were walking quietly side by side, yet one look at the two faces he knew and loved so well was sufficient—indeed, it was too much for his pent-up feelings.

A strong man, especially an Englishman, cannot bear to show any emotion in public, and therefore this strong, warm-hearted Englishman, when he had satisfied himself by that one look that all was well, instead of hurrying to meet the happy lovers, turned his back surreptitiously to wipe away the tears of joy that would force themselves to his eyes.

In a few seconds a little hand was laid lightly on his arm at the same moment that a strong one grasped his shoulder. Then he turned round, the tell-tale tears still in his eyes, and there was a short silence.

'What an ass I am!' burst forth Clement at length, as he seized the hands stretched out to meet his. 'Of course, I *knew* it would be all right; but now I see it all it seems almost too good to be true, and—and—— Hang it, Algy! you don't deserve your luck, you—you unbelieving, diffident idiot! Now let's go and tell Colonel and Mrs. Brabazon, and Mrs. Cartwright and William James, all about it.'

And, as a brown-eyed flower-girl approached them at that moment, he threw her a franc, and, seizing the bunch of roses held out to him, he thrust them into Hilda's hand, saying :

'Let us go and tell *everybody.*'

'What, even the croupiers?' said Hilda, with a happy smile, looking up into Algy's face.

'Especially the croupiers,' replied Algy, as he took her hand and placed it under his arm. 'I count them amongst my best friends now. There could be no public play without them, and you might never have noticed me if you had not seen me looking sad, and wearing my life out. At this moment I am at peace with everybody, and I feel as if Evy was looking at me and smiling his approval. Who knows? I may yet hit upon some means of getting back the old place. If hard work can do it, it *shall;* for I think, my Hilda, that the hope of seeing you at Hunting-ford would make me attempt the impossible. But that is a good deal too much to look forward to, and the present almost unmans me. I feel as if it must be a dream.'

'Oh, come, I say,' said Lord Clement, who, having recovered himself, is once more his own cheery self, 'this won't do. I foresee I am going to have a worse time with you now you are full of sentiment than when you were full of melancholy. Dream, is it?

Here is someone coming who will soon show you if it is a dream or not. Thank Heaven we are alone here! for I don't know *what* she won't do!'

Saying which he pointed to a path on the left, down which a little figure might be seen flying along, her hat just held by two pins at the back of her head. In a few moments Mrs. Cartwright arrives breathless before the smiling trio.

'Which shall I congratulate first?' she gasps out. 'You, Algy, because you have given us the most trouble.'

And her eyes are all ablaze with the fervour of her congratulation. Then she turns to Hilda, whom she enfolds in her arms, and keeps her there silently for a few seconds.

'Not much "dream" about this, eh, Algy?' says Lord Clement, as they watch the pretty and touching picture before them.

As soon as Hilda is released from that warm embrace, she and Algy instinctively take each a hand of their sweet little friend, and clasp it tenderly in their own.

'Thank you! Ah! how can I thank you?' says Algy huskily. 'If it had——'

'Oh, I know what you would say,' breaks in little Mrs. Cartwright; 'but we are in no mood for senti- ment at present—I'm just too wildly happy for that : I think I should like to scream—but look! here comes William James. He started with me, and he has only just arrived. Doesn't he look solemn, and won't

he just be shy ?   He won't know what to say, you see ;
for I don't give him much chance to learn.'

But William James was quite equal to this occasion.
He advanced, hat in hand, and, bending low over
Hilda's hand, imprinted a solemn kiss upon it ; then,
turning to Algy, he said :

' I know how happy you must both be, but I doubt
if even you are much happier than my little wife
here ;' and he looked at her fondly.

' Now I guess we are all right.   But you will want
to go together and tell the great news to Colonel and
Mrs. Brabazon ; so we will just leave you in peace
for an hour.   It won't be more, I'm afraid, for I don't
feel as if I could stop away any longer than that.'

Saying which the little American woman took her
husband's arm, and, motioning to Lord Clement to
follow them, left the lovers to stroll back to the
hotel.

It is almost needless to say that they were received
with the deepest affection by Hilda's father and
mother, who rejoiced with them on the happy termi-
nation to their strange courtship.

# CHAPTER XXI.

## A FAIRY GODMOTHER.

THE next few days were passed blissfully by all concerned in this little romance. Algy was generally building castles in the air, which invariably ended, somehow, in his becoming re-possessed of Huntingford; and Hilda, though never having known personally the joy and pride that attaches to owning a beautiful old family place, sympathized with her future husband in this, as in everything else that interested him. She was never tired of hearing about Evy, and the absolute unity of the lives of the twins until the fatal separation came. And if Algy drew a veil, as much as possible, over his beloved brother's weaknesses and shortcomings, Hilda was not the one to blame him. On the contrary, she loved him the more for his loyalty and devotion to the dead.

Mrs. Brabazon being still unfit to leave the warm climate of Monte Carlo after her severe cold, it was decided to remain on for the present.

As for the happy lovers, every place except Hunt-

ingford was the same to them, and Algy could now
pass the Casino without a shudder.

The prosaic question of settlements was freely discussed by all the party, and, thanks to the fairly good
luck that had attended Algy, the sum he had won,
added to his private fortune and Hilda's thousand a
year, enabled them to start life, if not with absolute
riches, at all events with quite enough to live comfortably wherever they might decide on pitching their
tent. Moreover, Algy looked forward to getting to
work again, either at the Foreign Office or wherever
a suitable opening might present itself.

In order to avoid delay, Colonel Brabazon had
already begun a correspondence with his solicitor,
and many legal documents touching on his daughter's
fortune, present and future, had already found their
way to the Hôtel de Paris.

It was therefore no surprise when, on coming into
their salon one day after a long walk, Colonel Brabazon
saw a blue official-looking envelope lying on the
table. He took it up, and was about to open it,
when he noticed that it was addressed to 'Miss Hilda
Brabazon.' The seal bore the names Wilson and
Fry.

'Wilson and Fry,' said the Colonel to himself,
putting the letter down unopened—'never heard of
them. This comes of having a daughter about to be
married. Well, I expect it is the first legal document
she has ever received, and I don't suppose she will
understand much about it.'

At this moment the door opened, and Hilda came in alone.

'Why, where's the other turtle-dove?' asked the Colonel, smiling.

'He is gone—I mean, Algy is gone with Clement Armytage to buy me a mysterious present; I am to know nothing about it till I see it, so they ordered me home.'

'Well, there is an important-looking letter for you. Pray open it at once; I am dying of curiosity to know what it is;' saying which he took up a paper, and, seating himself in his armchair, was soon absorbed in the latest political news.

Hilda gave one glance at the blue envelope in question, and then proceeded to place in water some lovely Gloire de Dijon roses she had brought home with her.

'Pleasure first, business afterwards,' she said to herself as she arranged the beautiful flowers given her by Algy, this fact naturally enhancing both their loveliness and their fragrance. 'How I hate these horrible money details! they seem to take away all sentiment.'

And she sighed as she put the last rose lovingly into the large china vase, also given her by Algy, and took up the offending blue envelope.

'What a regular clerk's handwriting! and yet I wish I could write as clearly as that,' she said, as she turned over the blue envelope, and read twice 'Wilson and Fry.'

Putting her hand to her mouth to stifle a yawn, she opened the letter, and read as follows :

'MADAM,

'We have the gratification of forwarding to you the enclosed letter from our late client, Miss Hilda Frances Dashwood, for whom we had the honour of doing business during the last thirty years. It was her wish that no notification of her death should appear in the papers, and that the enclosed letter should only be delivered to you after her cremation and the subsequent interment of her ashes in Woking Cemetery.

'These combined ceremonies having taken place on Tuesday, February 11, we lose no time in forwarding the letter in question to you, and beg respectfully to congratulate you on the princely fortune that has become yours according to the terms of Miss Dashwood's will. It is almost unnecessary for us to say that we hold ourselves at your disposal for the completion of the formalities necessary to place you in possession of it.

'We remain, madam,

'Your obedient servants,

'WILSON AND FRY.'

Hilda gave one look at her father, whose face was hidden behind the newspaper, then tore open the enclosed letter, which ran thus :

19—2

'MY DEAR HILDA,

'You will have heard of me from your parents, of that I have no doubt; whether you will have heard any good of me is another question, but that is of no moment now. I have been a selfish, obstinate woman for many years past, and now that I feel my end is near, I find myself, through my own fault, without a friend in the world. I can only blame myself, but that does not make me feel less lonely and uncared for, now that I look back on the past and think of what might have been.

'I will try and be brief in my explanation. Your mother and I were the dearest of friends when we were girls, but there was always a little jealousy between us. I was beautiful, accomplished, and an heiress; I can say all this now that my gray hair, wrinkled face, and unlovable nature have left me to end my days in sad solitude. At that time, however, I was desperately in love with a man who seemed to me all that was perfect; your mother warned me against him; she told me he only thought of my fortune, and she tried all she could to dissuade me from marrying him. I believed that she wanted him for herself, and we had a bitter quarrel; but your mother was right: he did only care for my money, and, finding a manufacturer's daughter with twice my fortune, he threw me over and married her.

'This lesson disgusted me with all men, and I became a thoroughly soured woman. Your mother,

on the other hand, almost immediately afterwards
met your father, who has proved, as you know, the
best and most loving of husbands. Well, when I
heard how happy she was in the prospect of her
marriage with the handsome and popular Captain
Brabazon, a fiendish idea seized me to try and break
off her marriage as she had wished to break off mine
—alas! in my case with too good reason, though I
had absolutely none to offer in hers.

'I wrote to her on the subject, and she answered,
begging me to come to her that she might try to
convince me that she was acting wisely as regarded
Captain Brabazon. Our interview was a stormy one
and I would rather not dwell upon it: for, although I
tried to convince myself that I was acting for your
mother's good, in reality I knew that it was jealousy
of her happiness made me attempt to persuade her
that the man she had promised to marry was a flirt,
and very extravagant. More even *I* could not find
to say against him. She listened to me with a smile
but assured me she knew what she was doing, and
had no fears for the future. I parted from her in
anger and disappointment at my failure, and when she
would have kissed me I turned my head away. But
as I left the room she said :

'" Remember, Hilda, no matter what has happened
or what may happen, I shall never forget our friendship ; nothing can shake that with me, and the day
that brings you back to me as you were will be a
very happy one."

'I did not answer, but left the room, and have never seen your mother since; though, from time to time, I heard of her brilliant success in society, and of her husband's devotion to her, these rumours only served to harden my heart against her. I heard that she had a daughter, but it was not until *last year* that I even knew your name.

'One day Mrs. Eyre, who had seen a good deal of you in London, was with me, and, being a kind-hearted woman, she tried to speak to me of my early friend, and to soften my heart towards her by telling me of her failing health and of the invalid's life she was compelled to lead—all to no purpose, however, until at last Mrs. Eyre said:

'"Are you aware that our poor friend has called her only child 'Hilda,' after you?"

'"Why after me?" I retorted; "there are plenty of other Hildas in the world!"

'"Yes; but not many girls named Hilda Frances. Besides, her mother told me that she had named the child after you in remembrance of the dearest friend of her girlhood, the friend for whom she had always kept a corner in her heart, notwithstanding the separation of years."

'Will you believe it?—my pride was too great to allow of my going to your mother to entreat her pardon.

'My solitary life had made me obstinate. Lonely I had lived, lonely I would die; but at least I could show that I appreciated your mother's kind thought of me by leaving the whole of my fortune to her Hilda Frances.

'So now, my dear child, you will be a very rich woman—I know that you are nearly of age, and I leave it to you absolutely to do as you like with. There is a sum of £300,000, invested in different securities, and my London house with all it contains. The jewels are at Coutts', and will be delivered to you through Messrs. Wilson and Fry, my solicitors.

'Hilda Frances, try and do better with your life than I did with mine ; think kindly of me if you can, and, above all, tell your mother that I bitterly repented my treatment of her, and that on my death-bed I, too, look back with regretful pleasure on our girlish friendship, which was the only happy time of my life. God bless you all !

'HILDA FRANCES DASHWOOD.'

Hilda read through the letter as if in a dream, but never withdrew her eyes from its closely-written pages ; and when she had finished it she pushed her hair from her forehead, and looked up for the first time. Her father had dropped his newspaper, and sat with his eyes fixed upon her face.

'I could not interrupt you,' he said in a serious voice, 'for you looked—I can hardly say how you looked as you read the last pages of that letter. What is it, my child ? What can have moved you so deeply ?'

Hilda silently gave him the letter. He took it in equal silence, and commenced reading, nor did he look up till he had finished the closely-written pages, written in a singularly legible, firm handwriting.

'Poor soul!' were his first words, his whole kind heart in sympathy with the lonely woman who had evidently died friendless, though the fault was hers, and the solitude of her own making. 'Poor soul!' he repeated once more. 'I always felt more of pity than anger for her. But now, my child, I do not want you to dwell on the sad part of Miss Dashwood's letter. You never saw her, and cannot, therefore, be expected to mourn her loss. She has left you the whole of her fortune. What is my little girl going to do with it?'

'I am sure I don't know, father,' replied Hilda, pushing her hair still further off her forehead, and walking up and down the room, a puzzled look on her face. 'You have always given me everything I wanted, and now I have got Algy I don't seem to have a wish ungratified. Ah, Algy!' she almost screamed, as she stopped short in the middle of the room. 'Algy! Huntingford! Father! father! don't you see? I can now buy back his old home that he loves so, and give it to him. Oh, say I can —say I can!' and the impulsive girl threw herself on the floor at her father's feet, and laid her head on his knee.

Colonel Brabazon smiled as he stroked the bright golden hair.

'You have been a long time finding out what to do with part of your fortune, child.   Why, it occurred to me before I had finished reading the letter.'

An eager, flushed face was raised to his, and Hilda exclaimed.

'Do you mean it?   May I?   Can I?   But, oh! Algy is so proud; will he ever consent to take Huntingford from me?'

'There can be no question of pride between you and Algy now, Hilda; but it is a good thing that this large fortune did not come to you before you were engaged, for in that case Algy's pride might have been a serious obstacle to your happiness, and you might have had to give up either him or the fortune.'

'And do you think I would have hesitated?' said Hilda reproachfully.

'No, I don't, you little goose!' replied her father, drawing her on to his knee.   'But I am very glad you will not have to make your choice.   Money is a fine thing, and just think of all the good you can do with it, and the happiness you can give.'

'Where is mother?   I do so want to tell her,' said Hilda, regaining her feet.

'She went for a short drive with the Elliots, and ought to be back by now.   She is still weak after her cold, so don't agitate her too much.'

Mrs. Brabazon entered the room at this moment, and looked askance at husband and daughter.

'What in the world has happened?' she asked

nervously. 'Has there been a dynamite explosion, or what ?'

Colonel Brabazon went up to his wife, and, taking her hand gently, led her towards her bedroom door, saying :

'It's all right, dear ; Hilda has some wonderful news for you. Go and take off your things, and rest a bit ; she will tell you all about it ;' and mother and daughter left the room together.

After the door had closed on them, the Colonel, instead of returning to his papers, walked up and down the room, his hands clasped behind him, thinking deeply. Three hundred thousand pounds is a very large sum to come into a family quite unexpectedly, and is calculated to give a practical man much food for thought ; and Colonel Brabazon was quite surprised when his wife came into the room, having read the long letter twice over, and laid her hand on his arm. There were traces of many tears on her pale cheeks as she said :

'My poor friend ! What a sad, sad end ! I wish she would have let me see her once more ; all could have been explained, and I might have been with her when she died. I never ceased to feel the deepest pity for her, and, as she did not succeed in making us think we were not suited to each other, you and I, we can freely forgive her, and think of her only with kindly feelings. But just imagine, our little Hilda a great heiress !' she continued, smiling through her tears. 'She has told me of her darling scheme, and is now longing to rush off and tell Algy.'

'Which is exactly what she must not do,' said the Colonel firmly. 'I have been thinking it all over, and the first thing we must do is to ascertain if the present owner of Huntingford is really willing to sell. Until we know that for certain, Algy must be told nothing. Do, dear, go and explain this to Hilda, while I write a note to Clement Armytage; he will be a great assistance to us in this matter, and we must see him at once.'

# CHAPTER XXII.

## THE OLD HOME REDEEMED.

ON receiving a note from Colonel Brabazon with the words 'Come here at once—good news,' Clement Armytage found his way as quickly as he could to the Brabazon salon, where the two letters received by Hilda were handed to him. After reading them with the deepest attention, he congratulated her with a pressure of the hand more eloquent than words.

'But you don't see,' cried Hilda, 'all that this means for me. It means——'

'It means Huntingford,' interrupted Clement; 'I saw that at once.'

'Of course you did, my boy,' said the Colonel. 'Small blame to you. This headstrong girl wishes to give the old place to Algy as a wedding present, and, knowing what we do of him, I cannot find it in my heart to gainsay her; but she also wishes to tell Algy at once, and there she is wrong, for if the present owner refuses to sell, the disappointment would be too bitter. I want you, therefore, to go over at once—

to-night even, if you can and will—in order to find out how the land lies. By-the-by, what is the man's name ?'

'Emerson P. Cotton.'

'Well, I think that you should write beforehand to Mr. Cotton, asking for an interview either at Huntingford or in London. Once alongside of him, five minutes will tell you what to expect, and the rest I leave to you: for I know you have the success of this project as much at heart as we have, and I make no apology for sending you off at once.'

Lord Clement was understood to say that he was ready to start for the Antipodes in an hour, if that was any use.

'England will do this time,' said the Colonel, smiling. 'But there is one thing more : Hilda will write by to-night's post to Messrs. Wilson and Fry, requesting them to take your instructions as to carrying out the purchase, should Mr. Cotton consent to sell ; and I will also add a few lines of my own to them, in order that they may know that Hilda's parents are with her in what to the ordinary legal mind will naturally appear to be a somewhat quixotic proceeding.

'I understand perfectly,' said Armytage, 'and will write to Mr. Cotton while my man is packing my things.'

'Remember,' were the Colonel's parting words, 'that we shall be on tenter-hooks until we hear from you, so write as soon as you have anything to say.'

'Ah!' pleaded Hilda, 'if it is good news, do not wait to write—telegraph to me.'

'Of course,' assented Clement. 'Anything satisfactory I will telegraph, and I *mean* to telegraph.'

As the door closed behind him, Hilda sank into a chair.

'How shall I live through these three or four days?' she moaned rather than said. 'I wish I could sleep until the telegram was brought to me. But what an ingrate I am, not to have remembered that Janie Cartwright does not yet know my good fortune They are both at home, for it is their "mail day," and they don't like to be disturbed ; but my news is good enough to protect me, and I shall chance it this time.'

Well it was that she did so, for not only did the unfeigned delight of Mrs. Cartwright add, if that was possible, to Hilda's own happiness, but that stanch, clever little woman was able to reassure her somewhat as to a danger which was to be apprehended.

'Supposing, after all, that Mr. Cotton refuses to sell,' said Hilda.

But little Mrs. Cartwright was never taken at a loss.

'There is no supposing about it,' she rejoined quickly, 'for the battle is half won by the fact which you tell me, that Mr. Cotton is not satisfied with his experience of the life of an English country gentleman, and the other half is provided for by the sentimental interest which he will feel in the romantic story unfolded to him by Lord Clement. We are a

primitive people, my dear, and slaves to sentiment ;
there's not a man of us, however hard he may be down
town, who will not do all he knows to make the course
of true love smooth.'

'Especially,' added William James, 'if he makes a
little bit on the transaction.'

'William James,' said his wife impressively, 'I
forbid you to calumniate your countrymen!  But '—
turning to Hilda—'you will get your telegram,
sure enough ; bet your boots on that, you doubting
girl!'

Notwithstanding this, the days that intervened
were full of preoccupation for Hilda, and this could
not escape Algy, who had already learnt to watch all
her moods.

'You are hiding something from me, my darling,'
he said, as they were strolling about on the morning
of the fourth day, 'and I connect it with Clement's
journey to England.  Is it that his inamorata has at
last consented to listen to his pleading ?  It is hard
that you should be in his confidence, and not I !
Perhaps you will get a telegram from him ; I should
be glad indeed to know that this prince of good
fellows is to be as happy as he deserves.'

'You are partly right,' replied Hilda; 'I *am* expecting a telegram from Clement, and when it comes I
will show it you at once.  Perhaps it may come to-
day—more likely not.  Still, I shall wait at home on
the chance.  Where shall I find you, if it comes ?'

'Upon Evy's seat ; I will take my book there, read

as much as I can, and probably build my usual castle in the air, while I am waiting for you—for you *will* come?'

'Indeed I will,' she said, as they parted.

She curled herself upon her sofa as soon as she got back, resigned to count the minutes until the telegram should come. She already thought of its arrival as certain, for Clement was adroit and determined, Janie Cartwright was confident, and in the end Hilda herself began to believe in her star.

Still, the minutes were leaden-footed, until at last the door opened, and the scene was enacted which she had so often pictured to herself within the last few days—a waiter entered the room, salver in hand, upon which rested the much-longed-for blue envelope.

'Une dépêche pour mademoiselle,' he said.

'Donnez,' she said, though rather unsteadily.

The telegram ran thus:

'Cotton consents to sell for the price he gave; the law work is quite simple, and in a few days Huntingford will be Algy's. I congratulate you both from the bottom of my heart.'

Hilda crumpled the paper up in her hand, and ran downstairs, and then towards Evy's seat. The pace at which she had come and her emotion made her heart beat against her side, and she had to stop to recover her breath when she came within sight of Algy.

He was evidently immersed in thought, for his book was on the seat, and his eyes fixed upon the blue sea beneath him. Still, he heard her at once; light as her footfall was, he would hear it 'were it earth in an earthy bed,' and he looked up at once.

'Have you got the telegram from Clem, my love, and is he engaged? I know that's why he went to England.'

'N—o,' she said falteringly. 'I have got a telegram from Lord Clement, but it is not about that. He went to England to arrange about a wedding present I wished to make to you, and—this is what he says.' And, opening her little hand, she showed him the telegram. 'Read it,' she added, turning away.

'Oh, my poor Evy!' were the words she heard sobbed out by Algy as he read, and, throwing her arms round his neck, she cried :

'Bless you, Algy, that your first thought is of Evy! He brought us together, he shall keep us together ; and, so long as we are spared, it shall be my pride that Evy's memory is always first in your mind.'

'But,' said Algy, 'I don't understand. How has this come about? What does it mean? Is it even possible?'

She gave him the two letters she had received, saying that they would explain, and again turned away, so as not to disturb him in their perusal. At last he looked up, very grave.

'It is an angelic thought of yours, my Hilda. To

20

what other woman would it have occurred? But can I allow you to do this for me? Can I possibly accept it?'

But this was too much for poor Hilda, and she broke down, saying hysterically :

'All right, then. I shall win my sovereign from father; for I told him that you would manage to refuse, but he answered, "No; I know your Algy better than you do. The knowledge of the happiness which his consent will give you would silence any scruples which his sensitive delicacy might conjure up, though there is no foundation for them whatever." And mother said, "Have no fear, child. Algy's devotion to his brother's memory, added to the knowledge that you realize what was his brother's dying wish for him—all that pleads for you, and he will accept with both hands." "No, no, no!" I cried. "He will refuse. I bet you a sovereign—I bet you a sovereign!" And now'—sadly, her excitement sustaining her no longer—'I have won.'

'Did your father and mother say this?' asked Algy slowly and very gravely.

'Every word of it,' she said. 'I think I have repeated their very words.'

'Then, my darling, you must pay that sovereign, for, with reverence and gratitude in my heart, I accept.'

And thus this battle between them ended, and their life of enchantment began.

Little more remains to be said. Messrs. Wilson

and Fry showed that they possessed more than that average legal mind with which the Colonel had hypothetically credited them; and once the sale was decided on, the rapidity with which it was carried through was a piece of conveyancing of which Lincoln's Inn Fields might well be proud, for from start to finish a month sufficed to replace Algy in possession of his old home.

It was a happy party that gathered together at Huntingford shortly afterwards; for Colonel and Mrs. Brabazon were there with two children to love instead of only one, and sweet little Janie Cartwright, proud of the happiness which her devotion to Hilda, and her energy, had so notably helped to create.

And yet a second bride; for, when Lord Clement turned from the care of his friend's interests to that even nearer to his heart, he found a maiden waiting for him upon the threshold, who silently placed her hand in his—and he understood.

# CHAPTER XXIII.

## A GREEN MEMORY

FOUR years after the events set down in the foregoing chapters, on a beautiful evening in July, a lady, who belonged to the neighbourhood of Huntingford, but had only very recently returned from a long residence in India, was strolling along a green lane not far from the old gabled house, when a vision of childish beauty met her eyes, almost startling in its picturesqueness; and she stopped to speak to the child, whose identity she guessed.

He was a little boy, with a face of great beauty, curly dark hair, and long gray eyes, his arms full of roses, and bareheaded, for his hat, which the nurse was carrying, was also filled with flowers.

'How do you do, my little man, and will you tell me what your name is?'

'Evy.'

'Evy? What a pretty name! And where are you taking all those lovely flowers?'

'To Uncle Evy, in dere,' he adds, nodding his head

in the direction of the churchyard. ' I picked dem all myself, and dose, too '—pointing to the hat the nurse was carrying.

' You must love Uncle Evy very much to give him such beautiful flowers.'

' I can't love him, because he is dead ; but I can love his mem'ry, for he was a dood, booful man, just like favver.'

The lady smiled sweetly as she stroked the shining curls.

' Who told you that, little one ?'

' Muvver.'

THE END.

BILLING AND SONS, PRINTERS, GUILDFORD.

# LIST OF NEW BOOKS

### PUBLISHED BY

# George Routledge & Sons, Limited.

## Price 7/6 each.

*Two Entirely New Books with all the changes to date. Full of Original Illustrations and Full-page Plates.*

**Every Boy's Book of Sport and Pastime.** Edited by Professor HOFFMANN.

**Every Girl's Book of Sport, Occupation and Pastime.** Edited by Mrs. MARY WHITLEY.

## Price £1 11s. 6d.

**THE D'ARTAGNAN ROMANCES OF ALEXANDRE DUMAS.** In 9 Volumes. Crown 8vo, cloth.

And in 9 Volumes, price 3s. 6d. each.

1. The Three Musketeers, vol. 1.
2. ——————————— vol. 2.
3. Twenty Years After, vol. 1.
4. ——————————— vol. 2.
5. Vicomte de Bragelonne, vol. 1.
6. ——————————— vol. 2.
7. ——————————— vol. 3.
8. ——————————— vol. 4.
9. ——————————— vol. 5.

**WOOD'S NATURAL HISTORY.** Three Volumes. Super-royal 8vo, cloth. New and Cheaper Edition.

# Price 21/-.

**EDGAR ALLAN POE'S WRITINGS,** *The Fordham Edition.*   In 6 Volumes, crown 8vo, cloth.

And in 6 Volumes, price 3s. 6d. each.

1. Poems.
2. Tales, 1st series.
3. ———— 2nd series.
4. ———— 3rd series.
5. Essays and Biographies, 1st series.
6. ———————————————— 2nd series.

**FIELDING AND SMOLLETT'S NOVELS.**   6 Vols. Crown 8vo, cloth, gilt tops.

**WOOD'S NATURAL HISTORY OF MAN.**   Two Volumes, Super-royal 8vo, cloth.   Cheaper Edition.

# Price 12/6.

**WOOD'S ILLUSTRATED NATURAL HISTORY OF MAMMALIA.**   With 18 Coloured Plates. Super-royal 8vo.

# Price 7/6.

Discoveries and Inventions of the Nineteenth Century.   11th Edition.   By ROBERT ROUT-LEDGE, B.Sc., F.C.S.

# Price 5/-.

Scotland for Ever! or, the Adventures of Alec M'Donell.   A New Book for Boys.   By Col. PERCY GROVES, Author of "With Claymore and Bayonet," etc., etc.   With Full-page Illustrations by HARRY PAYNE.

# Price 3/6 each.

**Little Hearts.** By FLORENCE K. UPTON and BERTHA UPTON, Authors of "Two Dutch Dolls." With 60 pages of Illustrations printed in colours. Fancy Boards.

## COUNTRY BOOKS.—*NEW VOLUMES.*

*Brought up to date.*

**British Butterflies.** By W. S. COLEMAN.

**British Birds' Eggs.** By the Rev. J. C. ATKINSON.

**Dogs.** By A. J. SEWELL, M.R.C.V.S.

**Common Objects of the Microscope.** By Dr. BOUSFIELD.

**British Moths.** By J. W. TUTT.

# Price 3/6 each.

**ROUTLEDGE'S CROWN CLASSICS.** Crown 8vo, cloth gilt, 3*s.* 6*d.* each volume.

*A New Series of the Best Standard Works, in large clear type.*

**Carlyle's French Revolution.** Two Volumes.

**Motley's Dutch Republic.** Three Volumes.

**Byron's Poems.** Three Volumes.

**Boswell's Life of Johnson.** Three Volumes.

**Shakspere.** Three Volumes.

# Price 3/6 each.

## THE "KING'S OWN" EDITION OF CAPTAIN MARRYAT'S NOVELS.

1. The King's Own.
2. Frank Mildmay.
3. Newton Forster.
4. Peter Simple.
5. Jacob Faithful.
6. The Pacha of Many Tales.
7. Japhet in Search of a Father.
8. Mr. Midshipman Easy.

---

The 23rd Edition of
Charles Mackay's A Thousand and One Gems
of English Poetry, with considerable additions.

## THE NEW KNEBWORTH EDITION OF LORD LYTTON'S NOVELS.

1. Pelham.
2. Falkland and Zicci.
3. Devereux.
4. The Disowned.
5. Paul Clifford.
6. Eugene Aram.
7. Godolphin.
8. The Last Days of Pompeii.
9. Rienzi.
10. The Last of the Barons, vol. 1.
11. ————————————vol. 2.
12. Leila, Calderon, and Pausanias.
13. Harold.

## Price 3/6 each.

### THE NOTRE-DAME EDITION OF VICTOR HUGO'S NOVELS.

1. Notre-Dame, vol. 1.
2. ———————— vol. 2.
3. Toilers of the Sea, vol. 1.
4. ———————————— vol. 2.
7. Les Misérables, vol. 1.
8. ——————————— vol. 2.
9. ——————————— vol. 3.
10. ——————————— vol. 4.
11. ——————————— vol. 5.

### THE STANDARD NOVELISTS. A Library of the 20 Best Novels of the 20 Best Standard Novelists.

*ORDER OF PUBLICATION*

Of the STANDARD NOVELISTS, to be completed in 20 Volumes :—

| | |
|---|---|
| SMOLLETT ... ... | Peregrine Pickle. |
| FIELDING ... ... | Tom Jones. |
| DUMAS ... ... | Monte Cristo. |
| SCOTT ... ... | Ivanhoe. |
| HUGO ... ... | Notre Dame. |
| DICKENS ... ... | David Copperfield. |
| COOPER ... ... | The Last of the Mohicans. |
| LYTTON ... ... | The Last Days of Pompeii. |
| AINSWORTH ... | The Tower of London. |
| LOVER ... ... | Handy Andy. |
| MARRYAT ... ... | The King's Own. |
| THACKERAY ... | Vanity Fair. |

# Price 3/6 each.

### THE STANDARD NOVELISTS—*Continued.*

| | | |
|---|---|---|
| AUSTEN | ... ... | Pride and Prejudice. |
| BRONTË | ... ... | Jane Eyre. |
| COCKTON | ... ... | Valentine Vox. |
| GRANT | ... ... | The Romance of War. |
| KINGSLEY | ... ... | Alton Locke. |
| LEVER | ... ... | Jack Hinton. |
| READE | ... ... | Peg Woffington and Christie Johnstone. |
| SMEDLEY | ... ... | Frank Fairlegh. |

**Life of Queen Victoria.** By G. BARNETT SMITH. Brought down to September, 1896, with 12 pages of Illustrations.

**The Fernandez Reciter.** Complete in One Volume (Popular Library).

## PRIZE BOOKS.—*NEW VOLUMES.*

Also in cloth, gilt edges, price 5s. each.

**A Child's History of England.** By CHARLES DICKENS.

**Every Girl's Book.**

**Sandford and Merton.**

---

**Carleton's Traits and Stories of the Irish Peasantry.** Complete Edition, cloth (in boards, 2s. 6d.)

# NOVELS.—250 Volumes.
## TWO SHILLINGS EACH.

**AINSWORTH, W. H.**

1 The Tower of London
2 Old St. Paul's
3 Windsor Castle
4 The Miser's Daughter
5 The Star Chamber
6 Rookwood
7 St. James'
8 The Flitch of Bacon
9 Guy Fawkes
10 The Lancashire Witches
11 Crichton
12 Jack Sheppard
13 The Spendthrift
14 Boscobel
15 Ovingdean Grange
16 Mervyn Clitheroe
17 Auriol
18 Preston Fight
19 Stanley Brereton
20 Beau Nash
21 The Manchester Rebels

The Set, in 21 Volumes, price 42/-

**AUSTEN, Jane.**

22 Pride and Prejudice
23 Sense and Sensibility
24 Mansfield Park
25 Emma
26 Northanger Abbey, and Persuasion

The Set, in 5 Volumes, price 10/-

**BRONTË, Charlotte E. & A.**

27 Jane Eyre
28 Shirley
29 Wuthering Heights

**COCKTON, Henry.**

30 Valentine Vox
31 Sylvester Sound
32 Stanley Thorn

**COOPER, Fenimore.**

33 The Deerslayer
34 The Pathfinder
35 The Last of the Mohicans
36 The Pioneers
37 The Prairie
38 The Red Rover
39 The Pilot
40 The Two Admirals
41 The Waterwitch
42 The Spy
43 The Sea Lions
44 Miles Wallingford
45 Lionel Lincoln
46 The Headsman
47 Homeward Bound
48 The Crater ; or, Vulcan's Peak
49 Wing and Wing
50 Jack Tier
51 Satanstoe
52 The Chainbearer
53 The Red Skins
54 The Heidenmauer
55 Precaution
56 The Monikins
57 The Wept of Wish-ton-Wish
58 The Ways of the Hour
59 Mercedes
60 Afloat and Ashore
61 Wyandotte
62 Home as Found (Sequel to "Homeward Bound")
63 Oak Openings
64 The Bravo

The Set, in 32 Volumes, price 64/-

# NOVELS—*continued.*

*HUGO, Victor.*

126 Les Misérables
127 Notre Dame
128 History of a Crime
129 Ninety-Three
130 Toilers of the Sea
131 By Order of the King

*KINGSLEY, Charles.*

132 Alton Locke
133 Yeast

*LEVER, Charles.*

134 Harry Lorrequer
135 Charles O'Malley
136 Jack Hinton
137 Arthur O'Leary
138 Con Cregan

*LOVER, Samuel.*

139 Handy Andy
140 Rory O'More

*LYTTON, Lord.*

Author's Copyright Revised Editions containing Prefaces to be found in no other Edition.

141 Pelham
142 Paul Clifford
143 Eugene Aram
144 Last Days of Pompeii
145 Rienzi
146 Ernest Maltravers
147 Alice; or, The Mysteries
148 Night and Morning
149 The Disowned
150 Devereux
151 Godolphin
152 The Last of the Barons
153 Leila; Pilgrims of the Rhine
154 Falkland; Zicci
155 Zanoni
156 The Caxtons
157 Harold
158 Lucretia
159 The Coming Race

*LYTTON, LORD—continued.*

160 A Strange Story
161 Kenelm Chillingly
162 Pausanias: and The Haunted and the Haunters
163 My Novel, Vol. 1.
164 ——————— Vol. 2.
165 What will He Do with it? Vol. 1.
166 What will He Do with it? Vol. 2.
167 The Parisians, Vol. 1.
168 ——————— Vol 2.

The Set, in 28 Volumes, price 56/-

*MARRYAT, Captain.*

169 Frank Mildmay
170 Midshipman Easy
171 Phantom Ship
172 Peter Simple
173 The King's Own
174 Newton Forster
175 Jacob Faithful
176 The Pacha of many Tales
177 Japhet in Search of a Father
178 The Dog Fiend
179 The Poacher
180 Percival Keene
181 Monsieur Violet
182 Rattlin, the Reefer
183 Valerie
184 Olla Podrida

The Set, in 16 Volumes, price 32/-

*MOUNTENEY-JEPHSON, R.*

185 Tom Bullkley
186 The Girl he left behind him
187 The Roll of the Drum

*PORTER, Jane.*

188 The Scottish Chiefs
189 The Pastor's Fireside
190 Thaddeus of Warsaw

# NOVELS—*continued.*